ESTHER'S PILLOW

MARLIN FITZWATER

Esther's Pillow

PublicAffairs   NEW YORK

BOOK DESIGN BY JENNY DOSSIN.

Library of Congress Cataloging-in-Publication data

Fitzwater, Marlin.

Esther's pillow / Marlin Fitzwater.—1st ed.

p. cm.

ISBN 1-58648-035-9

1. Trials (Assault and Battery)—Fiction. 2. Women—Crimes against—Fiction. 3. Women teachers—Fiction. 4. Kansas—Fiction. I. Title.

PS3606.I89 E88 2001

813'.6—dc21

2001019716

FIRST EDITION

1 3 5 7 9 10 8 6 4 2

For My Brother

ESTHER'S PILLOW

2001

I sat and watched as my father lay dying of Wilson's disease, a rare and incurable form of liver destruction caused by the build-up of copper in the body. My brother and I prayed for a painless departure. Amazingly, the process of natural death from the systematic shutdown of the body seemed well ordered and observable, much like the process of growing, and aging, only sped up in reverse, like the rewinding of an old movie reel. Dad consolidated seventy-six years of life into six months of dying. As the days passed, he grew weaker and weaker, gradually shutting down various functions, much like a computer shuts down at the end of the day, first the screen, then the hard drive, then the printer, until all systems are finally still—as still as death. At least that's the way my computer shuts down. I'm a teacher and my computer is very old.

In one of those stages of death, very near the end, my father babbled. He spent three days shouting continuously. He talked straight through the night, at the top of his lungs, and seldom in complete sentences. When we first heard him call for Jay we didn't pay much heed.

"Jay!" my father shouted. "Where are you? Where are you going?"

In an hour or so, he repeated the phrase. My brother sat quietly beside Dad, his hand resting gently on the old man's forehead, one thumb moving in concentric circles on Dad's temple. He said nothing as Dad rambled. But when Dad called for Jay a third time, my brother raised his eyes and asked, "Who's Jay?" There was no response from Dad, of course, and I had no idea who Jay was. Perhaps a friend or neighbor; there are so many in seven decades of life.

The Langstons don't get involved in other people's lives. My dad's father, Grandpa Ray, died in his nineties without ever uttering a harsh word, except once when a hired hand got careless, swung his hay hook for a bale of straw that Grandpa was leaning on, and put the hook clear through the calf of Grandpa's leg. He knocked Grandpa down. Blood soaked through Grandpa's overalls, yet all he moaned was, "Dammit Clint, watch out for that thing."

Another time, a neighbor arrived to help just as the last bale of straw was stacked in the barn. Even Clint commented that this neighbor never got anywhere on time where there was work to be done, but Grandpa said nothing. He offered a glass of tea and we all sat around, sweating, feeling real good about the work and the fact that the job was through. No, Langstons didn't fuss much with others. They kept a kind of detached attitude toward other folks. So when Dad cried out for Jay, it seemed out of character.

Dad only had one brother, a retired natural gas company executive named Edward, who lived in Dodge City. Apparently Uncle Edward and Dad had been inseparable as kids growing up in Nickerly, a town of only a few hundred people in central Kansas. Dad only took me there once, for a reunion of the Nickerly Presbyterian church. He talked in the car about playing basketball at Nickerly, about how everyone there used the two-handed, underhanded set shot, especially for free-throw shooting. When I was in grade school, Dad could hit that shot thirty times in a row in our makeshift hoop, a peach basket with the bottom knocked out, nailed on the side of the barn.

When Uncle Edward arrived for the funeral, he seemed much younger than I had remembered him.

"Your dad was a great left fielder," he said. "He could run and catch anything. Very fast. One time against Ellsworth, this ole boy hit a high one, and your dad started running. He actually jumped the fence, just a barbed wire cattle fence actually, and caught the ball. We had a big fight over whether or not it was legal. Your dad never said a word. Just walked back to his position and waited for the decision."

"Let me ask you something," I ventured. "When Dad was delusionary just before he died, he kept calling for Jay. Do you know who that could be? Maybe somebody from Dad's youth?"

Uncle Edward looked up toward the ceiling as if in contemplation, then down at the floor, then turned his head toward me. "It might be your grandfather's brother," he said quietly.

I thought for a moment. I had never heard Dad mention an Uncle Jay. I had never heard Grandpa Ray mention a brother Jay.

"I never heard of Jay," I said. "Was he a lot older than Grandpa?"

"I don't really know," Edward said.

"Where does he live?" I asked. "Of course, he would be dead now. But what about relatives? How come we've never heard from any of them?"

"I don't really know," he repeated.

"But why would Dad call out his name?" I asked impatiently.

My dad's brother started slowly. "Well," he said, "we don't really know much about Jay because Dad never would talk about him. My dad, your Grandpa Ray, just turned away whenever Jay's name came up."

"Why?" I asked. "What happened? Why didn't anyone ever mention any of this?"

"Well," he said, "we didn't know much. The story goes that Jay got in some kind of trouble. Some trouble with a girl. Then he passed some bad checks, and your granddad told him to leave Kansas and never come back."

My uncle leaned forward in his chair, a straight back with a stuffed seat in floral print fabric. I had found the chair on the loading dock of the local furniture store one afternoon after basketball practice—it must have been my junior year in high school—and asked the store manager if I could have it. It had a long scar along the inside of one leg, hardly noticeable, but the manager said he couldn't sell it. I gave it to Mom and Dad, and they set it out on the porch.

The porch had always served as a gathering place for evening conversation. Our little house was a typical cottage with the porch stretched across the front. The front door opened into a living room, then a dining room, then a kitchen, with two bedrooms along the side of the sitting rooms. Our house and those of our neighbors conformed to the dominant architecture in most small towns across America. We all lived in simple homes, built in the forties and fifties for middle-class families and modified over the years with porch boxes, bedroom additions, and finished attics. Despite the additions, the houses remained small. Ours had served us well for four decades. Now the old chair creaked when my uncle leaned forward, reminding me of the passage of time and the distance of my own travels.

"That's about all I know," Uncle Everett said. "I asked my dad, your grandfather, about it a couple of times, but he just wouldn't talk about it."

"Forgive me," I said, "but did he rape her? What happened?"

"I don't know," my uncle repeated. "I never really knew. I think she was a schoolteacher."

With each question, my uncle offered a few more words. It wasn't clear to me whether he knew more, or didn't want to know more, or just didn't want to tell me. But he was clearly reluctant to talk about Jay, and I decided to let the matter rest for a while. My family had obviously bottled this thing up for at least four generations. Dad had repressed the memory so deep that only death's calling could pry it to the surface.

After the funeral, after the aunts and uncles and cousins had departed on two- or three-hour drives to remote Kansas towns, a bouquet of gladiolus was brought from the funeral home and placed on the corner table in my brother's home. I collapsed into a chair across the room, my feet propped on a small footstool covered with a dark blue needlepoint of red and pink roses, and I dozed off. My dreams were sentimental and warm. I saw Dad riding his Farmal tractor, pulling the small International Harvester combine through the golden wheat fields along Holland Creek, the heat causing him to blur in the distance. As he moved away, the thermal winds turned his body into a shimmering mirage. From time to time he would stand up on the tractor, turn his head to see if the combine bin was full, then wave his wide-brimmed straw hat, a signal for me to drive the little Ford Ferguson and wheat trailer out to the combine, pull it right up under the downspout, and wait for Dad to start the auger. I drove the tractor with one hand so I could hold on to the water jug with the other. That jug had been around more wheat fields than I had. One side was caved in where someone had dropped it under a tractor tire. Mom had filled it with water and ice, which made the sides sweat in the sun, and when you pulled the cap off the small spout on top, the steel opening would almost freeze your lips. The jug was heavy, and you had to be careful not to put your mouth around the spout without having a good grip. A chipped tooth from this process was pretty common. I was just handing the jug to Dad on the combine when Gary woke me.

"Where do you suppose Jay is today?" Gary asked, shoving my feet off the footstool.

"He's history," I replied. "But he must have relatives somewhere. Somebody in our family must know something."

"I was cleaning out Dad's things yesterday," Gary said, "and came across this old suitcase." He placed a battered cardboard case on the footstool. "It's full of old pictures of us kids and Grandma and Grandpa. Maybe there's something in there."

My brother was naturally handsome, with all the rough edges still on. His hands were callused from daily work in the gas station, grease accentuating the creases in his palms, a faint smell of kerosene lingering in his clothes. His dark wavy hair, while thinning, reminded me of Dad, at least in the dusk of a long day.

Gary put down his cigarette. He normally smoked only in his garage or on the back steps of the house, but the funeral had put a barrel of pressure on him, to the point that he felt he deserved to smoke inside. He stubbed the cigarette out in a brown porcelain ashtray with a deer perched on one edge. You could grab the little antlers to empty the discarded butts into a wastebasket.

The suitcase was coming apart at one corner where a brass nail was missing from the hinge. Gary moved it from the stool to the couch, holding it between his hands like a giant sandwich, then setting it gently behind a pillow so the contents wouldn't accidentally spill onto the floor.

As he lifted the lid, the smell of mildew or mothballs, or at least something ancient, escaped. The pictures were piled with no order, corners sticking out in every direction, heaped large upon small. It was obvious someone had shuffled the deck many times over the years, no doubt looking for an aunt or long-forgotten cousin. Most of the pictures had a kind of Civil War tinge to them, as if produced on tintype. Some were edged in a kind of black lace around the edges, no doubt a part of the printing process. On top was a picture of Dad and Grandpa, wearing overalls and standing in a field of maize. They looked like my brother. All Langstons have thick wavy hair. Grandpa Ray had died at ninety-two with the great wave totally white, but solidly in place. Dad was gone at seventy-six with only a trace of gray at the edges and the wave slightly thinned. I glanced at Gary. His wave was rumpled from worry, but unquestionably a gift from the two men in the picture.

Gary picked up each picture gingerly, examined it for a few seconds, then handed it to me. They were mostly family shots, except for one postcard. Gary stared at it, a stone structure with turret rooms at each corner that stretched four stories high, giving the building a castle effect, with steeply pitched roofs between the turrets. The building was set on a wide dirt street with a few trees and an old car, perhaps a Model A Ford, parked in the corner. Gary flipped the card in search of a description or at least a post office cancellation. In the upper left-hand corner it read, "Nickerly County Court House, 1911." There was no writing under the postmark.

Gary handed me the courthouse and picked up the next picture. It showed an older man, surrounded by family, posed in front of a frame farmhouse. The man had white hair and a snowy beard, uneven at the bottom as if trimmed infrequently. His waistcoat was buttoned at the collar and open down the front, gaping as it crossed his ample midsection.

"That must be Grandpa Aaron, the dunkard minister—Grandpa Ray's dad—the Langston who brought us all to Kansas from West Virginia," I remarked. "Do you see Grandpa?"

"What's a dunkard?" Gary asked.

"He baptized people in the river," I said. "He dunked them."

Gary was squinting at the picture, trying to discern family faces. "This must be Aaron's family. Here's Grandpa Ray, and these must be his sisters . . . great beauties," he said with a snicker. "But look here on the end. Look at that wavy hair. These are Aaron's kids, all lined up, with Grandpa Ray at one end, and this kid on the other end . . . must be Jay," Gary announced triumphantly. "This is him!"

The wavy-haired young man in the picture looked to be about twenty. He had a long ruddy face, with a smirk frozen at one corner of his mouth, as if he didn't really want to be in the picture.

"He looks like a wise guy," I remarked.

"Always in trouble," Gary added.

Near the bottom of the box, with only three or four pictures left to consider, we found proof of Jay's existence. The background of the photograph was a pasture, open and barren to the distant horizon. Two men were standing in thick clover, with nothing around them to distract from the stark reality of Ray and Jay Langston. Jay's arm was wrapped around his brother's shoulder. It must have been their last picture together.

Gary turned the photo over. Someone had written in small careful letters: RAY and JAY. Nothing else.

We stared at the picture for long minutes, trying to fathom how someone like Jay could simply drop off the face of the earth; how we had never even heard about this handsome man with his arm around Grandpa's shoulder. I had been duped to the end by my own father, by all of the Langstons—aunts, uncles, and cousins—who had kept the secret. I felt foolish.

"This courthouse postcard gives me an idea," I said to Gary. "Let's go to Nickerly. I'm sure this old courthouse has been torn down. But let's go find out about Jay."

"You mean about his life?" Gary said. "His birth certificate, things like that?"

"Sure," I replied. "What about this woman and the bad checks business? Surely somebody remembers. Court records. Maybe the county historical society, assuming they have one."

"When?" he asked.

"Now. Tomorrow. I have a few days before going back to New York. You're off work for Dad's funeral. Let's go tomorrow."

.   .   .

It was a warm drive to Nickerly. Sun heated the outside of the windows, but the insides were cold to touch, forming a kind of cocoon around my family memories. I let my mind flutter. The miles passed unnoticed. On a Kansas highway the lines are straight, fence posts mark the distance, and the prairie grass sparkles like the ocean. I wondered how many years it took before my metaphors reversed, when I started comparing the prairie to the ocean, which I had never even seen until I was twenty-five.

I wasn't really like the rest of the Langstons. I had moved away from Kansas, moved away from them. Gone soft. There was a hardness in my family, more like stone, that gave strength to the soul of the Langstons, an internal discipline that could be vengeful or spiteful, but that rarely showed itself.

There was only one occasion I could remember when my father's iron will was publicly displayed, and it related to his in-laws, the other side of the family. When my mother's father died, my mother and her four brothers and sisters set about the task of divvying up the family antiques. The one thing my mother wanted was the family piano, the one she had learned to play as a little girl, had practiced on for hours; the instrument that had given her dreams of other places, taking her off the farm and out of the cycle of rural life with its bleak promises. Mom was in her fifties at the time of her father's death. She wanted to retrieve those memories of hope. But her sister, a far less accomplished pianist, had the same dreams and wanted the piano too.

It turned out that similar disputes erupted among the other brothers and sisters, to the point that they couldn't agree on the dining table, the buggy in the barn, the fine china, the primitive paintings, and all of the linens and quilts that Grandma had made in her later years. They argued and fought about who would get what. For weeks they traded letters, then agreed to a meeting, where they argued again and hurled insults long forgotten, dredging up schoolboy conflicts from forty years before. In the end, one brother said, "OK. Call Jim Shockey, the auctioneer. Sell every damned thing. If you want it, buy it, and we'll split the money five ways. I'm tired of arguing." Then he stomped out of the house and never spoke to my parents again.

I went home for the auction, primarily because I wanted to bid on some board games, particularly a chinese checkers board with the marbles in a coffee can, that Granddad, Gary, and I had played on every Wednesday night.

I flew to Wichita, rented a car, and drove straight to the farm where Granddad's three hay wagons—rubber-wheeled flatbeds that carried hay stacked six bales high—were parked in the front yard, covered with tools, wire, nails, pots, pans, porcelain, ashtrays, birdbaths, household goods of every description, and carpentry vises and grips of every kind. The auctioneer was giving his rapid fire, beckoning to all buyers to please give two dollars for a porcelain bird that Grandma had painted. I walked over to Dad, who was talking to my old grade school principal.

"Hi, Dad," I said, gripping his hand. My dad smiled and said, "Well, look who's here. I thought you'd be here earlier."

"My plane stopped in Chicago," I said. "Lost an hour. Has everything sold?"

"No," Dad said, "we're just about to move into the house. This outside stuff is about all gone. Walk around. See if there's anything you want."

I had missed the board game. It sold with a "lot"—that's auctioneer talk for a group of unrelated items—in this case a pickle jar, a bag of rusty nails, a hand ax, and a horse bridle that draped over all the items to denote the boundary of the lot. It went for three dollars and fifty cents.

As we moved into the house, I could feel a little tension, if only because it was so crowded. All the brothers and sisters were there. A half dozen antique collectors were fidgeting in the front, eager to pick up some cheap furniture in the hope that few of these farmers knew the real value of the china cabinets with curved glass or the oak dressers with hand-carved legs. The auctioneer kept his eye on them. He would run up the price if he could. He was paid on commission, and besides, the family had made it clear they wanted high prices.

As fate would have it, bidding began first on the piano. The auctioneer's staccato voice began the arcane ritual of selling. "Gimme fifty. Here now fifty-five. Beautiful piano. All the kids got lessons on this piano. Now sixty. Now seventy. Who'll give me eighty? Eighty-five?" And so it went, so fast that it took my ears several minutes to adjust, to figure out what he was saying, to know the bidding level. The first round included several neighbors, people who wanted the piano for their kids, especially if they could pick it up for fifty bucks or so. But the collectors soon raised the price to over one hundred dollars and that knocked most people out of the bidding.

My dad was determined to buy the piano for Mom. He hadn't been able to give her too many luxuries in life. Even after twenty-five years of marriage, Mom's wedding ring was still the most expensive item he had ever given her. So Dad held back, waiting for the bidders to thin, waiting to get a little closer to the actual buying price.

But my mother's sister had the same idea. She didn't turn the bidding over to her husband, the way most farm wives would. She screamed out her first bid at two hundred twenty-five dollars. Dad had already bid once. When he heard her voice, he turned to confirm the source, then caught her eye. He saw determination and confrontation.

I was standing next to Mom and she grabbed my arm, seeing the train wreck coming, seeing the fierceness in her sister's eyes and the pain of unresolved differences; she knew a fearful contest was at hand. She murmured something I didn't fully catch, "No, Dad, no." But it was a sorrowful plea, as if she knew Dad had to do it.

The price started climbing, in twenty-five-dollar increments, past three hundred, until the last collector dropped out. They couldn't make any money at that price. But the auctioneer kept going, changing the increments to a hundred, knowing that he had family against family, and that was alright with him. One of these people would pay dearly, but all the brothers and sisters would gain. He didn't flinch from the task.

As they passed four hundred, everyone in the room began to turn their heads from Dad to my mom's sister. Everybody knew them of course, knew their relationship and their circumstances. My aunt's husband worked for a grain elevator, was college educated, and made a good salary. They lived about ninety miles from Abilene, so people didn't know exactly how well they lived. But most felt they were a lot better off than us. They knew my dad was a farmer, my mother rode the tractor to help out, and most of our property was rented. They knew our cash flow was suspect, and surely my dad couldn't go too high.

I thought about telling Dad I would loan him, or give him, some money. But the room was so crowded I couldn't figure out how to do it so no one would notice. Also, I had never seen Dad so determined, so driven. A look of challenge blazed in his eye. The neighbors in the room started to edge away from him. And then the bid passed six hundred.

My mom's sister began to waiver. She looked at her husband. He shook his head, realizing this bidding had gone far beyond price and reason. He wished she had dropped out long ago, but he also knew better than to argue. Then my mom started crying, and her sister just looked at her with contempt, perhaps for being the weak sister, perhaps because my dad had chosen this ground on which to fight, perhaps because she really wanted the piano. But it seemed to me that all legitimate motives had vanished at about two hundred dollars.

My dad got the piano for six hundred and fifty dollars. When the auctioneer pronounced the item sold, the house fell silent. It was as if everyone in the room realized that a family had just destroyed itself. Also, they saw my father as they never had before; gone was the easy-going neighbor who avoided all confrontation, who let things slip easily away.

My mom's sister stormed from the house, leading her husband by the hand, marched down the sandy road to their car, got in, and drove away. I didn't see them again for many years.

But then the bidding started on my granddad's desk, a beautiful nineteenth-century rolltop, handmade of oak. Granddad had always worked assiduously at his desk, a silent studious figure of my childhood, who warned us never to touch anything on the desk, nothing.

All three of my mom's brothers began bidding on the desk, gently trading stories between themselves of times when they had to explain their report cards to Granddad at that desk. But when the bidding got to three hundred dollars, their friendly demeanor dissolved into silence, then frustration with the system they had devised, as they realized the money wasn't as important as the memories, and they would likely lose both.

My father stood quietly until only two brothers were bidding, at five hundred dollars. Then he raised the bid to six hundred dollars. There was an explosion of silence. Everyone turned to look at my father, and they knew. This was no longer about buying family heirlooms. This was a challenge, born of years of frustration between the families, of slights never recognized or confronted, of insults real or imagined, of a proud man who had always been made to feel inferior by his in-laws, of a proud man who had never seen his wife given credit for sticking with him in hard times. This was an act of defiance, and my father would not be deterred.

I watched all of this with amazement, realizing for the first time how little I really knew about my parents, about my family, realizing that it is possible to live around people and not live with them, to not see the pain and anger that crowd a person's chest. Only my mother knew the rage that was propelling my father, and she held my arm tight. Out of her tears had come her own determination to stand by her husband no matter what. She changed families that day, as we all must, and took charge of her own.

My father bought the desk and the piano, loaded them separately into his truck and my brother's truck, and left. No one said goodbye. Dad and the desk arrived home first. Gary was a few blocks behind with the piano. Dad parked in front of the house and was untying the rope that secured the desk in the truck bed, when he glanced up to see that Gary was turning the corner near our house. But it looked like Gary might be taking the corner too fast. The truck tipped and looked like it might roll, but Gary wrestled the steering wheel around, narrowly missing the curb. Just as he straightened out, the piano moved. It broke the ropes tied to the tailgate, slid about three feet to the back of the truck and never stopped. As it hit the pavement, it splintered into a thousand pieces. The black enamel was so old and dry that it just disintegrated; the wires sprang loose from every mooring and flew up into the yard; the keyboard snapped apart, sending black and white keys all over the street. Mom and Dad ran to where the piano hit the pavement. Nothing was there, not one piece of enough bulk to pick up. The piano had simply vanished.

Mom and Dad held each other, but they didn't say a word. They just turned and walked back to the house. As they passed the truck, Gary just shook his head.

"Clean it up," Dad said, "then come help me with the desk."

Dad wanted to put the desk in the attic, for reasons that escaped me at the time, but it was too big for the narrow winding steps to the attic. So he rigged two ropes through an attic window in the back of the house, and we raised the desk in three pieces up the side of the house and in the attic window. We put the pieces together in the attic, which wasn't a finished room. The ceiling rafters were bare, with thousands of roofing nails sticking through from the shingles. Several boards had been laid over the floor joists in the center of the attic, so the floor was only four or five feet wide. It was covered with dirt. We didn't talk much during the desk operation, except to warn each other not to step off the floorboards or we would go through the living room ceiling. As we started down the attic steps, Dad turned and said, "I never want to see that thing again."

When Dad died nearly thirty years later, the desk was falling apart, but I dusted it off and shipped it to New York, where I had it refurbished for about a thousand dollars. As my brother and I drove to Nickerly, we recounted the story of the desk and the piano, perhaps because we suspected we might encounter a similar story of family defiance, or at least one of hidden motivations we didn't clearly understand.

Interstate 70 races through Kansas as straight as an airport runway, with very little to distract one's attention. Even with the passage of countless storms, the trees seemed familiar from past trips; the same barns, faded and battered, still sheltered cattle and stacks of hay. At a distance, the small towns of Kansas look like clumps of trees, definable on all sides, surrounded by the prairie. From the interstate, Nickerly has one distinguishing quality, a spire that rises so far above the trees that it looks like a rocket, set on top of yellow Kansas limestone.

"Do you suppose that's the courthouse?" I asked Gary as we approached the town. "The one in our postcard? This must be it."

"I doubt it," Gary said. "That was 1911. Surely it's been torn down by now, or had a big fire. Most of those old buildings have burned down, even if the walls were stone."

We turned off the highway, moved down the off-ramp, turned left under the overpass, and landed right on the main street of Nickerly. It was wide, nearly twice as wide as most small-town streets, and spread out before us, with nothing to block the view at the other end. The street ran to infinity, out the other end of town, through the rye grass, and just kept going. On both sides of the road for less than a mile, the town of Nickerly was lined up like a string of limestone cereal boxes. And at the head of the parade stood the first building in town, a grand gathering of spires and steeples on top of several four-story turrets, with narrow roofs implying courtyards and a Victorian past of majestic strength. It took my breath away. And before I could even ask what it might be, Gary pointed to a stone marker in the yard that said simply "Nickerly."

The town itself was identifiable at a glance, a classic agricultural gathering where one general store had led to another until a main street was formed. Limestone gave this town a rather grand appearance, but the content reflected the necessities of farm life: a hardware store, two elevators to store and sell the crops, a couple of grocers, three banks, a couple of doctors and dentists, assorted insurance agencies, a high school, and enough wood frame houses for maybe three thousand people. But the jewel of the community had to be the courthouse.

Gary pulled up to the curb. There were no other cars around. We got out, stretched, took our coats out of the backseat to fight the chill, and just took a look around. Nothing moved. No cars. No people. Then down the block someone emerged from what must have been the bank. In most small towns there were usually at least three banks guarding the main intersection, often with three or four round concrete steps leading to a heavy oak door. The quiet of Nickerly's main street had a weight to it, as if burdened with history and customs of the past.

"Let's go find the county courtroom," I said. "Finding a court case with our uncle's name on it may take some time."

"Maybe someone will remember us," Gary said.

Gary had never left Kansas. He still lived by the murmurs of the land, where people remember families and places long after they have gone. Land was known as "places," the Romberger Place, for example, even though the Rombergers hadn't lived there in years. It was never clear to me what a family had to do to establish their name on a place. Certainly they had to own it, but they also had to stay at least a couple of generations, have kids that moved through the public school system, and have some incident that bonded the family to the land. We didn't have a Langston Place because we never owned land, but there might be one in Nickerly, where Great-Grandpa Aaron had owned a farm less than a dozen miles from the Nickerly Courthouse.

"I don't think we'll be remembered," I said.

On the first floor, someone had made a halfhearted attempt at modernization, probably in the 1950s, putting veneered mahogany wall paneling in all of the offices and magazine racks in the hallway with Xeroxed copies of conservation bulletins on the ten best ways to fight beetle grubs. A side staircase with worn swayback steps led to a three-story wall of heavy mahogany and a small sign reading: Clerk of the Court. We climbed to the first landing, turned up the second staircase, and were presented with a view directly into the courtroom: bench seats, walnut paneled walls, brightly polished tables for the defendants, wood captain's chairs for the jury, and a raised pulpit for the presiding judge. I stopped to marvel. The whole place looked like a movie set.

The courtroom was dark, but a light shined from the room labeled

Clerk. We turned the old brass doorknob, pushed our heads in first, and confronted a high counter that was clearly designed to keep people at bay. On the far side of the room, well protected by the counter and four desks behind it, sat Mildred Oaks, pale from too many years in the records room, respectably outfitted in a plaid wool skirt, beige blouse, and a brooch with the words inscribed: Order of the Eastern Star. She didn't look up. We took off our coats and hung them on the rack. She frowned, obviously concerned about our presumptuousness, and asked if she could help us.

Gary was getting excited. He poured out our story and asked about any court records that might mention a Langston. She shook her head. Gary asked if she had ever heard of the Langstons. "No," she said.

"I can give you the calendars," she said, obviously reluctant to engage in a discussion of family history. "That's about all I can do." She disappeared into a back room, presumably to retrieve the calendars. She emerged with a large, worn leather-bound book, so big that she cradled it in her arms and the edges went from shoulder to shoulder. "You might look through here," she said.

I noticed a computer on her desk. "Any chance you would have old court cases on computer?" I asked.

"I'm starting," she said a little defensively, "but I'm only back to 1984."

Gary shoved the calendar book across the counter and set it on a table in the corner. We sat down side by side, ready to begin our investigation. He opened the first page, and we stared at a beautiful script handwriting, a recording of every trial ever held in the Nickerly courthouse. First came the name of the prosecutor, usually the State of Kansas, then the names of the defendants. The date of the trial and number of the case were listed on the far right. The first page was yesterday. We started flipping back toward the 1920s.

As the years flashed by, it seemed less and less likely that we would find our name. Even if it were there, we might read right past it. 1911: We moved through the pages more slowly, starting in December. Then it popped out at us, almost as soon as we turned the page, like a neon sign blinking in a Las Vegas night: *The State of Kansas vs. Jay Langston, et al.*, November 20, 1911, 18486.

Gary turned to Mrs. Oaks, who had resumed work at her corner desk.

"Can we see the transcripts of the trial?"

She looked up and grumbled, "If we have them."

She emerged from the back filing room with four bundles of papers, folded in thirds, covered with dusty brown paper jackets, and bound with narrow gray ribbons. We unwrapped them carefully, and the names Jay Langston, Margaret Chambers, and W. W. McArdle appeared under the large printed heading: Arrest Record. Nickerly County, Kansas.

CHAPTER ONE

1911

Margaret Chambers burst out the front door and practically flew down the stone steps of the College of Emporia. She was clutched by a sudden, childish desire to twirl in circles, flinging her arms out from her sides and whooping loudly, but she caught herself, slowed her pace, and judiciously moved away from the College building. She had done it. She had taken her last test to become a teacher. She was through.

Margaret turned and walked past the small white wooden houses that framed the college grounds. About halfway down the block she came to the Wickham Lumber Yard bench, which had been placed along the curb as a rest stop for students, and which gave all visitors to the College a solid hint about where to buy their lumber and hardware needs. The bench was an advertisement. Many young people came to Emporia to attend the College, and their parents comprised an expanding market of customers who could take home a load of lumber or at least a barrel of nails for the year ahead. The Wickham Lumber Yard got good business from these visitors, selling them har-

nesses and yokes for teams of horses and buggies. The new automobiles gave this venture an uncertain future, but it still took horses to till
the fields and bring in the crops, and many people thought automobiles were simply a gadget for the rich anyway. Several of Wickham's
new customers had automobiles and horses, and remarked how much
they appreciated the new benches near the College of Emporia.

Margaret slipped onto the Wickham bench and took a deep breath
of the spring evening. It was her first chance to relax and think of
her future, of starting a new school year in Nickerly County, of returning to live with her family, especially her older sister Ileen who had
never left home, but who wrote her religiously for the two years it took
to get the teaching degree. It was a satisfying feeling, warm and secure,
to know that she had pioneered a new family achievement, a college
education. Emporia wasn't a four-year college, but two years were more
than enough to teach, and not many women had accomplished that.
Indeed, there were only three women among the fifty-seven students
at the College. And of the three or four county teachers she had met
in Nickerly, none had been to college. Most teachers had never even
graduated from high school, but had been picked by local township
supervisors for the job and given a certificate. Margaret closed her
eyese and relaxed, glad that she had worn her black jacket because it
picked up the remaining sun and warmed her shoulders.

There were the normal sounds of evening activity, a carriage down
the street rambling over the cobblestones and kicking up dust, two students chattering as they walked away from her toward the college. She
thought she recognized them but didn't care enough to really look.
Birds seemed to be all around her, darting into the branches, bouncing under the spirea bushes. That rustle in the shrubs must have been
a squirrel. They were reassuring sounds, the noise of a secure world
that suited Margaret like a handmade quilt in which every familiar
patch had been hand stitched, known by its source, loved for its memories.

When someone's hand appeared over her left shoulder, it barely registered on her mind, and it didn't frighten her. She had heard footsteps behind her, but that was normal on the main path between town and college. She gave a slight start when the hand gently covered her mouth, so gently she thought it was Martin, from math class, who was always kidding her, tapping her on one shoulder and darting around the other, but why didn't he say anything? She turned her head, innocently expecting the hand to be withdrawn with a greeting from Martin. But the fingers clasped more tightly, pulling her head back against a waistcoat. When she tried to twist her head away, a brass button dug into her cheek, hurting her. Even then, she was angry but not afraid. Some friend had gone too far.

There was no experience in Margaret's life for rough treatment, intentional or not. She had never known hostility, except perhaps when the grades were posted and she made superiors in every course. Then a few of the boys chided her about being "the brain," and she could see that they were jealous. Women were not attacked, certainly not molested. Rape was so unthinkable as to be unthinkable. Margaret had never been with a man, but she had kissed Ed Garvey Jr. the night before she left for college, and sometimes three or four girls would gather in her room to laugh and talk about school and boys and what it must be like to be married. From those meandering sessions she had learned about sex, or at least had listened to her friends' stories, many of which sounded like scenes from romantic novels rather than actual life experiences. From these social discussions Margaret had pieced together the basic physical aspects of love. But for her, love was still a synthetic vision of a couple walking in gardens of fragrant roses and honeysuckle. She dreamed of holding hands and expressing undying devotion, pledging to help each other and to share lives. She never really understood the word "lust," but she knew that sometimes her own body would feel different, like the night she kissed Ed Garvey and she felt light-headed, hot as if she might perspire, but not sure why. Her friends assured her that boys felt the same way, but they never mentioned that boys could be mean about it.

Margaret knew something was wrong because the person behind her never said a word, and there was a faint smell of something on his hand, maybe kerosene or ink. She could feel the rough weave of his coat scrape against her face. She tried to scream. Then another hand rushed to her throat, discovered the top button of her jacket loosened as she had left it, and moved down to force the second button through the eye of her blouse. The hand forced its way under her blouse, moving down. Then the fingers were on her breast, slipping beneath her brassiere, and then pulling out, one hand hitting her throat as the other left her mouth. She gasped for air. There was a terrible moment of confusion when she simply didn't realize what had happened. Everything was a blur. Her head was spinning, and she felt weak in her arms and legs. Coughing, she grabbed her skirt as she fell off the bench. She knew she had to run, but her legs just buckled as she tumbled forward. She struggled to her feet and stumbled forward onto the porch of the closest house. The door opened, and a porch light came on. Dusk must have arrived while she was dreaming. It was a woman's voice speaking, and Margaret could not see her, did not know her, but fell into her arms crying, "Help me, help me."

Mrs. Olsen had seen almost every girl attending the College of Emporia as they walked by her house each day. She said hello, and occasionally some girls would stop to talk. Usually lonely, they told her about where they were from and how much they missed their parents. She had seen Margaret before, so pretty with her sandy red curls that seemed to flow out of the ribbons, and her strong hands with long fingers. Mrs. Olsen had noticed her often because she was tall, at least in this community, and at five feet seven inches, usually could be seen bobbing above the other girls. She wore the standard black or gray skirt that almost touched the ground, flared over several petticoats, black lace shoes that covered her ankles, and a white blouse with starched collar that gave her a priestly look. There was little unusual about this costume, except for the fit. Her outer jacket was pulled tight and buttoned from throat to waist, a small waist no doubt accentuated by a corset and exaggerated by the size of her bust. With so many layers of clothes, almost all contours of the body were minimized, but the dimensions of Margaret's chest and waist were so in conflict that not even the most pious of men could resist a calculating glance, a moment of wonder that such a waist could hold so much above.

Margaret's nose was a little too straight and too long for most people to call her cute, a favorite term of the time, but Mrs. Olsen thought her a handsome girl anyway. She helped Margaret onto the couch.

"What's your name?" she asked.

"Margaret Chambers," she stammered.

"What happened?" Mrs. Olsen asked. "Did somebody hurt you?"

She asked the question in the most general way, not accusatory, and not reflecting any particular fear that might be lingering in the street. There was none. There was no fear of other human beings, of being robbed or beaten or raped, because those things simply did not happen. Rather, fear was derivative of natural phenomena, a horse that veered and kicked a pedestrian, a windstorm that shattered windows or felled a tree, one of those new cars that people seemed to have trouble controlling, or a rabid animal that might have wandered in from the nearby fields.

But Margaret was not thinking of any of those things. Her mind was jumbled, fearful but not understanding, knowing she had been violated but not sure how. The idea of a rough arm scratching her cheek, a hand over her mouth, a hand grabbing her, almost like in a fight, was so vulgar, so crude. She began to shudder at the thought, a stranger's hand had touched her breast, had so quickly invaded the sanctity of her clothing. She remembered laying them out this morning, when she was so happy—her beautiful lace petticoat that her mother had made, the finely starched blouse that she had pressed herself by heating the iron in the fireplace. She liked ironing because the fire was warm, and the result of her work left such a straight edge, such a fine orderly garment for presenting herself to the world. It seemed impossible that such a proper form could be so soiled.

She instinctively knew that she could not talk about it, indeed must never mention it to anyone. It was so shameful that anyone would pick her for violation. Her friends talked of boys stealing a glance at her ankles, and her best friends sometimes whispered that she had a wonderful figure. She could never answer the inevitable question—why her?—and did not want to. Certainly not to Mrs. Olsen. This kindly lady clearly had no idea what happened and would probably find Margaret's explanation hard to believe. Margaret suddenly realized that no one would ever see this boy, or at least she assumed he was a boy, surely no adult would do such a horrible thing. She knew instinctively this event could only reflect poorly on her, indicating some weakness that must have made her a victim, or even incite gossip that she had enticed the man, or that she had a secret lover. She almost gagged at the thought, clutching her throat, and tightening her stomach to steel herself against the possibility of sickness.

"Thank you," Margaret said without answering Mrs. Olsen's question. "I must go. I just saw something and it scared me. Thank you for helping me."

"My husband will be home soon," Mrs. Olsen said. "I'll have him walk you back to school."

"No," Margaret said. "Please. I'll be all right."

Margaret stood to test her legs, holding first to the arm of her chair, then to Mrs. Olsen's arm, realizing by the feel of her heavy coat that Mrs. Olsen must have been leaving the house as the attack occurred.

"It was just shadows," Margaret said, composing herself, and testing Mrs. Olsen again.

As if reading her mind, Mrs. Olsen said, "I didn't see anything dear, but in these times it could have been anything. Sometimes just the spirea and barberry bushes can be frightening. Are you sure you're all right?"

"Yes. Thank you," Margaret said as she pulled the door open, pushed the screen, and moved out to the porch. The Wickham Lumber Yard bench was just below the steps, empty and unthreatening, just a few pieces of wood on this now-empty street. She wondered if anyone else had seen what happened. She walked down the steps and started back to her room, carrying a stain on her breast that she could still feel, and the nudging of a guilt that she was somehow responsible. She hurried down the sidewalk, desperate for the security and privacy of her room.

Margaret Chambers had always wanted to be a schoolteacher. She thought often of that day, at age eleven, when she first saw the new Sunnyside School, a one-room building erected on a foundation of rough-cut timbers, that had been dragged to its site near Nickerly by a team of twelve horses. The school had been built on the Chambers farm, where Margaret's father had organized the neighbors and parents from the surrounding area to build their own school. Land for the school had been donated by the Murphys and accepted even though it was located in a neighboring township. The location was central to the four or five families that could be expected to send children to the school and within two or three miles, a reasonable walking distance, of every family. Often four or five schools would be located within three or four miles of each other, if that's how the family farms were situated.

Most of the adults and all of the children in Nickerly turned out to see the new school pulled to its permanent site. People began arriving at the Chambers farm on foot and on horseback in the early afternoon, ready to help move the school, or just to see the team of horses hitched to the building. As the Chambers team of six horses began their strain against the harness, their haunches settling down to give their hind legs traction, the small building began to move on its foundation, a pair of sleighlike runners. The timbers running down either side of the structure began to rise in the front, near the source of the pull, and drop in the back as the weight of the building shifted. Creaking sounds emanated from the freshly cut, green-wood joints, which slowly grasped each other in a wooden handshake that would never come apart. Then the new school started its forward motion, with Margaret's father leading the team in a slow but steady pace. The entire community walked alongside, watching the dirt and sand on the road eat away at the runners, until they had lost their round shape, and then they were flat on the bottom, smooth as glass, and wearing themselves thinner by the mile. Children began to speculate on whether they would last for the three-mile trip to the school site.

The building reached its permanent home in Murphy's pasture, a one-acre parcel donated by Sean Murphy, no doubt because he had six children about to reach school age, and because his pasture bordered the main county road from Nickerly to Lincoln. The school would be accessible to residents of Nickerly, as well as the dozens of small farms in the county. But there would be only seventeen students in the school, with at least one in every grade but sixth, which Margaret's mother attributed to the drought twelve years earlier when everyone was too depressed or too sick to have babies.

With the building secured by stakes driven through the ends of the foundation runners and into the ground, the men collected stones and rocks from the pasture and placed them under either end of the building, forming a loose foundation to catch the building if it settled and closing the underside of the school to possums, coons, and small children. Lastly, Ed Garvey's wagon arrived with the benches. Garvey operated the flour mill on the Saline River and was therefore the principal source of cash for Nickerly County crops. The mill was a congregation point for farmers, who pulled their wagons up to the bins, unloaded the wheat that had been gathered from the threshing machines, and received their pay in a small office behind the counting room. For many farmers, the mill was their major source of sustenance: flour. Every couple of weeks, most farmers would bring a load of corn or wheat from their storage bins and trade it at the mill for two 48-pound sacks of flour, which would supply bread, cakes, pies, and pancakes for several days. Ed Garvey held forth in the counting room of the mill every day, greeting the farmers as they came in, writing down their delivery, then walking outside for a visual inspection of the wagons, primarily to make sure the wheat wasn't wet or diseased by fungus. Most of the time, Ed sat at a square table in the middle of the counting room. Twelve-foot benches known as Garvey Benches stretched along two walls. Fully loaded, the benches might hold six or eight farmers lingering after their payments long enough for a discussion of the weather or a neighbor's decision to try growing oats, a seemingly foolish move when wheat had done just fine for the last thirty years. Whatever the discussion, everyone recognized the quality of Garvey's benches, wider than most because they were half a tree trunk, flat on the sitting side with the bark still on the underside. When Ed Garvey pulled into the school yard with his donation to the school, four new benches for the students, a cheer went up from the crowd of mothers who recognized the organization and rectitude that benches brought to a school. The challenge, of course, would be to make the students sit on them.

Mrs. Garvey, Ed's wife and the schoolteacher for as long as anyone could remember, beamed as the new benches were put in place. She had taught Nickerly students in the back of Tilden's dry goods store for seven years, or as long as it took to get Ed Jr. through at least the ninth and tenth grades, and into his father's business. She had intended to quit teaching after Ed Jr.'s schooling ended, but she stayed on a few more years. Now she stood at the front door of the new schoolhouse, arms crossed, overseeing every ounce of activity; directing the location of the benches; seeing that the shutters were level on the windows; and hanging the yellowed roll-down chart of the alphabet, the first building block of a Nickerly education.

Margaret, even at age eleven the tallest girl among her friends, stood in a circle of her schoolmates to watch these final touches being applied to a school that would be hers, with a name, Sunnyside, that she could call her own. The new school gave a feeling of independence to Margaret. It was a separate building, almost like a home, that she would share with other children away from the adult world. It was also the private domain of Margaret's idol, Mrs. Garvey, a figure of fortress-like qualities. She was a strong woman who knew the strange world of adults and thrived in it. She was independent. Margaret could never imagine Mrs. Garvey crying, as her mother often did. Margaret wanted to be just like Mrs. Garvey, and at age eleven she knew that this school would be the ticket. And that's what Margaret made of it. Often she walked home with Mrs. Garvey after school. They talked of distant places. After Margaret discovered that the Garveys had been to Wichita, she started asking her teacher about other cities. Her schoolbooks pictured a vastly different life in places like New York and Washington, where business wealth and political power had created a class of people that Margaret's father called, simply, "the rich." Mrs. Garvey had also been to Kansas City, and she told Margaret about hospitals and schools where thousands of people lived in small areas. It was Mrs. Garvey who first mentioned college, and Margaret took to the idea immediately.

In all those years of dreaming about getting away from Nickerly, it never dawned on Margaret that after going away, she might want to come back. But now she was doing just that. Mrs. Garvey had written to Margaret at the College of Emporia, informing her of her plans to leave Sunnyside and stay home with Ed and Ed Jr., who was just taking over the mill. Mrs. Garvey suggested to Margaret that she might want to come home and teach at Sunnyside. After the school board wrote to formally offer Margaret Mrs. Garvey's position, Margaret wrote her mother that she was coming home to teach. She had not seen the world, but she had met new friends from other towns in Kansas, and teaching would allow her to visit them in the summer and on holidays. She would actually have a job and earn her own money, money that could be used for all sorts of new plans. Going home seemed like the logical next step.

CHAPTER TWO

Jay Langston poked his brother, Ray, winked, jerked his thumb over his shoulder to signal a departure, then slid out of the last row of the Nickerly First Presbyterian Church with Ray following close behind. They knew their father could see them, but they also knew he was too wound up to stop his sermon. He would never disrupt the service to reprimand the boys.

It was spring and the front door of the church had been left wide open, an invitation to the fresh honeysuckle scents of the yard and the yellow splashes of forsythia along the side of the building. The boys slipped practically unnoticed out the front door as their father's voice rose in anxious pleading: "Oh, Lord, stop us from our worldly sins. Let our eyes rise to the golden glow of the sun and recognize the warmth of God's love. For while He forgives us, He will be a harsh judge of our sins. God will take his vengeance on those who dwell on worldly goods. He lifts our spirit and accepts our faith. He gives us hope and kindness. He leadeth us down the paths of righteousness. And I beseech you, do not turn away from these gifts. Do not seek pleasure

in the here and now, but seek your rewards in heaven. Live according to the gospel, a life of work and sacrifice that is its own reward."

Aaron's voice was warming to the task, rising but deep in tone, coming from his plentiful belly and emerging with a raspy tinge as the
syllables passed through the long white beard that seemed to hang
from various points on his face, as if stuck on by a schoolgirl using paste
and cotton balls. When the Reverend Aaron was in full throat, the
beard seemed to fill out, to puff up and take on a certain gravity as
he continued, "Just as God punished the enemies of righteousness,
so will He punish us, for all things are unto God, and He will take
the measure of our lives."

Aaron talked of love, but his God was a fearful force that measured and punished, and manifested himself more often in lightning
and thunder than in the shasta daisies that swayed easily among the
rye grass outside the church. Ray and Jay stood under a window, where
they could hear their father as clearly as if they were inside. The sun
brightened their faces and felt especially warm on the scar that creased
Jay's chin.

The First Presbyterian was their home church, but they didn't go
there often because the Reverend Aaron only preached there when the
regular minister was out of town. Usually, Aaron preached where there
were no walls, in a farmer's yard or along the banks of the Saline River,
where the "sacred waters flow, and the Spirit of the Lord receives all
those who accept Him as their personal Lord and Savior." He had
been raised a Quaker by his immigrant parents in West Virginia, but
after service in the Civil War, he migrated to Kansas and adopted
the church known as Church of the Brethren. Aaron had grown into
the ministry, working on various farms, attending church regularly,
and eventually being coaxed into giving sermons or Bible readings
when his family hosted a church service. He had watched Stonewall
Jackson ride through the ranks of his troops, beaten, tired, and torn by

the ravages of defeat and hunger. But the general's head was always high and proud. That's the way Aaron preached. And soon he was in great demand throughout the county.

Like many Church of the Brethren ministers, the Reverend Aaron was a dunkard. He baptized new members into the church by "dunking" them in the Saline River, a quite literal translation from the Bible's rite of baptism. Aaron's baptismal services were widely attended, often by non-parishioners who just came to see the spectacle.

In the image of Saint Peter himself, Aaron would walk from his carriage at the appointed time, fling his black overcoat to a nearby member of his family, and stride into the Saline River in a white robe, his arms outstretched, palms upward, preaching as he went. People crowded down to the water's edge. As Aaron reached the middle of the stream, he would turn and shout out his greeting: "Gather all ye sinners, for we are here to praise the Lord." And so the sermon would begin, winding its way through the Bible, into the wheat fields of Lincoln County, through the hearts and heathen souls of all those gathered, and leading to but one conclusion: the need for redemption through baptism.

After about an hour, Aaron would announce that on this Sunday, the children of at least one family in the community had reached the age of thirteen and had accepted Jesus Christ as their personal Savior. The children, usually two or three in number, would be led to the center of the river where the water was about three feet deep, shallow enough that Aaron could always keep his balance and his composure, but the children were gurgling in waves up to their chins and scared to death that drowning might be their first taste of eternal damnation.

Ray and Jay had only witnessed one disastrous baptism. Old John Finger was a brute of a farmer who was dying of internal forces widely believed to be whiskey-related. Old John saw his last days as a fear-

ful reckoning and went about the county paying off debts and apol-
ogizing to a neighbor whose dog he had killed years before for eating chicken eggs. When he stopped the Reverend Aaron in his corn
field and asked if he could be baptized, the Reverend was delighted,
seizing this opportunity to capture a soul long considered lost to the
saving arms of Christ. Aaron arranged for a baptismal ceremony that
very Sunday and waded into the muddy waters of the Saline fully
expecting to emerge with another dweller in the house of the Lord.
But when Aaron put his right hand behind Farmer Finger's back,
and his left hand, with a towel, over Mr. Finger's nose, and began to
lower him into the saving waters of the Saline, he failed to account
for Mr. Finger's sizable posterior, which shifted the combined weight
of their bodily twosome much lower than expected. As Aaron shouted,
"In the name of the Father, the Son, and the Holy Ghost, I baptize
thee, John, . . ." Old John Finger, so overwhelmed by all this transformation in his life, decided to actually give himself to the Lord, so
he simply dropped his behind, let his legs float free, and began bliss-
fully slipping into the loving arms of God, if not the supporting arms
of Reverend Aaron. Aaron shouted, "God," in a not entirely godly way.
His front foot, which was braced for the lowering, slowly slid along
the bottom of the Saline, and Aaron was suddenly on top of old John
Finger in four feet of water. Old John soon realized that some snag
had occurred in the process and began kicking wildly, just as three
members of the congregation, including Ray and Jay, rushed into the
water to help right the fallen angels.

Aaron, ever the trooper and always protective of the dignity of the
Lord, struggled to his feet, pulled down his muddied robes, and prepared to perform the dunking again, presumably following the rule
that a baptismal opportunity should never be allowed to slip away. But
Old John Finger was coughing, and sputtering, and scrambling
directly for the bank. He reached the shore, stomped to his team of

horses, climbed up on the buckboard, and headed for home. The Reverend Aaron, not wanting to shortchange either John Finger or the Lord, proclaimed that the baptism would be repeated next Sunday. Unfortunately, John Finger died that week. The Reverend Aaron preached wildly at his funeral of the great and benevolent life of this humble man, repeating several times that the baptismal performed the previous week, in spite of its somewhat abrupt execution, was nevertheless valid and that Mr. John Finger could expect all the heavenly rewards to which he was entitled.

Being a preacher in those years before World War I was not a particularly profitable pastime. The First Presbyterian minister, for example, was actually a circuit minister from Ellsworth who went from church to church according to a monthly schedule. He depended on the "love offerings" of the morning congregation for his cash rewards and the benevolence of individual parishioners for food and clothing. Farm families accepted many general obligations of life, among them the care and feeding of their minister. Every week at least one family was designated by the church to prepare a dinner for the minister. Most ministers ate pretty well, if not to their own taste. But their lives belonged to their flock, which set all the rules. The first rule was: A preacher could not live better than the poorest of his congregation. If a home was provided for the minister, it was usually a humble house, positioned close to the church, and seen by the community as theirs, not the minister's. It was a life beholden to the community, at a time when any luxury was an extravagance not to be tolerated by a minister of God.

The Reverend Aaron Langston avoided this servitude, and gave himself and his family a high degree of independence, by also being a farmer. He owned land just a few miles outside Nickerly, and raised his two sons and four daughters as farmers, as God-fearing members of the community, and as righteous observants of the societal restrictions of the church, not necessarily in that order. This combination of evangelism and farming resulted in a rather exalted position for the Reverend Aaron because he had his own source of income, and therefore in the minds of many, a special stature with the Lord. It was also true that baptisms and weddings—the two great acts in Aaron's repertoire—were genuine crowd pleasers. So the Langstons were a part of everybody's celebration, and they were well liked, in spite of the fact that Jay had once burned a neighbor's barn and was generally thought to be touched by the devil.

In addition, Aaron's wife, Ivy, was revered as the embodiment of her faith. She was a plain and sober woman, with a moon face that carried the farm wife's insignia—red cheeks and a sunburned chin underneath a bright white forehead protected by a bonnet. Always a bonnet. Black for church, calico with light blue flowers for working in the garden or the fields. Ivy's hair was pulled back, twisted in a tight bob, and knotted in place with a small black ribbon and a stick pin. Her shoes were plain with eight eyes for laces, one black pair for Sunday, and one brown pair for working in the fields. Both pairs had served long and well in the limited vineyards of her life.

Ivy Langston didn't smile much because she did not recognize or appreciate the ironies of life. When she did chance upon a humorous comment, she usually mistook it for derision or irreverence, two qualities she had worked hard to eliminate from her life. Her four daughters made her smile, for they were taller and prettier than their mother and it made Ivy proud. Her sons, on the other hand, tormented her. They always seemed on the verge of bringing shame to the family. Sneaking out of church, for example, was a mortal shame to her. But since Ray and Jay were in their twenties, and since they had been escaping their father's sermons for years, Ivy had just about determined that their souls were already lost to God's high standards.

When Ray and Jay were boys, she had sent Aaron for a switch several times to "tan their behinds" for disobeying the commands of the house. The boys soon learned to avoid her presence except in the most benign of circumstances. Sometimes Ray wished he could lay his head in his mother's lap, the way the girls did, but he had long since concluded that the accompanying lecture on the rightness of God's teachings was too high a price.

As Ray and Jay ambled away from the Presbyterian church that Sunday to investigate several Model As parked under a pair of cottonwood trees, Ray wondered why Jay had such a streak of orneriness in him. It was Jay who always wanted to sneak out of church during their father's sermon. It was Jay who always got them in trouble. When they were younger, their father would warn the boys to sit down in the hay wagon in case the horses became skittish. Jay always stood up. Or he would wait beside the road, pretending to be preoccupied with a flower until the team was moving, and then he would run and jump on the wagon. It was just such a move that gave Jay his slightly sinister physical appearance in later life. He had jumped for the wagon, misjudged the speed of the horses, and hit the ground, cutting a deep gash on his chin.

"I hear they hired Margaret Chambers to be the new schoolteacher," Jay said. "She was just behind us in school." Ray didn't respond.

"Three or four years," Jay continued. "I'm twenty-two and you're twenty-four. She can't be more than eighteen. Not much of a job anyway." Ray was quiet.

"She's a college girl now," Jay said, letting the scorn sound in his voice. College was too expensive, too far away, and too frivolous for serious people. Hard work provides the currency of life, and college was a detour, even a dodge from the reality of raising a family, life's most important endeavor. That's why so many girls around Nickerly started their families with a marriage at age thirteen or fourteen, hopefully to a young man about to take over his father's farm. It was not unusual for the boys of Nickerly to turn thirty-five, still unmarried, still working on their father's farm, and probably still virginal as well.

"You know, Ray, I think it's time for me to leave the farm," Jay said, switching subjects. "I don't like it. You're the farmer in the family. And Dad's got four girls to marry off. I'm going to Salina and get a job . . . maybe not 'til after the summer."

But Ray was still focused on Jay's earlier comments. "Well, I may just call on Margaret Chambers," he said quietly.

Jay was startled and stole a questioning look at his brother.

"Go ahead," Jay said, "but just remember her mother."

"What about her mother?"

"I hear that Margaret is hard to get along with," Jay said. "Independent. She once talked back to Judd Sexton. Refused to step aside for him in the general store, and then announced that she was first in line."

"What about her mother?" Ray asked again.

"Something happened over at the Haney place during their shivaree," Jay said. "You weren't there. Must have been ten years ago."

"What happened?" Ray asked. "I'm sure I was there."

"No, you weren't there, or you would remember," Jay said. "Nobody ever talked about it afterward, but I remember. While we were standing out in the yard, waiting for the Haneys to come out, Mary Chambers was in the bushes with Johnny Harwood. I don't know what they were doing. But Mary was married to John Chambers. And John Chambers caught them, grabbed Mary by the arm, and marched her right out of there. I was sort of hanging back in the crowd, beating my dishpan with that big ladling spoon Mom has, when the Chambers came charging through the dark. I saw Johnny Harwood head into the shrubs down by the barn, and I figured he hightailed it for home. He was just lucky that it was a wedding celebration and John Chambers didn't have a gun."

"I never heard that story before," Ray said.

Everyone liked a shivaree because it was a little daring, and one of the few community events with sexual overtones, not that they were ever talked about, of course. Ray didn't really know how shivarees got started, or what set of traditions they were based on. But the rituals were prescribed, and seldom varied, making a community shivaree almost as anticipated as the wedding itself.

Usually, the shivaree occurred within weeks of the wedding, when the marital experience was still fresh enough that most couples were assumed to be spending every night in sexual exploration. The arrangements were always the same: the community would gather around the newlyweds' home about nine o'clock, after it was dark and most couples were in bed. Then everyone would charge onto the porch, yelling and beating on pots and pans. The newlyweds would be caught in bed, traipse downstairs in their nightgowns, open the door to check on the commotion, and be surprised by all their neighbors.

Of course, they weren't really surprised, because the shivaree was as much a part of any farm wedding ceremony as the cake itself. And it had to be endured. Indeed, one young couple refused to come downstairs for their shivaree, preferring to stay hidden under their covers until their neighbors grew tired of beating on their pans, and their kids started crying because nobody came out of the house. After about an hour of grumbling about bad sports, the neighbors left, but the newlyweds were never treated the same again. Years later when the farmer in question became ill and couldn't put up his hay crop, a couple of neighbors suggested that the community come to their aid. A date was set for the haying, and no one showed up, not one soul, even the two farmers who first proposed the help. No shivaree, no help. People did not forget or forgive easily in Nickerly County.

At the Haneys' shivaree, the young couple fulfilled all their obligations. First the young husband brought a wheelbarrow out from behind the porch, where he had stashed it for this very purpose, helped his wife into it, still in her nightgown, and led a procession of all the visiting neighbors around the farmyard. It was a wonderful celebration, with everyone laughing and shouting, the men being the most excited because the young bride's nightgown exposed more of her throat than they had ever seen, and at least the faintest outlines of her breasts, unsupported by the rigid corsets of the day. No one ever spoke of this sexual aspect of the ritual, but it was evident to all that a certain titillation was the key to a great shivaree, especially the second traditional event: the washing of feet.

After the bride was helped from the wheelbarrow, she was carried by the groom to the front porch, where a small tub of water had been set up by the neighbors. She sat on the top step with her feet in the water, while the blushing groom knelt in front of the tub and washed her feet, massaging his new wife's ankles and toes, in what for many farmers might have been the most provocative public act they would ever see. Certainly, it was unlikely that Mrs. Haney would ever again show her ankles to such an assemblage. It apparently was at this point that Mary Chambers was overcome by the advances of Johnny Harwood. Johnny had put his arms around Mary's waist and was about to kiss her throat, when John Chambers came upon them. It's not clear that anyone actually saw this encounter take place, but the word spread quickly when the Chambers left the shivaree in such a hurry. The story was embellished over the years until everyone in Nickerly thought Mary Chambers and Johnny Harwood were having an affair in those bushes.

For the rest of their lives, John and Mary Chambers seldom appeared at social gatherings. They seemed to lock their shame in the most remote corner of their existence. It was often pointed out, for example, that the Chambers were nice people, but they didn't go to church. In fact, building the local school was the only positive point on the credit side of their community ledger.

"How come I never heard this story before?" Ray asked.

"Because no one talks about this sort of thing," Jay said, rolling his eyes at Ray's naivete. "We only talk in public about sin. Not the sinners. Dad preaches about adultery every week. It's one of the Ten Commandments. But we never talk about who does it. Every time I've seen Johnny Harwood since, I wonder what he's up to."

"But he's got three kids in high school," Ray said, "and Mrs. Chambers comes to town just like nothing happened."

"Well," Jay said, "something happened in those bushes that night, and it had to do with coveting thy neighbor's wife."

.   .   .

At that moment, the organ began the first chords of "When the roll is called up yonder." It was Aaron's favorite hymn, the prelude to his closing pitch. As the congregation finished the last chorus, Aaron's voice rose over the Cantor sisters in the front row, over old George Brown who thought his voice was a match for the Lord's, and he began his final words: "When the roll is called up yonder, will you be there?" Aaron pleaded in a singsong rhythm that rose and fell with the tune. "Will you be safe among the flock of God? Will you walk among the lilies in the presence of our Lord and Savior? If you have not accepted the Lord as your personal Savior, come forward today and accept Him. Come down the aisle now and accept Him. All this I pray in Jesus' name, Amen." And the "Amen" struck exactly as the last note of the song was hit by George Brown. It was a perfect performance.

Aaron always knew in advance, of course, if anybody would be coming down the aisle, simply because he knew everyone in the congregation. Aaron had worked on some of his neighbors for thirty years before he got them to convert, and even then it was usually because a family member was very sick, or dying, or had left home. Family tragedy always made people vulnerable to a reassessment of their station with the Lord, and Aaron never missed a chance to make his case. Jay suspected that was why preachers were so willing to visit the sick at home, knowing it was their best chance to add a notch to the ministry's scoreboard.

As the organ sounded the postlude, the Reverend Aaron hurried to his position out on the front steps, eager to assess the congregation's reaction to his sermon. Ivy and the girls joined him. The congregation liked to see Ivy at the Reverend Aaron's side, partly because it reinforced their view of a ministerial family, and also because Ivy's granite countenance reminded them of Aaron's unquestioned adherence to the tenets of the Bible; they simply could detect no frivolity in her face. Nor was she a threat to anyone. Devoid of any outstanding attribute—neither beauty nor talent in handicrafts or sewing—Ivy could not inspire envy. Indeed, she was the architect of the only chicken casserole to avoid at church picnics. Ivy saw cooking as primarily a bodily necessity, certainly nothing to tantalize or embellish with garnishes, herbs, relishes, or sauces. With six children to feed every day, the need for quantity far outweighed quality.

As the last of the congregation cranked up their Model A Fords, Ivy left Aaron's side and marched over to the boys. "I hope you'll come to the Funks for the picnic. Bertie says several families are coming, including the Garveys."

Jay nodded approval. He and Ray usually got together with their best friend Ed Garvey on Sunday afternoons, often down at the mill, just to talk or play baseball with whoever showed up. Today they would have to postpone their plans until after the picnic. On the other hand, Jay knew he didn't have to show up. It wouldn't be the first time he had skipped out on a family gathering.

CHAPTER THREE

When the Langstons arrived at the Funks' farm, Elmo Funk was still wearing his suit and dragging a weather-stained picnic table from behind the house. He positioned it under the sycamore tree, whose broad leaves with long limbs grew straight out from the trunk, forming a perfect umbrella. Later Bertie Funk would bring some blankets out for people to sit on, although most families brought their own designated picnic blanket, large enough to hold their entire contingent and colorful enough to be admired by their friends.

Ivy was making tea in the kitchen with Mrs. Funk when the Garveys arrived. Ed and Eunice had been the Langstons' best friends for thirty years, ever since Ed decided to build the mill. Aaron Langston had organized the neighbors to help put up the main structure, a two-story post-and-beam frame with brick exterior, and the lumbering water wheel that lapped up power from the Saline to turn the grindstones. There was never any talk of loans, or paybacks, or favors to be done. The community knew it needed a mill, and with their help Ed Garvey was going to build one.

Aaron opened the screen door, handed Ed a glass of tea, and motioned him over to the picnic table. The two men were comfortable together, having survived storms, weak crops, and worst of all, family deaths from diseases like chicken pox and tuberculosis. It was in the swimming hole near Ed's mill, a shallow basin of water formed by runoff from the water wheel, that Aaron and Ivy Langston's third son had drowned. There was never any blame for these occurrences, only a deep grief that the all-knowing hand of God had decided to strike in this time and place. But a Sunday picnic in the summer of 1911 was a pleasant occasion, marked by the warmth of the Kansas heat, dry and enclosing, safe and reassuring about the shoulders.

"Everyone says you gave a stem winder at the church this morning," Ed said.

"I noticed you didn't make it over," Aaron replied. "How's your leg?" Aaron always gave Ed a ready excuse, the arthritis in his leg, for not attending church, even though Ed hadn't been to one of Aaron's services in years and had probably never witnessed one of his evangelistic performances down by the river. But Aaron knew Ed was a religious man, hard in his interpretation of the Lord's teachings and unforgiving if he caught anyone cheating on the weight of his wheat. As a business practice, Ed may have given the Lord too large a role in his calculations. One farmer who tried to sell Ed moldy corn was banished from the mill forever and had to haul his feed more than twenty miles to the mill near Ellsworth. On the other hand, when the worst farmer in the county finally ran out of money and hope, left his wife, and disappeared into the badlands of Texas, Ed took in the abandoned woman and her ten-year-old daughter, Francis. Then the mother disappeared, and Ed paid for Francis to go to the orphanage near Russell. He had strong views about the right way to live, views guided by a rigid interpretation of the Ten Commandments, reinforced by the admonitions of his friend the Reverend Aaron.

"I read that Teddy Roosevelt is coming to Kansas this week," Aaron said. "The federal government is gonna build a monument to John Brown over at Osawatomie."

"That's typical of the government," Ed said. "The man blows up a town, kills a whole bunch of people, gets himself hanged, and we declare him a hero."

"They're gonna name a park after him, John Brown Park," Aaron said.

"Slavery was wrong," Ed replied, "but so is killing, and John Brown was crazy."

"Our former president is just back from Africa, where he killed more than 10,000 animals," Aaron said. "He's having trouble keeping busy."

"Old Taft isn't having any trouble," Ed said. "At three hundred pounds, we don't have to worry about him riding any camels around the world."

"He'd kill a horse," Aaron observed. "Break his back."

"I bet my white mules could carry him," Ed allowed. "They have backs of stone. Those mules can pull a plow in a line as straight as string, and do it all day long."

Aaron let the conversation sag, not having much to say about Taft or mules, but he did want to ask about school starting next month, and Ed was on the township school board.

"I see you voted for an eight-month school year," Aaron said. "That's a little hard for me. You know Ray is doing all my farming now, but I can't get Jay to stay home more than a week at a time, and there aren't many kids available. I need to hire some boys from Nickerly. How about a seven-month school year?"

"I understand your problem," Ed said, "but my problem is Mrs. Garvey. Everybody who comes in my place with a load of grain wants his kids for another month. But she thinks school is everything. Got that Chambers girl to go to college, then threatened to throw me out of the house if we didn't hire her to teach. We never had a teacher before with college, why do we need one now?"

"Always before we had your wife," Aaron said with a smile.

"I mean any of these schools around here," Ed said. "That Chambers family hasn't ever amounted to much, and it never will."

"Well, as long as she sticks to the basics, it shouldn't be too bad," Aaron said. "I never knew the Chambers to be church people, but Chambers built that schoolhouse a few years ago, so I figure his daughter has a right to teach there."

Aaron and Ed were sitting on the same side of the picnic table, Ed in his Sears overalls with gold buttons, two buttons on each side undone to allow room for his ample stomach. When Ed twisted his hips sideways to get his legs under the table, the side flaps fell open, as they always did, giving the children a glimpse of his cream-colored cotton underwear just under the tail of his shirt.

The two men looked out across Elmo Funk's land, open from the house to the two-story barn, painted a bright red and hiding all of Elmo's equipment. Elmo kept a clean piece of land, no rusted hay rakes or other machinery was within sight of the house. Like most farms, Elmo didn't exactly have a yard, but he had planted rye and brome grass around the house and barn. His horses had pulled the hay sickle cutter through it the week before, so that each blade of grass stood erect as if smeared with Wildroot. Using your horses to cut ornamental grass was considered a waste by most farmers, and downright extravagant by some. Elmo had even allowed Mrs. Funk to plant some geraniums in his vegetable garden, which showed a red splotch among the potatoes and cabbage, standing out to visitors like measles on a baby's back. The flowers only accentuated the starkness of the prairie, which ran uninterrupted from the barn to the horizon, a rolling shimmering brown in late summer. Trees just didn't seem to grow in these environments, although there was talk of a hedge apple tree that could grow anywhere, almost without water, that had been used to slow the dust storms in Oklahoma, and that might be planted along the roads to slow the southeasterly winds, generally thought to be the most destructive. No, this was flat land, where a jackrabbit could be seen for three hundred yards.

Aaron and Ed looked at the nakedness of the land and felt a sense of pride in the work that had cleared the trees, tilled the soil, and transformed the stones from the fields into fences that would last an eternity. The primary benchmarks for a productive life in Nickerly County were a well-kept farm and a full church. *The Nickerly Journal* carried some news of the world, which of course led to the discussion of Roosevelt and Taft, but most of the news focused on weddings, funerals, harvests, and decisions of the school boards and township supervisors. Fashions were prescribed by custom and by whatever was available at the local dry goods store. Travel was limited to day trips, mostly to Salina or Ellsworth.

Families never talked about what they wanted out of life because the answer was life itself. The Bible set forth a series of yardsticks for measuring the quality of a life and therefore gave it meaning. As the arbiter of biblical law, the Reverend Aaron was perhaps the strongest influence in establishing acceptable behavior. Worthy ambitions were most likely to center on a large family, regular church attendance, and daily devotions.

Ed Garvey set most of the secular standards for living in Nickerly County through the work of the mill, turning produce into baking flour and cash, the only two meaningful currencies. Wealth was measured in acres of land owned and bushels of wheat produced, but extravagance was carefully avoided. Few people displayed a new carriage, a parasol, or some other whimsical purchase that indicated a trip had been made to Salina. These frivolities were normally enjoyed in private because the right hand of the Lord, the Reverend Aaron Langston, was quick to remind everyone of the sins of sloth, avarice, pride, and anything sensual. Thus the only rewards for achievement related to the strictness of personal behavior. The more you repressed your behavior, the greater the achievement.

There was an element of pride, however, that slipped into one of the most basic elements of farm life, butchering. Every year the Langstons, like most farmers, butchered one cow, one pig, and one sheep, thus providing them with a year of meats, kept in the Nickerly ice house.

The ice house operator was also the butcher, a small quiet man named Jack Butter, who had killed, opened, and dressed most of the meat in his ice house. Some farmers did their own, but Jack was known to cut his animals leaner than most farmers could, and then save more fat for soap or other by-products. Also, Jack gave a 10 percent discount on storage at the ice house if he was the butcher.

Butchering was an all-day event of some celebration in the farm community. Ray and Jay would often attend their neighbors' butchering, and neighborhood kids of every stripe and size would come to the Langstons for theirs. The butchering had its own set of rituals. Jack Butter would station the heifer just below the block and tackle hanging from the crown of the barn. He would tie the rope halter to the barn door, then step back for the prayer. Aaron blessed the harvest and the animals, ending his prayer with "Bless this food for its extended uses." Then Jack Butter would walk over to the cow, and with one clean and fast stroke, plunge his knife into its thick neck. Its front knees would buckle. Slowly the huge beast would twist and turn toward the ground. Its hind legs would become like stone, simply falling to the side. A large pool of blood would form, but almost before the tail hit the ground, the head was severed, the throat was fully cut, the pulley hook was inserted, and Jack, Aaron, and Ray were putting all their weight on the block and tackle to raise the cow off the ground and expose its belly for Jack Butter to do his work. It was all so fast and methodical that the cow never seemed to be in any pain. It was as if the cow knew its destiny and accepted it. For the Langstons, it was a celebration, with Ivy getting ready to save and store and use every spare part of the animal, giving thanks for their abundant good fortune. The butchering was a harbinger of family meals, good health, and freedom from hunger.

As Jack Butter made his first thrust into the torso of the cow, it fell open from throat to tail as if unzipped, the entrails tumbling out in different colors. The children gasped. Then Jack reached into the smorgasbord of intestines, pulled out a kidney, cut it off from the stomach, and tossed it out in the dirt. Aaron kicked it around with his foot a little, to soak up the wet blood and other fluids, then put it to his lips and inflated it as easily as a penny balloon.

"Here, boys," Aaron said, as he tossed it to the ground, and gave it the first kick. Thrilled with their new soccer ball, the children kicked the kidney around the yard and down by the granary, as Jack finished the butcher. Several days later, the kidney was still down by the corn field, dry as dirt and covered by flies.

Butchering contained the kinds of lessons that every child had to learn, and they did so with some enthusiam. School, on the other hand, was a necessary evil to most families and viewed in practical terms. Of course, there was a growing demand for a mathematical expertise—at least if anyone wanted to know the changing prices for corn, hogs, and wheat—but seven or eight years of school seemed more than enough to master the most important lessons: to memorize the Ten Commandments and learn to make moral decisions. Aaron and Ed both assumed that the new schoolteacher understood these principles of education; it was her family history that concerned them.

"We'll see how she does," Ed said. "Wait till the first Literary, then we'll see what happens."

CHAPTER FOUR

Margaret Chambers knew it was Ileen because the screen door didn't slam. It was allowed to close gently, as if slowed by the body of a cat slipping and twisting through the opening. Ileen Chambers walked softly in the world and doors closed gently behind her.

Ileen maneuvered through the mud room, sidestepping the milk bucket and her father's rubber overboots with the tin clasps. She noticed that her parents' coats were gone from their nail hooks and realized she must have plenty of time before the Literary. Wherever her parents were, they would not miss Margaret's first Literary as a teacher. Ileen was seventeen and had not gone to Literary since she was in high school, providing her mother with another explanation for Ileen's lack of a husband: lack of exposure. But why did she need exposure in a community where she already knew everyone?

"Is that you?" Margaret called out from her room.

Ileen did not answer until she was in the bedroom. They had shared it all their lives, and the evidence surrounded them: a vase from Aunt Jane, a faded sampler blessing the home, and a Sunday school watercolor that Margaret had done twelve years ago. The watercolor was pretty, a daisy with bright colors. Margaret's mother remarked on it every time she came in the room, so the girls kept it on the wall even after they became tired of it. A birdhouse with a red roof sat beside the china lamp. Margaret always said the painted blue jay on the lamp shade was the only admirer that birdhouse ever had, and probably so since Margaret took the house out of the tree just a week after her father had hung it on a low limb. She saw the neighbor's cat creeping down the limb; the house had been in their room ever since. Margaret had once read a French saying that marriage was like a birdhouse, those without want in and those within want out. She wasn't sure if she remembered the saying right, or exactly what it meant, but she thought about it a lot, especially when she became dissatisfied with her surroundings. It always seemed to her that she wanted an escape, but then she wanted a return to safety as well, like coming home to teach, even though she didn't seem to have the patience for all the rituals of the job, like Literaries.

"Ileen," she said, "I've been going to Literaries all my life. I remember sitting on the front steps of Mt. Pleasant School when I was in about fourth grade, while all the adults were inside eating, and three boys about my age, maybe a little older, asked me if I wanted to go on a snipe hunt. I was so excited."

"You didn't fall for the old snipe hunt, did you?" Ileen asked, laughing. "I thought you were too smart."

"I bought it for the same reason every kid buys it," she said. "I wanted those boys to like me. Ed Garvey was one of them. I don't remember the other two. But I remember sitting out in that grass, holding that stupid paper bag, and waiting for the boys to drive those snipes into my bag. And I remember waiting in the dark, just able to see the school past the mulberry bushes, and I remember being scared to death that some snake was going to get me before the snipes got there. And then I saw the door of the school open and a shaft of light came out that hit those boys full in the face, while they were laughing and sitting on the same steps where I had been, and I knew I had been tricked. I hated those boys. I ran inside to mother and they laughed at me all the way. I have never liked Literaries since."

"Oh, Margaret, you're so dramatic," Ileen said. "Those boys were harmless. And now Ed is one of our most important citizens. Practically runs the mill."

"It's not that," Margaret said. "It's like the birdhouse. I feel trapped. Do you know that Jerry and Berry Quick are going to play their marimbas again? They're grown men. They've been playing those twin marimbas for twenty years. We used to think they were going to be great musicians, giving concerts around the world. Now they're just old bachelor farmers playing in barns."

"Oh, Margaret," Ileen said with a kind of shushing sound, "you're the only one who thought they would be traveling around the world. The rest of us knew they were just farm boys in overalls who liked playing the marimbas."

She let the moment slide, then added, "You probably thought that old man who played the harmonica and the accordion was going to the Kansas City symphony."

"Hush, Ileen," Margaret said. "When did you get so sarcastic? And where did you get the Kansas City symphony?"

"I don't know," Ileen said. "I've always liked the music, even the spoons player. You know I saw Dad trying that down in the barn once. I walked in and he had three spoons between the fingers of each hand and he was beating them against his knee, and I think he was even singing. Daddy can't sing. But they had just been to a Literary, and he thought he could do it."

"At tonight's Literary," Margaret proclaimed, "I am the main attraction, and I don't even want to go."

"You're not my main attraction," Ileen said, grinning. "I want to see those new Swedish boys you were telling me about, the blonde ones who just moved onto the Bonebreak place."

"Ileen, they're still in school. Too young for you."

"I'm only seventeen, and I'm going to get married. One year doesn't matter much."

"Just remember," Margaret said, "there are four schools coming together tonight. I'm the only new teacher in years, and the only one who's been to college. These people never change. Everybody sits around in the desks. Then we have Mrs. Darden introduce the teachers, then we have the Quick brothers, and the spoon players, and old Ab Grogger playing the bones, and then little Jenny Arnstead gives her reading. Then we set the date for the next Literary, adjourn, and then we have the covered dish dinner . . . a lot of baked beans and potato salad."

"Margaret, why are you teaching anyway?" Ileen said.

"I love teaching. The kids are wonderful. It's just these meetings with parents I can't stand. Literaries are the only entertainment in this community. I understand that. They're fun for the children and their families. They're just not fun for the teachers."

"I can't believe you don't like the whistling Solomon family, with all those grandkids lined up, just a whistling and yodeling their hearts out," Ileen said with a giggle.

"We've been watching that family so long the oldest boy is seventy-three," Margaret said, joining in the humor. "But that's what makes it so hard to have fun around here. Everyone but the Solomon family is repressed. We don't sing anything but hymns. Don't dance. And the Reverend Aaron makes it sound like joy in any form except work is bad."

"Margaret," Ileen countered, "you've got to work your way into heaven. That's what the Bible says."

"Well, I want to dance . . . to have fun like we used to in college," Margaret said. "I'm not just working to get into heaven. I want to meet a grown man as handsome as those Swenson boys and live in the city, and go to plays and dances and parties. Maybe I'll just take that Swenson boy with me."

"Margaret, you don't mean that. That Swenson boy is your pupil."

"I know that," Margaret said, "but he does have an eye for me. You know what I mean, Ileen. I'm going to teach for five years and then move to Kansas City. You can come with me if you want."

.   .   .

There were 133 one-room schools in Nickerly County. Ostensibly, the reason for this was so that the children could walk to school, especially in winter when roads were difficult and hooking up the buggy for a short ride to school simply seemed extravagant. But a more compelling reason was parental control, over the teacher and over the curriculum.

Mt. Pleasant was a larger school than Sunnyside, principally because it was closer to Nickerly and served a larger population. Mt. Pleasant was named for the picture of a mountain printed inside the textbooks selected for 1903. The mountain's snow-crested peak was so pristine and sparkling that it reminded the school mothers of God's beauty. Even though the closest mountain was in the Rockies, some 500 miles away, and no one in the Mt. Pleasant School had ever seen a real mountain, it seemed the perfect name for a new school. Several of the mothers looked at the Mt. Pleasant picture and proclaimed that they would one day visit that place.

The school had twenty bench desks that ran the full width of the school, and twenty bench seats of the same length, meaning all the children sat in rows, side by side, an arrangement conducive to foolishness such as pencil poking and ankle kicking. Although hand holding had never been allowed, children would group together in the yard to laugh and tease about the latest school romance. Teachers watched this sort of thing carefully, and the admonitions against touching by the Reverend Aaron were a fearful reminder that such behavior was not allowed. For most children, of course, it was not desired anyway, and some of the boys placed their rulers on the bench as a reminder to any girl to keep her distance.

On Literary night, the parents squeezed onto the benches, but the "ruler" division erected invisible barriers between families. It was crowded, and the farmers folded their arms over their stomachs so that their shoulders and hands wouldn't accidentally touch. For several of the heavier farmers and their wives, maintaining the margin of decency could be quite taxing, to the point where farmers would turn in their seats, crossing their legs away from their neighbors and putting their arms around their wives' shoulders, thus eliminating the possibility that anyone, even for an instant, could imagine any untoward touching.

The easiest way to avoid this contortionist purity was simply for the men to sit together in the back of the room and the women to sit together in the front. As many of the Nickerly families came from Quaker ancestry, they were quite familiar with the separation of men and women in public places. Indeed, although it was now a source of liberal pride that most churches had moved away from the practice of forcing men and women to segregate, it was still a voluntary chastity that was widely practiced. Also, men and women had different things to talk about in terms of their farm duties. Some families liked the Literaries, however, because children were among the few subjects that men and women could talk about, and in many cases it was the only time a farmer even found himself in the company of a woman, or at least a woman other than his wife.

So it was not unusual to see the first three rows filled with the women of the Civic Improvement Association, although there did seem to be a special intensity about their introductions, as each lined up to meet Margaret Chambers, the new teacher at Sunnyside. Margaret was wearing a dark blue wool dress that protected her against the cool air of the autumn prairie evening. The dress had bright white trim about the neck and sleeves. On her right shoulder, like a star against a blue bird's wing, she wore a golden brooch, as large as a silver dollar and curved like a seashell. The brooch glittered like a piece of broken glass that catches the sun. Every introduction brought the patrons of the community face-to-face with this undefined challenge, this bit of rebellion.

In fact, all of the women were a little frightened of Margaret, for reasons that few understood. Ileen had noticed it years before. Even when Margaret was in high school, other women shied away from her on the street. When she walked into a group of adult women, they drew back like a clutch of hens, as though sensing danger in their midst. Even now, as the ladies drew closer to Margaret to welcome her to the school, some of them got a spooked look, like a horse's eye when it catches the flicker of a passing shadow, skittish and fearful of a rock in the field. Ileen could never understand this reaction. Perhaps it came from Margaret's reputation in school for perfect papers or from her physical maturity that had always seemed on the verge of being out of control. As a child Margaret's long legs were hard to keep hidden. But there was also an innocence about Margaret that kept the women from gossip, from assigning any malicious motive to these lapses in decorum. It was as if Margaret could not be blamed for an uncontrollable gene her ancestors had bred beneath her bonnet.

"What a beautiful brooch," Mrs. Garvey said to Margaret, knowing that the ladies were already looking askance at the bright piece of jewelry and hoping to relieve the stigma by openly and specifically addressing the matter.

"Thank you; I won it at school," Margaret said. Margaret had won the brooch her first year at Emporia, as the only female member of the debate team that argued the merits of Theodore Roosevelt's efforts to bust the railroad trusts. The team sponsor had given writing pens to his team for years, but in honor of this break in the gender barrier, he had selected a simple brooch from the local jeweler. Margaret had worn it tonight as a symbol of intellectual achievement and because she liked the sparkle it gave to her dress.

Mrs. Garvey could see that the womenfolk had a somewhat different interpretation, and was determined to help Margaret with a clear statement of her approval. But her chivalry didn't prevent Mrs. Tucker from staring straight at the brooch as she said hello to Margaret. A look of condemnation was spread across her face like the pain of tight shoes. The brooch was brazen. It boasted of a superiority to Mrs. Tucker and most of the other ladies there, from a woman judged to have no right to superiority by all the normal standards of social ascendancy. Margaret's claim to superiority could only come after she had taught for thirty years in the community, or if she married a farmer and raised a dozen children, or if long days of backbreaking work in the fields had yielded honest wealth, or if she demonstrated piety through faithful service to the church. These were the normal pathways to social acclaim and community praise. Anything less than a lifetime of commitment was a superficial attempt at recognition, a temporary and sometimes scornful presence, like the patent medicine salesman who stepped down from his square rig and prancing horse to offer cures for every ailment, then moved on down the road and out of mind.

Margaret caught the look in Mrs. Tucker's eye and instinctively stepped back. Then, recovering herself, she leaned into the introduction with the confidence she had learned in college and she did a remarkable thing: she stretched her arm forward to its full reach, opened her palm and there for all the room to see, she offered to shake Mrs. Tucker's hand.

Jay Langston, who hadn't taken his eyes off Margaret since he first caught sight of the auburn curls that flowed over her shoulders, noticed the exchange with Mrs. Tucker and exclaimed to the men huddled near him, "The new teacher shakes hands."

"She thinks she's a man," said Ed Garvey. "My mother has treated that girl like a daughter, helped send her off to college, and now she comes back thinking she owns the place."

Margaret realized there was a flutter in the room, but she held steady, her gaze fixed and her smile as broad as Tiny Tucker's bosom. Mrs. Tucker was not prepared to be on the defensive and had no idea how to respond. She was a private person in a world where people did not draw attention to themselves in public, certainly not by shaking hands, which women just did not do, and not by sharp words or wild gestures either. She turned and walked to her seat, head down, realizing her humiliation and vowing to exact an appropriate vengeance, just as soon as God made his wishes known. Margaret Chambers had committed the sin of pride, and Tiny Tucker had no doubt that she would soon feel the wrath of the Lord.

The handshake attempt brought the room to order as quickly as if someone had tapped a spoon on a glass, and the evening's formal festivities began. The teacher at Mt. Pleasant School, Mr. Talmage Grimes, welcomed the parents and friends to the first Literary of the year.

Mr. Talmage Grimes was only twenty-three. He had completed just one year of high school, the minimum requirement for getting a teaching certificate from the State of Kansas, and he had spent nearly four years helping his father in the local grocery store before leaving in a family dispute and deciding on a career in education. He found himself well suited to education, patient with the children, studious in his preparations, and serious in his ambition. As a man, he enjoyed the preferential benefits of a higher salary and community recognition. He was in his third year of teaching, and he was earning thirty-six dollars a month, well above Margaret's starting salary of thirty-one dollars and fifty cents. He introduced Margaret briefly as the new teacher at Sunnyside, whose family had resided in Nickerly for many years.

Margaret had thought about her introduction to the community carefully. Although this was an evening of socializing, she wanted to express her seriousness of purpose and to educate the parents as to their children's curriculum. This first Literary might be the only one of the year for the menfolk, especially if the remaining ones occurred during a snowstorm or at harvesttime.

"Good evening," she began, "I'm delighted to meet you all, even though I know most of you from living here, and I thank you for coming. I want to take this moment to tell you about our new eighth-grade graduation test. It will be given to all proposed graduates, and since we don't have any eighth-grade students this year, I thought you would like to take the test, just to see how smart our children have to be to graduate."

The audience was not prepared for levity, and missed the attempt entirely.

"These questions were developed by the State of Kansas," Margaret continued, "and will give you a clear idea of what your children are learning. Now, here's the first question on the exam: Name the parts of speech and define those that have no modifications."

Margaret paused for emphasis, and to let the parents think about the question. But most of the fathers in the room, still having nightmares about questions they couldn't answer in grade school, thought she might be waiting for one of them to stand up and answer. They started slumping on their benches, pressing closer together, and looking at the floor. All the repressed fears of being called upon as a boy suddenly resurfaced, striking a resentful anger.

"She isn't going to make us answer, is she?" Ed Garvey whispered to Jay Langston.

"Who does she think she is?" Jay responded, suddenly thinking this teacher was not someone he wanted to tangle with, in spite of her curls.

"Let's turn to geography," Margaret said. "Name and describe the following: Monrovia, Odessa, Manitoba, Hecia, Yukon, St. Helena, Juan Fernandez, Aspinwall, and Orinoco."

Jay swore under his breath. "I know Denver and the Yukon," he whispered. "The rest I never heard of."

"Those will give you a hint as to how tough the test is," Margaret concluded. "I think it will be a useful measure for achieving graduation."

There was silence. The men breathed a sigh of relief that the possibility of questioning was over, and the women clasped their hands in their laps, a stern show of sympathy for the discomfort of their husbands. Only Mrs. Garvey offered support, smiling at Margaret and mouthing the word "good."

"Thank you," Margaret said, and took her seat beside Mr. Grimes.

CHAPTER FIVE

Easy Tucker pulled his wheat wagon, led by two dappled mares, onto the scales at the Garvey Mill, tied the reins to the front of the buckboard seat, and jumped to the ground. The horses were sweating from the pull, and Easy swatted aimlessly at the large flies circling their haunches. He patted the left horse's front shoulder to let him know the trip was over, then waved to Ed Garvey's shadow in the window of the elevator.

The August morning sun cast a glare in the window, so Easy couldn't be sure whether it was Garvey senior or junior behind the scales. He opened the door with a rush, befitting his celebratory mood, and hardly noticed the handful of men seated on benches around the room or leaning against the back wall.

"Hello, Ed," Easy said. "This is the last of it. Got my boy out there plowing today."

"Good to see you, Easy," young Ed Garvey said. "The boys here were wondering if you'd be in this morning."

Ed Tucker had farmed near Nickerly all his life. And as sure as weevils like the wheat, Ed liked the feel of cold hard cash for his crops.

The threshing machine was hardly out of the field before Easy had every scoop of wheat in the elevator and every dollar in the bank, not that he left it there long. His philosophy was that every year's work earned him at least one extravagance, and this year he was planning on a new car.

Ed Garvey studied the scale before him, moved the weights to the far right, then jotted a figure on the back of a letter from the Kansas Grange.

"Easy," Garvey said, "I suppose that horse and wagon outfit weighs the same as yesterday, or do we need to weigh it again?" In order to weigh the wheat, Garvey normally weighed the wagon fully loaded, emptied the wheat, then weighed the wagon empty, and subtracted the difference. It would save time just to use the weight of yesterday's wagon, since presumably it hadn't changed overnight, although Ed Garvey Jr. knew his father wouldn't approve of this practice.

In addition to his love of cash, Easy Tucker had a number of eccentric qualities, including the fact that he could never remember anybody's name. He had no trouble with numbers or places, and he had done pretty well through the seventh grade, which was as far as his family let him go, but he couldn't always tell you Ed Garvey's name, even though he sat beside Ed all seven of those educational years. It was very embarrassing, and more than a little frustrating, and so he got to calling everybody by an all-purpose nickname of one kind or another. This was a perfect solution because every man in Nickerly had a nickname, from Cavity Ben Johnson who had no teeth and was called Cav, to Red Romberger who had bright red hair and freckles. Easy Tucker hit on a solution to his problem when one day he accidentally called his best friend Lucky, and it worked—Ed Garvey responded. From then on, Easy Tucker simply called everyone either Easy, Lucky, or Speedy. When his friends realized what he was doing, they mockingly started to call him Easy. The name stuck.

Ed Garvey calculated the weight of the wheat, opened the dark green accounts book, and made an entry for Easy Tucker. His right hand followed a strip of leather from his belt to his pocket, where it dislodged a key that opened the wooden cash drawer beneath the table. Ed counted out the cash into Easy's right hand and said, "Thanks for your business, Mr. Tucker."

Jay Langston, leaning against the iron stove in the middle of the room, watched and waited for the transaction to take place. Business was business. Then he piped up, "Easy, you gonna buy a car with that money?" He didn't wait for an answer. "No matter. That money will be gone by Christmas anyway."

"No, it won't," Easy said. "No, it won't." But Easy knew it might. He was usually broke and begging for a loan by Easter. Most families, like the Reverend Aaron and Ivy, sold a little of their wheat in August for cash to buy school clothes or a new roof for the house, but kept the lion's share in a granary to be traded for flour during the winter. Every month Aaron would take a load of wheat to the mill and trade it for two 48-pound bags of flour. Ivy would bake all of her breads, pies, cakes, pancakes, and biscuits for the month out of these two bags. Most farmers husbanded their resources this way so that no matter what else happened, the family always had food. Not Easy. He said he wanted his money to grow, at 1 percent in the bank. Unfortunately, he seldom left it there long enough to benefit from his financial strategy.

"I bet you take that money right down to the dance hall, take a fling around the floor when Mrs. Tucker isn't looking, and lose the whole pile," Jay shouted so all could hear. The other farmers chuckled, until they noticed that Easy wasn't smiling.

Easy had a quick temper, or at least that was his reputation; few of the men at Garvey's had actually seen him angry. Easy was built like a block of cedar, with a square face and large forehead and one peculiar feature: he had no nose, at least not that you could see. His nose looked like a bite of pancake from the front. It was so flat against his face that sometimes people would work their way around to his profile just so they could see if he really had a nose. The story went that one year at the county fair, Easy was stopped near the sheep pens by a complete stranger who asked if he really had a nose. Startled, Easy stepped back from the stranger as if stung by a bee. Then he realized that several folks had heard the question and had stopped to look. Easy felt the blood rushing up through his shoulders and past his collar. Then he turned slightly away from the stranger, lifted his right fist, and sent it with slingshot velocity right onto the man's nose. The nose flattened with a crunch, sending blood flying in all directions. People ran, screaming and shouting that Easy Tucker had gone mad. Satisfied that now there were at least two people in the world with a pancake nose, Easy found Mrs. Tucker over by the baked goods exhibits and took her home without saying a word. The joke around the community was: If you make fun of Easy Tucker, you soon look like Easy Tucker. So the men at Garvey's Mill let the matter of money drop.

Hank Simpson, who ran a bakery on Nickerly's Main Street, had dropped by to join the boys for a bottle of pop. Usually, a small group of farmers gathered at his shop in the afternoon, especially on rainy days when they couldn't work in the fields. Rainy days were set aside for stocking up at the hardware and dry goods stores. On nice days, when business was slow, Hank left the store to Mrs. Simpson and wandered on down to the mill.

"Easy," Hank said, "you better keep that boy plowing noon and night 'cause it's almost time for school. Another two weeks and you lost him to that Chambers girl."

"Not if my wife has her way," Easy said. "She says the new teacher has been showing more than ankle to that oldest Swenson boy."

Club Wilson spoke up from the end of the bench, "I think that Chambers girl is a bird. You touch her and she'll fly away so fast."

Club Wilson's family owned more land in Nickerly County than anyone, thousands of acres by some accounts, with teams of draft horses that could plow twenty acres a day, and barbed wire fences running along stone posts for uninterrupted miles. They also owned the quarry that produced the limestone for all the buildings in town and the fence posts around the farms. Hundreds of men were employed by the Wilson Quarry. They set the dynamite charges and drilled the holes for spacers that would crack the stone open like peanut brittle, not always perfectly straight but close enough for construction purposes. The Wilsons probably had more money than the Garveys, but it hardly showed, mostly because the Wilsons kept to themselves. Club broke his leg in high school, playing football in a pick-up game one evening after class, and hobbled around in a leg cast for nearly six weeks. After the cast was removed, his friends started calling him Club because he tended to drag one foot. The name stuck long after all evidence of the broken leg had disappeared. In fact, most folks no longer remembered how Club got his name in the first place.

"I don't think she's so much," Club said rather sheepishly. "Too tall for me."

"Not too tall for Talmage Grimes," Jay broke in. "I hear she slips over to Mt. Pleasant ever so often for a little lesson sharing."

Joe Tanner hadn't said anything because the conversation seemed so meaningless. But he could feel the group stirring with uneasiness as the subject turned to women. He had been involved with a girl once, nearly ten years ago when he was nineteen, and she had told him she loved him, just before she ran off with one of the boys from the quarry.

"I'm leaving," Joe said, standing up. "I got no use for women of any kind. Trust in the Lord, I say, 'cause he's the only one that won't leave you when you need him." Joe walked through the group and out the door. His departure quieted them for only a moment.

"This is a serious matter," Easy said. "It's our kids going to that school. No telling what that Chambers girl is teaching them. She don't go to church. Her folks don't go to church. And you can ask Johnny Hargrove what her mother is like."

A general silence fell over the room as the men considered this new accusation. If this was a call to action, it was slow to be recognized. But Easy had put a question before the group that required a response, and Club was the first to offer a rational solution: "If you boys want to get rid of her, why not just have the school board fire her?" he said. "You guys run the school."

"No, we don't," Ed Garvey interrupted. "My mother does and she loves that Chambers girl. I'm not sure she's so bad anyway. I don't believe half that stuff they say about her."

"Maybe you don't believe it 'cause you don't want to," Joe said.

"That's crazy," Ed said. "I don't like it any better than you if she's corrupting the morals of our kids."

"Hell," Club added, "she's been to college. You know she's trying to talk those kids into leaving Nickerly County. First thing you know, we won't have anybody to work the fields or the quarry. We won't be good enough for our own kids."

"Boys, I've known her family all my life," Piney Woods offered. "The Chambers live just up the road. They may not be God-fearing people, but they aren't evil. We can't get her fired."

"Piney," Club said, "I heard your wife just the other day tell you to stay away from that Chambers girl. Just as you went into the hardware store."

Piney was embarrassed. He was as tall as a pine tree, with a long face and coal-black hair that lay across his head like wet seaweed. Because he didn't seem to have any hips, his pants were hitched high, and cinched tight. He wore wire-rim glasses that his grandfather had left him. The glasses had helped Piney, his father, and his father before him through at least three grades of school. They should have been replaced long ago, but since the diagnosis was the same for all three generations of men—they couldn't see the windmill in the cow pasture—they were passed down from one generation of Woods to the next. The remarkable thing was that the glasses survived three generations, unbroken and with only a few deep scratches, even though Piney's face was so narrow and his ears so small that the glasses kept slipping off his nose.

Despite his homely appearance, Mrs. Woods loved Piney with a passion, and she suspected most other women of secretly sharing her sentiment. Ever since the first Literary, when she caught Piney staring at Margaret Chambers during the introductions, she had imagined a spark of interest between them. Of course, there was no such illicit romance between her husband and the schoolteacher. But jealousy is a passion of its own making. The more Mrs. Woods thought about the possibility of someone else sharing her Piney, the more certain she became that something had to be done to stop Margaret Chambers.

Piney dismissed his wife's concerns as so much women's talk, but he did notice a new attentiveness in Mrs. Woods, and when she had touched his leg three nights in a row, it occurred to him that her preoccupation with Margaret Chambers might not be such a bad thing.

"Oh, Mrs. Woods is always saying that," Piney said. "She says there's something going on with that Swenson boy. Now that ain't right. God's hand will fall hard on any teacher that takes a boy. I find it hard to believe."

John Buckhorn sat quietly through the discussion, mainly because he had never heard any of these accusations before. He was single, lived alone in his family's home on the edge of Nickerly, and had known Margaret Chambers all his life. Indeed, he probably knew Margaret better than anyone at the mill, and he did not recognize the picture they were painting.

"John," Ed said, "do you think we could run her out of town, get her to leave on her own?"

"What?" John asked. "What are you talking about? Why would she leave?"

"What if we told her to leave?" Ed said. "Just told her we don't approve of her carrying on, told her to get out."

"You mean scare her?" John asked.

"Sure," Ed said. "Let's tar and feather her."

.   .   .

The theme for this month's meeting of the women's Civic Improvement Association was blueberry pie and family history. Each member would bring a pie recipe and an old family photo. The recipes would be shared and written down, while the pictures would lead the family history discussions. Tiny Tucker, Easy's wife, opened the meeting with a prayer.

"Dear Heavenly Father," she began, "thank you for another month of blessings in which our community has prospered. We have reaped the rewards of your attention to our needs, and we pray that we may be worthy of your goodness."

Tiny was making an effort to keep her prayer short. She had been accused in the past of rambling in her pleas to the Lord, and while no one wanted to be critical of this most sacred conversation with God, Tiny had opened her eyes once during her prayer at the meeting two months ago and saw that Heneretta Woods, Piney's wife, was fast asleep, a fact Tiny took as personal criticism. Tiny was angry with Heneretta for weeks, but at the next meeting she did shorten her opening prayer, and today she would try to be particularly succinct.

"Lord," she began, "as we bless you for this bountiful harvest, we also beseech you to deliver our community from the demons among us, raise our hearts above the mundane affairs of the world, and allow our eyes to shine on the goodness of the Lord. Lead us, Heavenly

Father, onto the paths of righteousness, for there are those among us who threaten our families and our children. Hold us close to your heart, oh Lord, as we struggle against the devil and his disciples."

Tiny could hear some shuffling among the seven members of the club present, but she kept her eyes firmly closed. "Dear Father, our children today are threatened by dark and sinister forces," she continued. "Soon they will begin school again and every day face the dangers of worldly sin. Help them, oh Lord, to resist temptation, and help us, oh Lord, to rise up and throw off the sinners, to lift the demon from our midst, to support those who would rid our community of the infestation that plagues our youth, and give us the strength to stand and be counted for the Lord. I ask in Jesus' name, Amen."

The women of the association opened their eyes and said nothing. They stared at Tiny as if she had lost her senses. Tiny looked around the room, feeling that some explanation was necessary, but not wanting to acknowledge that she might be alone in her antipathy for Margaret Chambers.

"All right," Tiny said, "who wants to read her recipe first?"

Tiny was intimidating. Her dress was long and gray, reaching to the floor, and tied with a drawstring about the neck. Her body was completely protected from intrusion by the most heavily starched costume in Nickerly. Her face was a landmark, as strong as stone, vaguely like a bronze bust that seemed too big for its pedestal. She had a long and slightly hooked nose that implied Roman ancestry, large brown eyes covered by dark hoods of eyebrows that suggested a manliness of character. She ran the Tucker family with an iron hand, making sure that Easy was involved in every farmers' organization in the county. She understood the power of information and organization, and even supported the women's suffrage movement, although this was not a subject for public discussion in Nickerly. Tiny had sent a check for three dollars to the Topeka organizers of a protest march for women's right to vote, although she never told Easy she did it.

It was not easy for Heneretta Woods to speak up in any way that might be construed as contrary to Tiny Tucker's view, but she was so perplexed by the prayer of welcome that she blurted out, "Tiny, what were you talking about?"

"Let's trade these recipes first," Tiny said, collecting one from each member, then redistributing them so that everyone received a different recipe. As she moved about the small living room with its two settees, a rocking chair, and two cane backs, she noticed the wall tapestry of farm women in beige and maroon dresses, picking up armloads of wheat. The women carried the wheat in aprons tied about their waists, dropping them in large stacks for feeding into the thresher. Next to the tapestry was a picture of Jesus in brown tones, framed in rosewood. Tiny marveled that Jesus was such a handsome man, with his well-trimmed beard and long satin-smooth hair.

As she sat back down in the rocker, she started, "I mentioned to Easy last night that something needed to be done about the Sunnyside schoolteacher. We've all heard the stories."

"I haven't," Heneretta said. "What on earth are you talking about?"

"That Swenson boy," Mrs. Tanner whispered.

"Not only that," Tiny said. "Where have you been, Henny? Didn't you see her at the Literary? And the way she flirts with our men? She shows no respect."

"Is she a good teacher?" Henny asked, hoping to find a positive aspect to the young woman's character. Henny always sought out the good in people, even arguing at last month's meeting that Joe Tanner had served his country as an Indian scout, and it didn't matter if he drank too much; he had killed people and needed the drink to clear his conscience.

"We can always find good teachers," Tiny said, "but we can't allow the morals of our community to be destroyed. These are our sons and daughters."

"Let's go around the room and read our recipes," Henny said, realizing that Tiny was not to be deterred from her mission. "I have some questions about my crust."

·   ·   ·

John Buckhorn started for the door of the Garvey Mill office. "I think I better go home," John said. "I don't have anything against Margaret Chambers. She has always done right by me."

"Wait a minute, John," Ed said. "You won't have to do anything. Just take her out. Tell her it's a dance at the Robinson's barn tomorrow night. We'll do the tarring."

"Wait yourself," Jay Langston interrupted. "This is moving too fast. Where'd you get this tar and feathers idea?"

"I read about one in the Ellsworth paper a few weeks ago," Ed said. "Happened back east. In Ohio. Girl was caught with a married man, and his wife's whole family tarred and feathered her, told her to get out of town, and they never saw her again."

"That seems a little excessive," John muttered.

"Why?" Ed said. "If it had been a man with somebody else's wife, they would have shot him. Besides, a little tar will wash right off and she'll be good as new."

"Wash off!" John exclaimed. "My brother tarred our roof, and he thought he'd never get that stuff off. Had to pour kerosene all over his arms and legs, scrub himself with lyso, and he still had black marks on him." There was silence as this splash of reality landed on the party.

"Well," John Buckhorn continued slowly, "I'll go along, but I won't take her to the dance. You better get somebody else for that." He moved slowly through the group and out the door.

CHAPTER SIX

Herb Forchet leaned back in his weathered captain's chair on the boardwalk in front of his barbershop, closed his eyes so as not to be distracted by the candy cane barber pole beside the door, took one last swat at the gnats that hung like fog in the Kansas summer, and slept. The residents of Nickerly went about their business by moving around Herb without disturbing him, knowing that the barber business was good on Saturday and very slow on Wednesdays. Weekends were for getting cleaned up and ready for church on Sunday. For most farmers, that included taking a bath on Friday evening, putting on clean overalls on Saturday morning, and getting to the barbershop about noon. The time didn't really matter because the whole day was set aside for talking with neighbors, shooting the bull with the city boys at the barbershop, and visiting the hardware store for any new products, like buckets with rubber handles or saws with new teeth configurations that could cut a log in minutes.

Jay Langston was going through town on his way home from the mill when he spotted Herb Forchet at rest. He had known Herb and the Forchet family for years. They had operated a lot of businesses in the community, usually service businesses like the laundry. For a time they ran the only French restaurant in western Kansas, or so they billed it. But the Forchet heritage in French cuisine was pretty weak, and their fancy name didn't help much in Nickerly. Indeed, there was some prejudice against any kind of foreign food in Nickerly, and the promise of French cooking didn't do any better for the Forchets than the time egg rolls were introduced on the menu at the Sunflower, Nickerly's most successful restaurant for the last fifteen or so years. But the Forchets had always been good workers, usually leaving their own businesses in failure, then hiring themselves out to the more successful farmers. Young Herb, however, liked to talk and to gossip and the barbering business was right up his alley. He wouldn't admit it, of course, but he particularly enjoyed the smell of Wildroot hair creme and the bottled sweet water he used as aftershave. He also liked being his own boss, sleeping in front of the store, and cutting hair. He didn't mind at all when Jay Langston called out to him from across the street.

Jay walked toward the slowly arousing barber and inquired about the weather, speculating that the heat could break anytime.

"Hello, Jay," Herb called out, "come in, and we'll turn the fan on."

"I don't need a haircut, Herb," Jay said. "Just on my way home when I saw how busy you were."

"Midweek business is slow," Herb said. "Harvest is over and everyone got a haircut last week. This is a time to spend your money or eat cantaloupes under an elm tree. Good time to have a girlfriend, too."

"I'll tell you what," Jay said, "the boys at the mill need somebody to take Margaret Chambers out. They want to scare her off. Think she would go out with you?"

"What are you talking about?"

"Well," Jay started, "just about everyone in town agrees that Margaret Chambers tried to do something with that Swenson boy. Don't tell me you haven't heard these stories."

"I can see she's got a pretty waist, and I heard she lost her teaching license over in Saline County," Herb said. "But I never heard about the Swenson boy. What happened?"

"Seems she gave him a ride home from the Literary, in her carriage, and a little love sparked between them. Tiny Tucker says all the kids know. That Swenson boy is ga-ga over the teacher."

"So what?" Herb said, shifting in his chair.

"It's not right," Jay said. "The boys down at the mill think a little tar might send her packing. But we need somebody to get her outside of town."

"So you want me to take her out, then you'll tar her?" Herb asked. "I been out with Margaret before, a couple of years ago, and we didn't hit it off too well, but I'm game. I'll give it a try."

"Call her up," Jay said. "See if she'll go tomorrow night."

"Where will I take her?" Herb asked.

"I don't know," Jay said, suddenly realizing he had no concrete plan. "Tell her it's a dance. An invitation dance at the Robinsons' barn. She'll go to that."

"But what happens?" Herb said. "How do they scare her?"

"You charm her," Jay said. "Stop the buggy out by Twelve Mile Run, and the boys will come along. Give her a kiss or something."

"But what will they do?" Herb pressed again.

"I don't know," Jay said, "maybe put a little tar on her. Tell her to get out of Nickerly County."

Herb squinted up at Jay to see if he was fooling, but Jay just flashed him that crooked smile. Herb thought the plan sounded possible. He didn't really like Margaret Chambers. The last time they were out, to a school picnic, he caught her from behind near the coat closet and put his arms around her waist. If a couple of kids hadn't been there, she might have raised a real ruckus. As it was, she turned and pushed him away, saying he was fresh, and she wanted to be taken home. That had been over a year ago, but it still seemed like there was some unfinished business there. Also, he remembered the smallness of her waist and the fullness of her breasts, memories that still stirred more than a casual interest in being with her again.

"Call her up," Jay said. "If she can go, tell Ed Garvey and he'll take care of everything."

CHAPTER SEVEN

Easy Tucker was rummaging through the Garvey Mill storage shed, looking for a can of paint thinner to mix with the roofing tar he brought from home, when he felt the first murmurs of pride about getting Margaret Chambers out of the county. Mrs. Tucker was almost pleading when she placed her hands around Easy's arm earlier that afternoon and told him to be careful with that roofing tar. In her sternest voice, she said, "Edward, you and the boys make sure that girl understands. We can't have her in our school."

Easy was so in love with his wife of seventeen years, he thanked God every night for sending her to him. He knew he wasn't a handsome man, and he had heard the snickers throughout his youth about his pancake nose. He was painfully aware of all the aspects of his humiliation; he minded terribly when girls moved to another seat rather than sit beside him. It often happened in church or at Literaries. When mothers and daughters would suddenly find themselves near him, and move to another pew. But Tiny had never flinched from his company. The first day they met in church in Ellsworth, she had led her family of brothers and sisters into the church pew, watching Easy

Tucker every step of the way past the maroon songbooks and sat down right beside him. Once during the service their shoulders touched, and she did not pull away. Easy Tucker was in love from that moment on and would have walked to Colorado to prove his affection. Indeed, his neighbors said the real reason he turned all his crops to cash so quickly was just so he could buy things for Tiny Tucker. If she was threatened, he was threatened. And if she wanted Margaret Chambers out of their community, he would see that it happened. He was only too happy to bring the roofing tar to Garvey's Mill.

Easy found the thinner in the corner of the shed under a stack of feed bags, bound with twine string. He thought they might have a use for the bags as well, so he tucked them under his arm. The paint thinner can was only about half full. That was alright since he only had a one-gallon pail of tar anyway. He had poured the tar from a ten-gallon drum into an open pail, and it had already started to jell during the trip from the farm to the mill. He had to get some thinner into the tar quickly or it would be too thick to handle, despite the 90° August heat.

Easy climbed into the back of his wagon and was pouring the thinner into the pail of tar when Jay Langston rode up. Easy gave the tar a quick stir with a tree limb, motioned for Jay to go inside, then picked up the bags and followed Jay through the screen door.

"Howdy, Easy," Jay said with his usual swagger. "Got everything ready?"

"I got the tar," Easy said. "The only problem is, that stuff's so damn thick I don't know if we can use it."

"Hell," Jay said, slipping into language he could never use in front of the Reverend Aaron, "we're not trying to keep her from leaking." All three laughed. "We're not trying to cover the roof," Jay continued, trying for another laugh. "We're just going to throw it on her, dump the feathers, and beat it."

"Wait a minute," Ed Garvey cautioned. "We have to do this right. We have to make sure she knows we want her out of town."

"Hell," Jay repeated, "everyone in town knows what we want. Three of the boys called me this afternoon. As I was coming through town, Tiny Wilson yelled at me to say, 'Club will be there.' Everybody knows. I'm amazed Margaret Chambers doesn't know."

"Hank Simpson is coming on his new motorcycle, with one of his cousins from Russell," Ed Garvey said. "They both got bikes. I hope they don't scare the horses. Joe and Piney will meet us here if they can get here by eight. We have to be at Twelve Mile by eight thirty."

"I just hope we can depend on Herb to do his part," Ed continued. "I went over it with him this morning, but he halfway likes that girl. Plus he gets so nervous, I don't know if he can get her out to Twelve Mile Run or not."

Jay Langston hiked up his trousers, grabbing the silver belt buckle he had won at the County Fair two years ago and pulling it up until his trouser cuffs no longer touched the ground. Jay's face was red from working in the sun during harvest and a wild shock of brown hair hung over the side of his forehead. Even his mother said he always looked like he was up to no good. While his face was slightly crooked, it had an angular quality that girls liked, and he often bragged about going to neighboring towns for square dances. But he also had a reputation for meeting girls, promising to take them on a picnic at some future date, and then not showing up. The word was that he had to stay away from Ellsworth for nearly a year until some of those promises were forgotten.

"What's Herb gonna do?" Jay asked.

"He's supposed to stop the buggy down by those cottonwood trees at Twelve Mile, take Margaret off for a few kisses, and then we'll teach her how girls are supposed to act in Nickerly County."

.   .   .

Margaret Chambers laid out her newest dress. It wasn't that she wanted to impress Herbie Forchet so much, but an "invitation only" barn dance was an important event. No doubt they'd hired a local square dance caller, probably Everett Fenton and his boys from Tescott. Besides, she had learned in college that it always paid to wear your best in public, especially if you might meet other boys.

She admired the dress as it lay on her summer lace bedspread—pink with pleated sleeves that gathered just above the elbow, and a white apron that hung from her waist to her ankle. The dress had a high neck with no collar but a red rose embroidered at the throat where the top button hooked. It was light as a breeze, but the evening promised to be quite warm, and she could take a shawl for riding in the buggy. She had ordered the dress from the Parisian Cloak Company in Kansas City, based on a flier that the company had sent to the Nickerly Dry Goods store.

She picked it off the bed and held it to her shoulders as Ileen stepped into the room.

"Oh, Margaret," she said, "it's so beautiful. I can just see you whirling around the room. Although not with Herbie Forchet."

"It's just for one evening," Margaret said. "This could be the last dance of the summer."

"You mean the only dance," Ileen smiled. "You know mother doesn't like these dances."

"School is about to start," Margaret said, "don't ruin my good time. In a few weeks I'll be grading papers instead of going to parties. I look forward to school, but I hate for summer to end."

"I like the fall," Ileen said. "There are more church activities. We start choir practice next week, and I want to be a soloist."

"How can you sing with all those old ladies?" Margaret continued, turning up her nose, trying to decide whether to wear her brown or black shoes. "I wish I had a pair of shiny shoes, real party shoes, to wear."

"That's why people talk about you, Margaret. You're always drawing attention to yourself. Showing off."

"Ileen, I'm not showing off. I just want to dress up. The way we did at school."

"I'm not sure you should even go to this party," Ileen said. "Why hasn't anybody in town mentioned it?"

"Because it's private," Margaret said. "Herb says Ed Garvey is going, and he didn't know who else."

Ileen got up from the edge of her bed and moved to her dresser, a stand with six drawers that her father had made to fit between her bed and the window in the middle of the wall. A mirror with a wooden frame and fluted edges leaned against the wall on top of the dresser, her lone claim to privacy. Everyone shared the bathroom, and Margaret had her own mirror attached to her low dresser. But Ileen's dresser was her private treasure chest. Her mirror had reflected all the raw emotions of her adolescence, especially those moments when she had tried to be pretty, when she had stared for long minutes at her pale face and asked when one of Nickerly's young men would find her attractive.

"Margaret," Ileen said, turning to her sister, "I want you to take this with you." She held out a six-inch silver hatpin with a large pearl on the end.

"Thanks, Ileen," Margaret said, "but I don't need that. I know Herbie Forchet. And even if he did something vulgar, I couldn't use a hatpin. I wouldn't know what to do with it."

"You mean my older sister, who's been to the College of Emporia and who has taught school for a year, couldn't defend herself with a hatpin?" Ileen teased. "Here. Just take it for me."

"Ileen, you're so dramatic," Margaret said, taking the pin in her hand. "I don't have anything to wear it on."

"Just put it in your purse," Ileen said. "I'll feel better."

.   .   .

"Should we wear masks?" Jay Langston asked.

He passed the small brown jug of whisky to Easy Tucker sitting nearby on the wooden benches. Ed Garvey Sr. kept the jug in the closet for an end-of-the-day swig—fortification against Mrs. Garvey and her demand for an accounting. Sometimes farmers stopped by about dusk, knowing Ed and his jug were always available. Of course, the whisky was a gift to be offered, never to be taken. Ed Garvey Sr. was the richest and most powerful man in the county, and his jug was a kind of scepter to be used in granting camaraderie status to select friends and neighbors. The only person brave enough to dip into the jug without Ed Sr.'s blessing was Ed Jr., and he did so knowing that he had better not leave the jug empty. Tonight, Ed Jr. felt the tar party group might need a little fortification, and around six thirty, he brought out the jug for the first round of swigs. By seven thirty the whisky was being consumed in ever bigger gulps, and Ed felt the group had better get going while they were still level-headed.

"Why don't we wear these feed bags?" Easy suggested. "Just cut the eyes out."

"Are you crazy?" Jay shot back. "They say 'Garvey's Mill' in big red letters. Everybody in the county will know who did it."

"No, they won't," Ed chimed in. "Everybody in the county has these sacks. It could be anybody."

"Bring 'em along then," Jay said as he headed out the door. The three men walked to the wagon, already hitched to one of the Garvey mules. Jay took three bags out of the bundle, opened his pocket knife with the bone handle, and cut small holes just above the word "Garvey's." He tossed the first one to Easy.

"Here," he said. "You may have to make the holes bigger."

Easy thought that might be a reference to his wide, flat face, but he let the remark pass and tried on the bag. It was perfect. He folded it lengthwise and tucked it into his belt. He also had Tiny's bonnet, which seemed preferable to a feed bag.

"Did you bring the feathers?" Ed asked as he unhitched the mule. No one answered. Ed looked up at Easy. "Didn't I tell you to bring the tar and feathers?"

"Gosh, I'm sorry," Easy said. "I forgot."

"We'll stop by the Ennis place," Ed said. "It's on the way." All three jumped up onto the seat in the front of the wagon, and Ed guided the mule away from the mill, onto the road that ran under the small railroad trestle for the Sante Fe line that passed straight through Nickerly. As they neared the Ennis house, Esther was in the front yard waiting for them.

"Good luck, boys," she shouted.

"We're gonna get her out of the county tonight," Easy said.

Ed brought the mule to a stop, leaned forward in his seat to talk past Easy and Jay, and asked, "Can we borrow a pillow, Esther? We forgot the feathers."

Esther ran back in the house without saying a word.

"Does everybody in town know what's happening?" Jay murmured to no one in particular.

Esther emerged from the house, letting the screen door bang behind her, and threw the pillow up to Easy.

"This should do it," she said. "I hope you teach her a lesson."

"We'll do that," Ed said as he urged the mule forward. It was almost dark, and they wanted to be well hidden before Herb and Margaret arrived.

The boards on the wooden bridge across Twelve Mile Run were well worn with age and splintered by the hooves of cattle driven across them on a regular basis. Some of the nails had been jarred loose, and shrinkage left sizable gaps between the planks, creating a washboard effect for buggies and wagons. It was only a mile and a half to the bridge from Nickerly, but since picking up the pillow from Esther Ennis, the boys didn't have much to say, suddenly realizing that so many wheels had been put in motion, so many people involved, that they could not back out.

Jay Langston felt a rumble in his stomach as the wagon wheels rolled across the bridge, bouncing his insides with every plank, reminding him that he hadn't given much thought to how his family might react to the events ahead. He guessed his father would approve; he had heard the Reverend Aaron condemn the conduct of Miss Chambers as blasphemy, a sin against the will of the Lord, and as a disease that should be bled from the community. It seemed clear that Jay's role tonight was pretty much what his father was talking about.

By the time they reached the intersection at the top of the hill, it was Kansas dark, which under cloud cover is as black as an Angus, with rural electricity still a rare commodity and farmhouses so far apart that window lights look like fireflies. But on a clear night, the open prairies and sparse tree lines have just the opposite effect. There is nothing to obstruct the glow from the moon and the stars; they hang above the landscape like lanterns throwing great shafts of illumination across the fields, exposing rabbits in full gait and all manner of night creatures scurrying across the clods turned up by the plows. Shadows dart about like martins, so fast you cannot follow them to their point of origin, and cows stand along the horizon like dolls at the Nickerly carnival. It was in this light that Ed Garvey could make out the forms of Cavity Ben Johnson, Red Romberger, and Club Wilson, their wagon parked down the road nearly a half mile, no doubt so as not to alert Herb and Margaret. There were three or four other figures with them as well.

Ed pulled his wagon up to where the three were standing and whispered hello. Cavity Ben took the bridle to steady the mule while Ed climbed down.

"Where are they?" Cavity asked.

"Can't be far behind," Ed whispered. Voices could carry for miles across the open prairie; indeed Ed was sure they would hear the buggy before they could see it, especially when it hobbled over the bridge. He privately congratulated himself for planning this whole thing with the bridge, a kind of early warning system. Then he got a look at Easy Tucker, who had slipped behind the wagon and seemed to be changing his clothes.

"Holy cow, Easy," Club exclaimed, "what are you wearing? Is that Tiny's dress?"

Easy didn't reply. Ed walked over to get a closer look, pinching the excess cloth about Easy's waist and remarking, "You and Tiny don't seem to be the same size."

"Shut up, Ed," Easy said. "Wait till you see my hat." Then he swung his left arm from behind his back and held up Tiny's fishing bonnet, a huge floral print affair that folded over her head like a tarpaulin over a stack of wood. The bonnet puffed over Tiny's entire head so that when she sat on the bank of the Saline, fishing pole in hand, waiting for the catfish to bite, she looked like a giant mushroom. Easy hoped it would have the same effect for him.

"I see you picked up some friends," Ed said, turning to Club. "Howdy boys." He motioned for the four men standing back a few yards to come over to the wagon. Ed knew them all, of course, Ab Polk, Emil Emig, Yohan Swenson, and Quenton Reynolds. Yohan and Quenton both had children in the Sunnyside School, and they couldn't like what was being said about relations between Margaret Chambers and her students.

The mule heard the rumble first, raised its ears, then its head, and let out a loud mulish scream at the unknown intruder. Ed grabbed the harness and settled the animal down, then listened himself as the far-off noise moved slowly in their direction.

"Must be the motorcycles," he said. "Hank Simpson must be just starting out from town. Sounds like more than one cycle. Must have his cousins with him."

Everyone turned toward town to listen, but the sound was new to them, and they couldn't tell if it was two or three cycles. Even the new Model A Ford engines all sounded different, and Ed wasn't sure he had ever heard a motorcycle engine before. But that must be the roar, and it sure sounded like more than one.

"I hope they're ahead of Herb and don't pass him on the road," Club said. "Those bikes will scare his horse right into the ditch."

.   .   .

Herb Forchet had forgotten just how pretty Margaret Chambers could be, especially on a warm summer night when the sun had just vanished, the locust hum was starting to tone down for the night, and the dust had settled on the roads. He helped Margaret into the buggy, offering his hand, and feeling the strength of her long fingers as she stepped on the metal stirrup and bounced onto the leather seat. She carried a plaid shawl over her left arm, thinking she could cover her head if the breeze threatened her hair, or wrap it around her shoulders if it got cold on the trip home. Her pink dress was finely starched and splendidly crisp, so fresh that it gave Herb a moment of anguish about his assigned task. She did not seem like an evil girl. It was true that he had tried to put his arms around her on their last date, several months ago, but it was only because he heard that she liked it. Joe Tanner had told him that she liked to be kissed, that every boy who had ever taken her out had kissed her. He was still angry that he should be the only one she rejected, but maybe tonight would make up for it. At least tonight all the boys would see her in his arms and know that he was as good as everybody else.

"Do you know anything more about who's coming to the dance?" she asked.

"No, Margaret," Herb said, "I expect several of the boys from Ellsworth will be there. But I know you and I will have a good time."

Margaret glanced at him cautiously as the rig moved away from her house and down the road. "Now, Herbie," she said, "don't you try anything with me like last time. You said this was just a square dance."

Herb laid the whip to his horse lightly, not wanting to continue this conversation, and the rig leapt forward. It didn't take long to reach the Twelve Mile Run bridge, and Herb slowed the horse to a walk just in case one of the boards was missing or broken. As they crossed, Margaret leaned forward, squinting into the night. It was quite bright, and she could vaguely make out the outline of something in the road.

"Look, Herb," she asked, "what's that ahead?"

"I don't know," he said, recognizing an opportunity to bring his horse to a stop and make one last pass at Margaret before meeting the boys. He leaned forward with her, feigning an attempt to see down the road, then put his arm around her shoulder.

Margaret jerked away. "Don't," she said rather loudly. "If that's all you want, you can take me home. Now get this buggy moving or take me home."

His rejection now complete, Herb moved to the edge of the seat, relishing the comeuppance Margaret Chambers was about to get; she would soon wish she had treated him better. He once again applied the whip and smugly waited for his friends to appear.

As they neared the top of the hill, Herb spotted a group of men crouched behind some scraggly mountain laurel bushes in the ditch along a crossroad. He had never noticed a crossroad at that location, even though he had been on Twelve Mile Run several times. It must be just a wagon trail used to gain entry to the pastures on either side of the main road. As they got closer, a mule and wagon suddenly pulled out of the shadows and stopped in the center of the road. Two men were in the wagon and several more were running behind.

Herb jerked on the reins so hard that the horse bucked in front of them. Margaret grabbed Herb's arm for support.

"What is it, Herb?" she stammered. Several of the men wore Garvey feed bags over their heads. "What do they want?"

Herb sat still, not knowing exactly what to expect. But he recognized Ed Garvey's voice telling him to get off the rig. He jumped off the buggy, and Garvey caught him off balance, knocking him down with a shove that scraped his face in the sand. Then other hands grabbed his coat and shoved him into the ditch beside the road. "Stay there," someone shouted.

Herb touched his nose and realized it was bleeding. Then he looked up and saw the guns. One man stood holding the bridle of the horse; three others were holding pistols aimed at Margaret; and one man, he assumed to be Garvey, was pulling Margaret off the rig.

As Garvey grabbed Margaret's arm, she screamed, "What is this? What are you doing?" He yanked her off the seat with such force that she stumbled. Her dress caught on the stirrup and tore as she fell to the ground.

Two men grabbed her by the elbows and pulled her to her feet. She thought of fighting or screaming. She tried to wrench free, but a large man wearing a poncho and straw hat reached down and grabbed her ankles, pulling her feet out from under her. They held her in the air for a moment, as if uncertain what to do next. Margaret thought she recognized the dress on one of the men, but it was so ill fitting she couldn't be sure. Their breath smelled of whisky.

"Take her around back," the first voice said. And the three men carried Margaret around behind the buggy and lowered her to the ground. The man in the poncho started to let her go, but she struggled, and he tightened his grip.

"Why are you doing this?" she cried.

"We want you out of the county," the voice said.

Then another man with a feed bag appeared beside her. It was Jay Langston, holding a milk pail at least half full of a thick black substance. Another bag was stuffed in his belt, hanging almost to the ground. Then the man in the dress bent down and slid his fingers under the neck of her dress.

"Oh, no," she screamed. Her mind flashed back to college, to that dark evening when the unseen hand had moved along her throat and under her blouse. She gagged and she struggled again. That only seemed to anger her attacker. He jerked the red rose at the neck of her dress like a handle, and Margaret's ears filled with grunts and snarls. She gave a powerful kick, but then her body froze as she felt his powerful arm yank forward, ripping her dress straight down the front.

Easy didn't realize the force of his adrenaline, and the dress tore all the way to Margaret's waist. Then he grabbed her bodice, not knowing exactly what it was for or how many garments might be involved, and he ripped again. But this time his eyes saw Margaret's breasts burst forth. As his hand slashed downward, his little finger and the side of his hand brushed against her hardened nipple. It was like a branding iron had scorched its imprint on his hand, and he drew it back instantly. He rubbed his hand against his leg, but the burning would not go away. He thought maybe his hand was cut, but he could see no blood. He reached down frantically and rubbed the side of his hand in the dirt, but even the road sand would not eliminate the gnawing at his little finger. He set the bucket of tar on the ground and grabbed his right hand with his left. He was shaking.

"What the hell are you doing?" Garvey yelled. But Easy didn't answer. He just stood up and stared off into the dark, clutching his burning finger. Garvey yelled again. Then Easy Tucker just turned and staggered off into the night.

Jay Langston picked up the tar bucket, tore the feed bag off his head, and dipped it into the tar. He then made one big smear down the middle of Margaret's chest and stomach. Then he reached down and lifted her skirt. Club Wilson was still holding her legs and he gasped.

"Don't you let go, Club," Jay hissed.

Then Jay reached for the waist of Margaret's pantaloons and pulled them down to her knees. He started for her panties, then stopped, reached again for the well-soaked feed bag in the pail of tar, and swabbed her thighs and legs.

Margaret had quit struggling. Her mind was numb. She did not understand why this was happening. Her head reeled. She felt the warm tar on her legs, then collapsed on the road. The man stood over her and poured the rest of the pail on her stomach and dress. The whole process took only a few moments.

"Where are those damn feathers?" Garvey shouted.

Margaret could hear footsteps as someone ran toward the buggy, then the pillow was in front of her, just a white cloud pouring down on her, soft and fluffy. Then everything was black.

People were shouting to get out of there. Her feet were dropped. The hands holding her arms began to drag her body, then she was lifted into the air and tossed onto the seat of the rig. She could hear the horse dance with nervousness as people ran away. Horses were moving. Engines were revving. Wheels were sliding in the sand, but Margaret never looked up. Her body was sticky and burning, her clothes covered with a black glue that would not wipe away.

Herb Forchet crawled out of the ditch when it was clear everyone was gone. He wanted the darkness to cover his shame. He realized how small he must appear, hiding in the ditch, crying over his own cuts, willing to sacrifice his sense of civility and manhood for the approval of his friends. Yet they did not admire his actions this night. They despised him for his weakness, and he knew it. They had thrown him into the ditch, like wastepaper. He stumbled to the buggy and climbed into the seat beside Margaret, whose face was still buried in the leather.

"Please help me," she cried. "Please take me home."

"I will," Herb pleaded. "I'll take you home."

He took her by the shoulders to help her sit up, and saw what they had done to her dress. Margaret held the front together with both hands, but black tar was everywhere, on her dress, her face, in her hair, on the seat of the buggy. Her pink dress was unrecognizable, wrinkled and torn, with feathers sticking to the fabric, making her look like a wounded bird who had been caught in a thunderstorm and thrashed by hail. She was torn apart.

Margaret couldn't figure out how to put herself together. She just held her stomach and pleaded to go home. Herb found the reins of the rig and turned the horse around in the road. As they straightened out, he asked again if he could help.

"No," she whispered. Then she remembered the hatpin in her purse. She leaned over and felt for it under the seat. She took the hatpin, remembering Ileen's words and wishing she had used it on Herb Forchet, or any one of her attackers, but now she just wanted it to hold her clothes on. She pulled her dress together across her breasts, and threaded the hatpin through the material with two dips. Then with her hands free, she began to pick the feathers from the tar, scraping them against the edge of the wagon to pry them from her fingers.

As Herb worked his horse up to a trot, Margaret looked up for the first time. Then she froze with fear. Not a hundred yards ahead of them were four more men, walking down the middle of the road toward them.

"No," Margaret cried, "they're coming back. Whip up the horse! Whip up the horse!"

Herb was in no position to question her instructions, and he had no idea why these boys would just be arriving. He laid on the whip, and the boys jumped out of the way as the buggy tore past.

"Who was it?" Margaret asked. "They were wearing head scarfs."

"I don't know," Herb said, not knowing and not wanting to know. He only wanted to get back to town, and then as far away from Nickerly as fear and shame would carry him.

CHAPTER EIGHT

When Margaret's mother poked her head inside the girls' room at milking time, the moon was still hanging outside their window like a golden locket. Margaret and Ileen looked so angelic with their soft faces sticking just above the covers that Mrs. Chambers gently closed the door so their father would not disturb them. It wasn't until two hours later, nearly seven o'clock, that she opened the door again to rouse the girls for breakfast. The sun was splashed over Margaret's forehead, bleaching out her eyebrows and leaving the lower part of her face and hair in tender shadows that gave no clue to the turmoil of the previous evening. But when Margaret stirred, her mother noticed a strange redness on Margaret's cheeks and around her hairline, a roughness like a raw sunburn after a long day in the fields. Mrs. Chambers crept closer and lifted her hand toward Margaret's face, ready to check for fever or some other malady, when Margaret's eyes opened. They showed a sadness Mrs. Chambers had never seen before, and then Margaret started crying; long slow uncontrollable sobs that Mrs. Chambers could not understand, so she held her daughter, raising her from the pillow, slipping her arm under Margaret's hair, and holding her face gently against her own. She caught a pungent whiff of kerosene and lye soap.

"What is it, Margaret?" she asked. "What's happened?"

She did not hurry her daughter. She knew that when Margaret stopped crying, she would talk, and then they would know what to do. She rocked Margaret slowly from side to side.

Ileen awoke and started to speak, but her mother motioned with her free hand for her to be quiet, so she sank back into her bed, frowning as she remembered her admonitions of the previous evening, but thankful that Margaret was home safe. She was surprised that she had not heard Margaret come to bed. She had waited up for her sister, reading by the fireplace until almost eleven o'clock, then going to bed, expecting to be awakened by Margaret. But that had not happened, and now Margaret was crying in her mother's arms.

Mrs. Chambers was a gentle woman, who prayed often even though she seldom went to church. She read the Bible daily. Her church homilies were a guiding philosophy, for herself and her family. She instructed her girls in the way of the Lord, and admonished them to live humble lives of servitude to God and family, the way she had lived her own life. She was not particularly strong, not a leader, or even a joiner of organizations like the Civic Improvement Association. Those were for other women with rich husbands and too much time on their hands. Mary Chambers didn't resent those women, because she wasn't a resentful person. She had spent all of her life in God's shadow, living on the promises of a loving Savior and doing her best to cast aside the worldly sins of ambition, greed, vindictiveness, and jealousy. If there were ever a confrontation, she would back down. And if she were shortchanged by one of the patent medicine salesmen who sold elixirs on the sidewalk, she would never complain, telling her husband that the man undoubtedly needed the money more than she did. For those who knew the story of her dalliance at the shivaree so many years ago, it was as if the fire in her personality was exorcised that night, the humiliation with Johnny Harwood having left her with a guilt that rendered her forever meek. But she had made the best of it, turning meekness into goodness.

When Margaret finally stopped sobbing, she looked up at her gentle mother, and wondered if she could tell her what had happened, not because her mother would not be sympathetic, which of course she would be, but because her mother would have no idea what to do. Retaliation of any kind, a public reckoning of any kind, was simply beyond her. Her mother's natural inclination would be forgiveness. That would not be Margaret's course, but right now all she needed was sympathy and support, and her tale came tumbling out.

"Oh, Mother, it was so horrible," Margaret began. "Why would they do it?"

"Just tell me what happened," Mrs. Chambers softly urged. Ileen lay stiff in her bed, afraid for her sister and for her mother, suspecting some vicious attack by Herb Forchet. Would her mother think Margaret doomed to hell by some sin of the flesh? Or worse, that the sins of the mother had been repeated and guilt would wash them all into a sea of shame? Ileen thought of her own shame, then realized how selfish that would be and pushed it aside. She would support her sister, no matter what.

Margaret, ever the schoolteacher with the organized mind, walked through the story from the beginning: the phone call from Herbie Forchet, the buggy ride, being waylaid, the horrible feeling of tar being applied to her body, and then the long night of cleaning before coming into the house.

"I stayed up until eleven," Ileen commented from across the room.

"I was home before that," Margaret whispered. "I asked Herbie to let me off down the road. It was still light out, from the moon, and I could tell that you were still awake, but I didn't want to scare you.

"I went along the hollyhocks by the side of the house and out to the barn. The cows were out so there wasn't any noise. Mother, I just couldn't let you see what happened. My pretty new dress. It was horrible."

Mrs. Chambers said nothing. She sat stunned, on the edge of the bed. "But why?" she finally managed to stammer.

"I don't know, Mother," Margaret said. She was relieved that her mother wanted to know, to understand the men's motives, because Margaret already knew that she herself would be seeking those answers.

"I went to the back of the barn where Father keeps the horse blankets," Margaret continued, "and took off my clothes. My legs and chest hurt so bad. They were so sticky. And it was in my hair."

The words were rushing out, as if the expression of events had to be cast aside with her soiled clothing.

"I threw my clothes on the straw by the gunny sacks. There weren't any rags, so I took a gunny sack and soaked it in kerosene. I just splashed kerosene on my chest and legs. It felt cool at first, but then it started to burn, and I was scared it would just make things worse. The tar started to wash off. I even put kerosene in my hair, where they had touched it. Oh, Mama, it was so horrible."

"Then I found the lye soap that Daddy sometimes uses, and I climbed in the water tank by the windmill. I know it must have been cold but I didn't even notice. I scrubbed and scrubbed with that soap. You know I've always been afraid of that tank because that's where the cows drink, and it has that moss all over the bottom. But last night it felt so soft and clean. The moon was shining in the water and I could see myself. If I didn't move, the water was still and I could see that I wasn't really hurt. I just felt such shame. Why did they do this to me?"

"Don't you worry about that," her mother said. "We're just glad you're home."

"I put my clothes in a gunny sack," Margaret continued. "It's still in the barn. I left the blanket just outside the back door and came to bed. I was so thankful none of you woke up."

"Don't you worry," Mrs. Chambers said again. "Your father will find the blanket and your clothes. He'll burn them later. No one need ever know about any of this."

"Mother," Margaret said, "everyone will know. All those boys. What will I do?"

"Don't worry about that today, darling." It was the first time Margaret's mother had used that affectionate term in years, since Margaret was a child. When she was seven, Margaret was playing in the barn, climbing through the stanchions where Father milked the cows, moving the sliding boards that yoked the cows while they were being milked, when she spotted a stray cat crouched in the corner. Cats and dogs wandered in and out of the farm on a regular basis, sometimes staying a day, sometimes a year, but in the end always moving on. Margaret treated them like the hoboes who came to the back door for food or a day's work. The Chambers were known as people who didn't turn strangers away.

Margaret knew the cat with the dirty yellow fur and crooked black stripes across its back was the most common form of stray, without pedigree, color, size, or any distinguishing characteristic to suggest a natural lineage. It was dark in the barn, even in midday, and shadows played against every wall, hiding the cat's ears as they lay back against its head, and masking the angry hump of its back as it raised against the wall. Then it leapt at Margaret, clawing her arms and sinking tiny sharp teeth into her hands. Margaret drew back but the cat clung to her, somehow tangling its claws in her wool sweater. Margaret screamed and ran, bumping the door of the barn that was kept closed by a large spring, knocking the door open, and finally dislodging the cat from her sweater. She ran into the house, screaming for her mother, who finally calmed her down, washed the cuts and bites, and ordered Father to find the cat and shoot it. After she had wrapped bandages around Margaret's arms, she helped Margaret to bed and held her just as she was doing now, repeating, "Don't worry, darling, it will be all right."

Margaret could not understand the motives of the tar party any more than she could those of the cat.

Ileen brought her a glass of water. As Margaret raised up on her right elbow to accept the glass, Ileen caught sight of the deep red scratches on her chest and the bruises that were turning black on her breasts. Ileen instinctively put her hand to her mouth and backed across the room to her own bed. Margaret noticed the reaction but said nothing. She raised the glass to her lips, turned to look out the lower corner of the window, and saw the small fire burning in the cow pen. She handed the glass to her mother and fell asleep.

.   .   .

Easy Tucker stumbled in the back door of the farmhouse he and Tiny had shared all their marriage and quickly switched off the single lightbulb that hung over their kitchen table, hoping his wife wouldn't notice his red and swollen eyes. Worse, he still couldn't erase the irritation on the side of his right hand. It wasn't pain, or a pinch, or any kind of burning sensation—just a presence that seemed tied to his brain, so that when he felt the itch he saw her breasts shining large and full in the moonlight. When he had the vision, the feeling pulsated on the outside of his little finger, like a festering leprosy that had been diagnosed but couldn't yet be seen. He stuffed his right hand in his pocket and made a tight fist in the hope of squeezing the feeling away, then sat at the table, trying to gather his senses before facing Tiny.

When Easy looked up, she had filled the doorway. "Is she leaving the county?" Tiny asked. "I prayed for you all evening. You were the instrument of God's vengeance this night, Ed, and I know you carried out his wishes. I pray that we will be rid of her evil for all time, Ed, and that will be the Lord's will."

Easy said nothing.

Tiny could see that something was wrong. She walked around the small table and ladder-back chairs to place her hands on Easy's shoulders, feeling the shudder that moved across his body. "Are you all right, Ed?" she asked. "What's wrong with your hand?"

Easy jerked his hand from his pocket and shoved it onto the table. "Nothing," he said. "I'm fine."

"Tell me about it," she said. "What happened?"

Tiny reached over Easy's shoulders and placed her hands on his cheeks; she felt the wetness of tears and the pain that had stretched his skin, like the freezing and thawing of the earth that leaves crevices in the spring. The walk home from Twelve Mile Run had left Easy's face broken and rough.

As large as Tiny was, and as rigid as her belief in God could be, she was still a gentle woman who had salved Easy's wounds, physical and psychological, for seventeen years. She knew when his tears touched her fingers that something had gone terribly wrong; Easy was a common man of good sense, but he seldom cried, and Tiny was worried.

"Tell me, Ed," she said.

Easy just shook his head slowly from side to side. Then he dropped his forehead to rest on his left arm, and his back began to shake with convulsions. Tiny felt more helpless than she had in a long time, probably not since her children were sick with the fever. They had recovered, but she never forgot those terrible days when she could not help them as they shook and coughed; her only recourse to trust in the Lord. The Lord had responded and her faith was rewarded. Nevertheless, it hurt her to see Easy's body so consumed by grief.

Easy could feel Tiny rubbing his shoulders and it gave him reassurance. He raised his head from the table and began to tell the story, not in sequence, but in blurts and coughs that focused on his pain.

"Oh, Mom," he said, using his most endearing name for his wife. "She was so young, about like our own kids. I tore off the front of her dress. I saw her . . ." And his voice faded into sobs.

Tiny's hands flew to her mouth. She said nothing, but her face started to harden as she realized that she had never really thought about the process of tarring and feathering. Why tear off her dress? Somehow she just assumed the tar would be poured on the outside of her dress. Maybe just on the apron of her skirt. Not on her face. Why tear off her dress?

"She kept saying, 'Why me? What do you want?'" Easy said.

"Well, I hope you told her," Tiny answered.

Easy said nothing, but he was regaining his composure. He straightened his back and used his shirttail to dry his eyes. It had helped to blurt out what had happened, even if he didn't fully understand why. He looked down at his right hand. The itch was still on his finger.

Tiny said nothing as Easy looked up. He stretched his legs under the table and let his muscles relax for the first time in hours.

"Ed," Tiny began, "did you see her?"

Easy knew what Tiny meant, but he said nothing.

"Did you tear her dress off just so you could look at her?" Tiny said slowly. "Did you break a commandment of the Lord?"

Easy wasn't sure what he had done. The question made him stop and consider his guilt and shame. He knew that lust was wrong. But lust wasn't adultery. Had he broken a commandment? He didn't "covet his neighbor's wife"—this Margaret was just a girl. But it was definitely wrong to look at a young girl's breasts. It was a sin. A terrible sin that he recognized the moment it happened. He wondered if Tiny knew that her anger and questions were actually easing the guilt because he couldn't specifically identify the sin. He guessed not.

"How could you?" Tiny screamed, staring at him. "How could you let yourself be lured into a mortal sin by that vile woman? You put your hands on her. You touched her. You tore her dress and exposed her body. Shame on you, Ed Tucker. The Lord will strike you for this. I sent you out in the name of Christ to rid our county of this shameful, evil woman, and you fell under her spell. You will know the Lord's vengeance, Ed Tucker." Then Tiny turned and ran to their bedroom, slamming the door behind her.

Easy sat at the table and with his left thumb, he began to scratch the outside of his little finger. Quietly, he began to cry.

.   .   .

The next morning, Ed Garvey Jr. slipped out of the house without breakfast, not wanting to face his mother, not knowing whether she knew about the tar party. He needed to talk with his father. He rode directly to the mill, arriving just after dawn when the world seemed incredibly peaceful. A few meadowlarks ushered in the brightness of another summer day. Ed noticed a slight dampness still on the wheels of the wagon parked behind the mill office. He had pulled the wagon behind the building last night, unharnessed the mare, and rode her home. She was still lathered from the fast pace of getting away from Twelve Mile, and a line of white sweat was spread over her haunches like froth along the beach after an ocean storm. Ed had looked her over this morning in the barn but didn't bother to wash her down. She had been put up wet before. Instead he rode the stallion to the mill.

This morning, everything seemed to be in place. Ed took the used tar pail out of the wagon and dropped it from the edge of the water wheel into the deepest part of the river, a sinkhole that slowly deepened with each turn of the wheel. He watched as the pail filled with water and sank down into the darkness.

Ed Sr. arrived about seven thirty, seemingly in high spirits, wearing a brand new denim jacket he had picked up in Salina. He wasn't surprised to see his son already in the office, sorting out the books for the day ahead. Ed Sr. had run into Club Wilson's dad the previous evening and had heard about the plan for the tar party. Now he wanted a firsthand report.

"Hello, son," he said, "I understand you boys were up to a little mischief last night. How'd it go?"

"I think we got her out of this county forever," Ed Jr. said. "She knows we won't tolerate her kind around here."

"That's good, son," Ed Sr. said, lowering himself onto a bench. "Now we won't have to fool with that damned school board. I wish your mother wouldn't find out, but I'm sure she will. You just leave her to me. We had to get rid of this teacher, and everybody knows it. Hell, you'll probably get elected mayor for all this."

"You don't think she'll go to the sheriff, do you?" the son asked.

"Naw, the sheriff wouldn't do anything anyway. He knew yesterday what was up, and he didn't do anything. Besides, he'd have to arrest half the town, and for what? Putting a little tar on that girl. No law against that far as I know. I wouldn't worry about it. Our biggest problem now is we have to find a new teacher."

"I worry about Herb."

"Who's Herb?"

"You know, Dad. The barber, Herb Forchet. He drove her buggy. He looked scared out of his knickers last night. Plus we gave him a bloody nose."

"Why'd you do that?" Ed Sr. asked.

"We had to make it look real. He was supposed to take that Chambers girl off the buggy before we got there, but they were having some kind of argument, so we had to throw him off in the ditch."

"You didn't hurt her, did you?"

"No. We tore her clothes a little to put the tar on. But she's all right."

"You tore her clothes," Ed Sr. repeated slowly. "Why didn't you just pour the tar on her dress?"

"I don't know," Junior said. "We didn't talk about it. Easy just grabbed her dress and ripped it down."

Ed Sr. didn't really want to hear any more. He was really quite proud of the boy, not usually one for leadership in most matters, and in this case he had put the whole plan together. Of course, he knew some folks might look a little askew at tearing off the girl's clothes, even if they did want her out of the county. Even the Reverend Aaron might have trouble with that. But he could take care of Aaron, and the sheriff, if need be.

"I noticed the wagon out back has a little tar on the floorboards," Ed Sr. said. "You might want to clean that up a little."

Ed Jr. got the message. He closed the red ledger, shoved it back in the top drawer, and moved to the door. Just as he reached for the knob, the door opened in front of Club Wilson.

"Oh, sorry, Ed," Club said. "I just came over to tell you that Herb Forchet has left town."

"What do you mean?"

"Barbershop is locked. Buggy is gone. Looks to me like he never even went home last night."

·   ·   ·

The Reverend Aaron and Ivy Langston, sitting at their kitchen table, poured themselves a glass of warm milk only minutes out of the cow. All five of their holsteins had been milked before sunup. Jay's brother Ray had drawn them the general outlines of the previous night's activities while they were milking. Ray hadn't participated, but he knew what happened, and when he looked in on Jay that morning it was confirmed. Jay's clothes were rumpled on the floor at the foot of his bed, and a small feather was lodged in the cuff of his trousers. Ray walked directly to the barn, stood between the holsteins fat with milk, and spoke over their backs to his parents, each sitting on a "t" stool with a pail between their legs. Ray didn't know the details, but he knew the plan, and he rushed it out with the barest of details. The Langstons listened without comment, then Aaron spoke with unusual quiet. "Your mother and I will take this up with Jay after milking." No more was said until the couple sat down at the kitchen table.

"Mother," the Reverend Aaron began, "I have preached often on the sins of the mortal. I have asked our congregation to be ever aware of their sinful ways, to follow the lessons of God, to teach their young that the laws of God are the laws of man. And I believe the Lord will punish all those who break his laws; he will have mercy, but he will not be restrained. If the Chambers girl is guilty of taunting our boys, or leading them into temptation, then she should be removed from the school."

Ivy was a hard and unforgiving woman in matters of betrayal to God, and she agreed with her husband in every aspect of his ministry. But she also had five daughters and had heard their prattle about boys and teachers and their other friends at school.

"I worry about Margaret's mother," Ivy said. "In spite of that incident years ago, and in spite of their not going to church, I think she is a good woman. She wouldn't hurt anyone. I hope Margaret wasn't hurt." Ivy also understood how a personal comment once made can never be taken back, how a moral mistake once made can never be erased from memory, and she knew that Mrs. Chambers had closed herself off over the years rather than face any reminder of shivaree night. Ivy could not imagine compounding that pain with the knowledge that her daughter had been tarred and feathered.

"We'll know soon enough if Margaret was hurt," Aaron said, pouring another glass of milk.

They hadn't bothered to make pancakes, or fried eggs, or scrambled potatoes, or any of the normal breakfast dishes. Ray had stayed in the barn, eager to avoid the discussion about to take place in the house, and the girls were still in bed. So the house was still when Jay padded out of his bedroom and into the kitchen, wearing an undershirt and trousers, but no socks or shirt. He was still waking up, unshaven, and hoping for a quick drink of water from the cistern pump to clear his throat. But the minute he stepped through the kitchen door, he knew it could be some time before he finished dressing.

"Sit down, son," the Reverend Aaron said. "Tell us about your activities last night."

"We had us a tar party," Jay said casually, leaning against the door-jamb. "We showed that Chambers girl a thing or two."

"Whenever we take the Lord's will in our hands," Aaron said, "we must be sure of our righteousness. Do you know her trespasses?"

"Yes, Dad. Everybody knows her trespasses. She tried to seduce that Swenson boy. And she teases everyone. You know how she looks at people. Wearing all that fancy jewelry."

"We know her sins of pride and arrogance," Aaron said. "But it is also a sin to bear false witness against another. Do you know all these things to be true?"

"We didn't hurt her," Jay said. "We just poured a little tar and some feathers on her and told her to get out of Nickerly. She wasn't hurt. I helped put her back on the buggy myself."

Ivy's face was known to set in a frown that would outlive stone, but when she heard Jay's comments, so unadorned with remorse or concern for the girl's family, a slight crack moved from the left corner of her mouth around the corner of her chin, betraying a deep moral conflict between the purpose and the methods for enforcing moral purity. Although she would never acknowledge it, she also had considerable doubt about her son's newfound zeal in enforcing the tenets of the Bible. She believed in the thoroughness of his moral upbringing, a process that had involved hours of lectures, Bible readings, and religious studies. But the fact that he let these admonitions slide so easily from his bearing worried Ivy. She had hoped for some show of remorse at having to inflict this unusual punishment on the Lord's behalf. But it was not there. Her son was pleased, even proud, of his actions.

"Everybody in town was in on it," Jay said, beginning to feel that a more secular defense was needed. "Must have been fifteen guys there. And we got the feathers from Esther Ennis."

"I don't need to know the details, son," the Reverend Aaron said. "I'll pray for you. And you better pray that that Chambers girl is all right. Now get dressed before the girls get up."

Jay shifted his weight off the doorjamb and turned on his heel. He smiled to himself. The inquisition had been easier than he expected, presumably out of deference to the religious value of the tar party's actions. But he was a little concerned about his mother's reaction, especially that vaguely hesitant expression that had fluttered over her face. He wasn't used to seeing his mother uncertain.

CHAPTER NINE

W.W. McArdle, the county prosecutor, walked quickly along
the dirt road in front of his newly rented home, one of only four houses
on Fourth, and the only one in Nickerly available for rent. He counted
his steps from home to the courthouse, saying a number with each
footprint he made in the soft black soil. The street had been graded
with a horse-drawn blade, but every rainstorm left ruts in the road
from the wheels of wagons and carriages. W.W. swerved every few
steps to keep from twisting his ankle, but he never lost count.

The little town of Nickerly had lettered its streets in one direction, and numbered the cross streets, a miniature version of the sec-
tion roads that measured the farmsteads every mile. W.W. wanted
to know exactly how far he walked to work in the morning so he could
advise clients on distance. It was only a hundred paces from home
to courthouse, and maybe three hundred paces from one end of town
to the other, although he hadn't had a chance to walk it yet. This was
his first month in Nickerly and moving his wife and daughters from
Topeka to a prairie town of a few hundred people left him little time
for walking tours.

He took the courthouse steps two at a time and bounded into his office, setting his briefcase on his dark walnut desk. He moved to the two double-hung windows behind his chair and raised the roller shades, allowing a block of morning sun to form on the desk. W.W. was still apprehensive about this move west, but it helped that his wife was starting to appreciate the slow pace of Nickerly life. He remembered how she had questioned the move, having grown up in Kansas City. But now they had a church, the First Presbyterian, and Mrs. McArdle had been invited to join a Bible reading group. It seemed his family was assimilating rather well.

W.W. was less certain about himself. He liked the prestige of being county attorney. His classmates at law school often talked about the long climb in building a legal reputation, the boring probate cases that formed the basis for most private practices, and the struggle to secure clients. But here in Nickerly, W.W. seemed a celebrity from the beginning. His name was in the paper. People even stopped him on the street just to shake hands. Yet he wished he felt more comfortable with farmers and their clipped conversations about grasshoppers and cattle diseases. It wasn't a perfect fit for W.W., but he was trying to learn the local customs. Last week he even stopped by the blacksmith shop to watch a red-hot plowshare being hammered into shape. He admired the smithy's quick, self-assured movements, his deft handling of the scorching metal. The smithy had a unique talent, and so did he. W.W. was proud of being a lawyer.

Margaret Chambers and her mother paused at the base of the steps and looked up the limestone front of the Nickerly County Courthouse, past the varnished oak doors, past the long windows on the first floor, past the conical roofs of the corner towers, to the clock tower in the middle of the building. It was almost noon before Margaret had convinced her mother that she had to tell the sheriff what happened, and it took another hour for her mother to explain that the sheriff wouldn't care, that he was friends with the men who tarred her, and that too many community leaders were involved. So they decided to talk to the one person they didn't know, the young county attorney from Topeka, who had arrived in Nickerly only a few months ago.

Margaret had tearfully recounted her story again for her parents, even the part about her dress being torn and the man in the bonnet who walked away. Her mother gasped at each new revelation, feeling her daughter's pain, the crudeness of her attackers, the shame of her physical exposure. Margaret's father sat stone-faced. He was furious at the cowardice of his friends and neighbors, but within him dwelled a deep fear of the community's judgment and such a heavy shame that he could not muster a stronger defense of his daughter.

Margaret saw that weakness in her father's eyes and knew that if she sought justice of any kind, she would likely stand alone. She would be the accuser, not the victim. But she had her mother. And in her mother blazed a fierceness and an understanding of her situation that came from years of being unable to fight back, unable to challenge the shivaree rumors. For it took more strength than any in the family realized for Mrs. Chambers to endure that injustice, to sleep through the anger and rise each morning to face a condemning community. Margaret knew now where her courage came from, and she knew her mother would stand beside her in the "Office of W.W. McArdle."

Mr. McArdle's office was on the first floor, across from the county clerk's office, only two doors down from the district judge, and within twenty steps of the county courtroom, a solemn and elegant chamber at the end of the hall. Margaret knocked gently, pushed the door open, and held it for her mother. Then they both stopped to face the county attorney.

W.W. McArdle looked up from his desk but said nothing. Not many women had visited him since he took office. Most of the legal affairs of the county were conducted by men, and most of the trials brought to him for prosecution involved violence by men against men. He knew that women were taking a greater interest in public affairs, even marching in the streets of Topeka for suffrage, but he had no idea what these two women could want.

"Are you Mr. W.W. McArdle?" Margaret asked. "I read about you in the paper, and I need your help."

"I am," he replied. "Please come in."

As Mr. McArdle rose from his desk, Margaret took stock of him. She did not know what lay ahead of her, but she imagined that at a minimum she would have to face her attackers, and she hoped for a strong shoulder to lean on. The man in front of her did not look too promising. Mr. McArdle appeared to be less than thirty years old, with a narrow build and slightly hunched shoulders. At least his clothing seemed professional. His white shirt was heavily starched, accented by a thin black tie. He wore finely pressed black pants, highly polished shoes, and a pair of round, wire-rimmed spectacles. He looked to Margaret like a professional man should look, and a far cry from the businessmen of Nickerly who seldom polished their shoes. His voice was somewhat high, but she had only heard five words, and they were uttered with a precision that appealed to her. He had thin features, with black hair parted in the middle, but his saving grace was a smile that materialized the minute he stood up.

"I'm Margaret Chambers," she said. "And this is my mother. I have been tarred and feathered, and I want to punish the men who did it."

The smile vanished from W.W. McArdle's face.

"Please sit down," McArdle said, ushering the two women to the wooden captain's chairs in front of his desk. As he moved around the desk to his own chair, he took an appraising glance at the straight-talking young woman before him. He didn't know the Chambers, or many other people outside the courthouse. But the name Margaret Chambers did stir some recognition, perhaps a gossip item from one of his secretaries, or perhaps a mention by his wife after church. He couldn't recall the exact context.

"Tell me what happened," he said. "Don't leave anything out."

Margaret took a deep breath and carefully recited her story with total fidelity to the truth, as she knew it, but there did appear to be a lot of blank spaces, particularly the whys.

"Forgive me, Miss Chambers," McArdle said, "but why did these men do this?"

"They said they wanted me to leave the county."

"But why? Did these fellows all have children in your school? Do you know any of them? Any personal grudges?"

Margaret's mother reached between the chairs and touched her daughter's hand.

Margaret's firmness began to weaken. She had steeled herself for the painful recollection of the attack, but she still hadn't come to terms with her feelings toward the individuals. It was easy to hate Herb Forchet, and she blurted his name out quickly. He had tricked her, used her, and made advances that she rejected. But the others were harder to classify.

"I don't know why," she murmured.

Margaret looked at the floor. Her hands registered a faint tremor, as she thought of Mrs. Garvey and what her accusations would do to their family. But if justice was to be done, she had to reveal everything she knew.

"Ed Garvey, from the mill, and Jay Langston, the preacher's son, and another man in a dress and bonnet that I didn't recognize," she said. "There were others, everywhere. I couldn't see them. There were horses in the dark. And a roar, like one of those cars. And then more men on the road wearing head scarves. I didn't know any of them."

As Mr. McArdle listened, his anger began to grow. This was not a childish prank, or even an adolescent mistake. This was a crime perpetrated by grown men, married men, leaders of the community.

And it didn't really matter why, or what, Margaret Chambers had done. These men had assaulted her, had violated her, and they had to be dealt with by the law.

"Miss Chambers," he said slowly, "if you're certain you want to proceed with this, I'll need you to swear to charges against these men, and I'll have the sheriff arrest them. I think we should start with Mr. Forchet."

"What will happen?" Margaret asked. "Will they go to jail?"

"First, we'll have to investigate this matter," McArdle answered. "Then we'll see what kind of charges need to be brought. Do you know where Mr. Forchet is?"

"I understand he left town that very night," Margaret said.

"Well, let's start there."

McArdle took a sheaf of paper from his desk drawer. At the top, in large script, were printed the words "State of Kansas, Warrant— General Form."

"Whereas," McArdle wrote, "an information has been presented and filed against Herbert Forchet, charging that on or about the 7th day of August A.D. 1911, in the County of Nickerly and State of Kansas, one Herbert Forchet did then and there unlawfully assault, beat, and wound one Margaret Chambers, contrary to the form of the statute in such cases made and provided and against the peace and dignity of the State of Kansas, therefore:"

The rest was preprinted. It was an order to the sheriff to arrest, forthwith, Mr. Forchet, and secure his appearance before the judge of the District Court of Nickerly County to answer for the charges.

McArdle pushed the warrant to the front of his desk for Margaret to read. She shuddered slightly at the legal formality of the charges, but her expression never changed. Neither did she look at her mother, who had gently started to cry. Margaret nudged the warrant back with a soft "Thank you."

McArdle rose from his desk and walked the women to the door. As he was closing it behind them, Margaret suddenly turned and said, "Why doesn't it say anything about the tar and feathers?"

"Sadly," McArdle said, "there's no law against that."

.   .   .

Jay Langston rushed into the mill office early the next morning, out of breath from the short ride at a high gallop, hoping to find Ed Garvey Jr. alone so he could give him the news. But inside the office, standing behind the counter, were Ed and his father, obviously agitated and angry. When the door broke its jamb, the two fell silent, but their last words were still on their lips, like a drop of coffee from the last sip. It was the kind of awkward silence that shrinks a room, and Jay could feel the walls.

"You know," Jay said simply.

"Everybody knows," Ed Jr. said. "I heard it from three people before I got two blocks this morning. By noon, everybody in town will be here." He meant everybody involved in the tar party.

"You boys quit stammering," Ed Sr. said. "That Chambers girl deserved exactly what she got. You boys did the right thing, and this town will back you up. I'm going to talk to the sheriff today and straighten this thing out. It'll never go to court. I'll spend every last dollar I have to see to that."

Jay could see that the Garveys knew more than he did about the arrest of Herb Forchet. "What's going to happen now?" he asked.

"We don't know for sure," Ed Sr. said. "That Chambers girl went to the county attorney and filed charges against Forchet, and the sheriff arrested him on the way back into town last night. That fool got scared and went to Topeka for three days."

"Well, now he's back, and in jail," Ed Jr. said. "And I bet he's talking pretty fast about all the rest of us."

"Hell," Ed Sr. said, "who cares? You boys were carrying out the will of this community. Besides, far as I know, it's not illegal to tar and feather anybody anyway. If she had left town the way you told her to, there'd be no fuss at all."

Unfortunately for Herbert Forchet, however, County Attorney W.W. McArdle went home from his meeting with Margaret Chambers, kissed his wife at the door, hugged his two small daughters, then collected them on the sofa for a family conversation. The more he told his wife of the Chambers story, the more personal it became, and the more determined McArdle grew. He wanted his wife to know that pursuing this case could affect the family. It could hold them up to ridicule, cause their neighbors and friends to turn against them, cause people to talk about them and shun them in church. But McArdle was certain it was right, and the closer his innocent daughters pressed themselves to his sides, the more his outrage grew over the assault on Margaret Chambers. He would prosecute every last one of the men who participated in this barbaric act. McArdle went to bed eager for the next morning's interrogation of Herbert Forchet.

CHAPTER TEN

Mrs. Ed Garvey was mad as a hornet. She was so mad that she just sat at the kitchen table, clutching a mug of cold tea and staring vacantly at the tiled wall. She was thinking hard, wondering how things had gone so wrong. Her mind was racing back through time, scanning for some sign, some mistake she had made, some explanation for the events of the last few days. She reached back to the deep past.

Eunice was raised an only child. Her father, like many others in the county, had come to Kansas after the Civil War, homesteading 160 acres of bottomland along the Saline, living in a dugout etched in the side of a hill that came to be known as Garvey's Bluff. One of her earliest memories was hiding behind the spirea bushes to watch Ed Garvey ride by on his pinto pony. Ed's farm was only two miles down the road. As they grew older, Eunice laughed with Ed at church picnics and endured his teasing as if they were brother and sister. From the first beckonings of womanhood, she loved him. Their marriage wasn't the beginning of their lives together, it was just a milestone, another step in an already intense relationship. Eunice was fourteen,

Ed twenty-four. And the marriage had worked. They had forged a partnership, sharing the same ambitions and the same ardent sense of morals, religion, and duty.

Ed and Eunice Garvey were fiercely loyal to their friends, the community, and to their business. They had started the mill together some ten years after their marriage, when the farm was prospering and the future seemed boundless. It was hard work, but their crops increased every year as Ed added more land to his holdings. Ed had a way with money. He wasn't afraid of it. He was willing to borrow from the bank in order to take risks. And Eunice encouraged him, assuring him of her support regardless of the consequence. They built farm and mill together, becoming rich and influential in the process. It seemed that nothing could come between them.

But that loyalty was challenged now as never before. Mrs. Garvey had not known in advance about the tarring and feathering of Margaret Chambers, or she surely would have stopped it. And although she had heard about the attack that morning from the clerk at the dry goods store, only now was she starting to assemble the facts of what had happened, mostly from the ravings of Tiny Tucker and Mrs. Club Wilson. They had stopped by that afternoon, when Eunice was cutting some mid-August zinnias from her small flower bed along the foundation of the house. Zinnias like the heat, and the August sun had burned a brightness into every petal.

When the two women appeared at the gate, they didn't interrupt until Eunice had filled her apron with long-stemmed colors.

"Eunice," Tiny began matter-of-factly, "I assume you know about getting Margaret Chambers out of the county."

"I know," Eunice answered sadly. "Everybody in town is talking about it." She was walking toward the house, with both hands holding the corners of her apron. Mrs. Wilson hurried around her to open the screen door. But Eunice stopped cold, turned to her two old friends, and said, "Why didn't you tell me before this happened? My own husband and son. Your husbands. All conspired behind my back because you knew I would have stopped this terrible thing."

As the three moved into the house, Eunice dumped the flowers into her chipped porcelain sink. Tiny stopped at the end of the table. "Eunice," she said, "we know you have a soft spot for that girl, sending her to college and all, but she's evil. We've all heard about that Swenson boy, and you saw her at the Literary. She's not one of us. I don't want our kids going to school there, until she's gone."

"Now, of course," Louise Wilson said, "we don't know what's gonna happen."

Eunice did not look up from her sink.

"We just came by to say we are going to fight that girl if she has our men arrested," Tiny said. "My husband sits at home now, cursed by the body of that woman, cursed by her evil. He just holds his hand and walks around aimlessly. I don't know what to do with him, but I sure know where that woman should be. She should be in jail, not poor Herbie Forchet, or anybody else."

"I don't feel that way, Tiny," Eunice said calmly. "But I won't argue about Margaret now. Our husbands have done a terrible thing. I don't know what I'm going to do."

Tiny and Louise Wilson edged toward the door. When Eunice didn't raise her head or turn to say good-bye, they just pushed the screen open and left.

Eunice felt guilty for not going straight to see Margaret to offer her support, but first she had to talk with her husband and son. She made herself busy around the house but had no interest in cleaning, and certainly none in cooking. Finally, she sat in her rocker by the fireplace, the same rocker she had known as a child, crawling into her mother's lap. It felt comfortable in an uncomfortable world.

Ed and Ed Jr. walked in the house just before dark. Ed didn't like to argue after dark. Arguments always seemed bigger if they couldn't be reflected against the backdrop of the day. A disagreement over whether or not to go to church—and Ed usually didn't—could be angry and mean at night. But if they walked to the barn in the middle of the day to argue, the tension soon fell away. Disagreements simply did not hold up against the world he and Eunice had already conquered. Ed desperately wanted to take Eunice for a walk to talk about Ed Jr. and Margaret Chambers.

But Eunice had the house in readiness. She had not cried over this incident, because she seldom cried, but also because she didn't really understand what had happened. She was simply angry that her men could let something like this get out of hand. And she was going to demand answers. She loved Margaret Chambers, she had schooled the girl like a daughter, had urged her off to college, and brought her back to teach. Her men knew this. They had known Margaret since she was eleven or twelve. They knew the Chambers family. It was just inconceivable that this could happen.

Ed and Ed Jr. entered through the back door and looked at the woman now perched on a kitchen stool, her back straight, her hands clasped precisely on the old oak table, her jaw hard. They saw a stony determination in her face, and also a glint of confusion and fear.

"I'm sorry, Mom," Ed Jr. blurted out. "But she deserved it."

Eunice said nothing. She folded her hands on her apron, a habit more than anything else, and looked into the faces she had trusted all her life.

"Did you do this thing?" she asked.

Ed sat down slowly but forcefully, folding his hands on the table in front of him. "Junior here and some of the boys set out to teach that Chambers girl a lesson and get her out of Nickerly County," he said. "You know what was being said about her. We can't have that kind of person teaching school."

"The Lord sayeth thou shalt not bear false witness," Eunice said.

Her voice was level, and she let the words out slowly, enunciating each one carefully. "And surely our neighbors have borne false witness against Margaret Chambers. I do not believe what they say. Margaret is a strong girl, that I taught, and I do not believe she is corrupting the morals of our children or our community."

"Mother," Ed Sr. said, "you know the Civic Improvement Association does not agree with you. Just last week Tiny Tucker prayed for deliverance from this woman. And nearly every family in town knew what these boys planned to do."

"They aren't boys, Ed," Eunice continued. "They are grown men, with families, with responsibilities. I am as faithful to the Lord as most, but I do not believe the wrath of God goes to the shaming of an innocent woman. This is 1911. We don't burn people at the stake, whatever their transgressions."

"Eunice, don't you lecture me," Ed said. "Our boy did the right thing, and I will defend him with every penny I have. The community will stand up for him. We will prevail over this girl no matter what you think."

"Ed, this is not a matter of prevailing," Eunice said, seeming to understand the situation perhaps better than even she realized. "Herb Forchet has been arrested, and he has named every one of you in on this. Fourteen men. Fourteen men, and not one of you had the gumption to stand up and say, 'This is wrong.'"

Ed Jr. shuffled in his chair.

"This was not wrong, Mom," he said. "Ask anyone in town. Margaret Chambers tried to seduce that Swenson boy. She flirts with all the men. She doesn't know her place."

"You don't know any of that," Eunice said. "That's town gossip."

"What about her mother and Johnny Hargrove?" he countered.

"That was twenty years ago, and we surely don't know what happened that night. Probably nothing." Eunice was flabbergasted at this accusation. "That was twenty years ago, and you still bring it up.

We see the Chambers family every week. They helped build our school. They raised two fine girls. They are honest and decent people, yet you bring up that silly shivaree. And for that you want to tar and feather their daughter."

Ed decided it was time to change the conversation, move away from what had happened, which couldn't be changed now anyway, and consider the present.

"Eunice," he said, "the sheriff will be here tomorrow for Junior. I have hired John Engle to represent us, and he's going to get the best lawyers in this state to help us. My boy will not go to jail for this. We should be proud that our community has stood up for its Christian principles."

Eunice hadn't really considered the possibility of jail. "What will the charges be?" she asked. Her voice was quiet and low.

"The sheriff says this new county attorney, McArdle, is going after everybody," Ed said. "That little weasel of a Frenchman is sitting in jail right now claiming that our boys made him do it. The sheriff went out to Twelve Mile Run this afternoon to look the place over. They'll be down at the mill tomorrow. But I don't believe there's a jury in Nickerly County that would ever convict these boys of anything."

The knock at the door was faint, but clearly discernible, even through the fog of family argument. Nobody moved. They sat still, silent, not believing that anyone would be coming to the house after dark. Then Ed Sr. heard the knock again and pushed his chair away from the table. Ed Jr.'s shoulders sagged as the air slid out of his body like tension suddenly gone from a wire fence. He felt limp. His father opened the door. It was Easy Tucker.

"Your wife was here earlier, Easy," Ed said, without even waiting for a greeting. He just wanted to get rid of Easy and return to his conversation.

"Can I see you a minute, Ed? Outside?"

Ed looked helplessly back in the house, catching Eunice's eye. Although her expression never changed, Ed turned and walked outside. Easy took a few steps away from the house. It was the first time that Ed noticed Easy's hand, tucked behind his hip, and it looked in the dark like he might be wearing a glove.

"Ed," Easy said, looking hard at the ground, "if anything happens to me will you take care of Tiny?"

"Sure," Ed responded. "But this is going to blow over. Don't you worry. Now go on home." Ed turned to go back in the house.

"Wait," Easy said. "I already sold the lake to Jack Butter down at the ice house, just in case I need a lawyer. But will you see that he gets the ice if anything happens?"

"Sure, Easy, but you'll be here."

Easy sold his ice every year to Jack Butter. Jack came to the farm in the coldest part of winter, usually February, to cut the ice with long handsaws. He hired a half-dozen farmers, who often sought part-time jobs during the winter, to work two saws and load the ice squares onto sleds pulled by mules or horses. Jack dragged the ice to the ice house, stacked it layer upon layer, with sawdust between each layer to insulate against a thaw, and then sold it throughout the summer in three-foot squares. By the end of the summer, when most of the ice was gone, the sawdust was four or five feet high in the ice house, and just finding the remaining ice took some serious digging. Ice was a valuable commodity, and Easy's lake had provided ample income ever since Jack Butter's ice house was built.

"I just want to make sure everything is right," Easy said, and turned to leave. It looked to Ed like Easy grabbed his right hand with his left as he turned, but it was too late to ask about the glove, and Ed wanted to get back inside to his more immediate problem. When he stepped back in the kitchen, no one had moved. Ed sat back down at the table.

"What was that all about?" Eunice asked, smoothing her apron with both hands.

"Easy is worried," Ed said. "You know how he is about Tiny. Very protective."

"What's Tiny done?"

"Nothing, he just wanted me to know he's already sold his ice to Jack Butter."

"Dad," Ed Jr, interrupted, "did you see his hand?" Ed Jr. had stared through the screen door as Easy and his father talked. He tried to imagine the last time he saw Easy, wearing a dress and sunbonnet, tearing Margaret's blouse, then wandering off into the night. He wondered what was going on in Easy's mind. Easy was such a complex character, quick to temper but long on compassion. He had once pulled a neighbor out of a threshing machine after the man's arm caught in the drive belt, tearing it off. Easy carried the man to his wagon, drove him to the small hospital in Nickerly, and stayed with him for three days while the doctor sewed up the stump and kept him from dying.

"Easy seems real upset," Ed said, "but I told him to go home and not to worry."

"Can you say the same for us?" Eunice asked sharply.

"What does John Engle say?" Ed Jr. inquired, going directly to the point.

"Engle says this will never go to trial. There is no law against tarring and feathering. And Margaret Chambers is a tart. Our boys were carrying out the wishes of the community and the will of God. You've seen how this girl walks down the street, inviting men to flirt with her. I hear she's been with half the men in Ellsworth."

"Margaret is not a tart," Eunice said forcefully. "And if you boys try to destroy her, after all you've already put her through, I'll be on her side."

"Now, Eunice," Ed Sr. said, "don't get worked up. Let's talk about this tomorrow when the sheriff comes."

"When is that?" she asked, surprised.

"At dawn," Ed said. "He said he'd be here at dawn."

CHAPTER ELEVEN

Temple Dandridge strode into the newsroom of the *Kansas City Star* and announced to his colleagues, more than twenty editors and reporters bent over scarred wooden desks in a newsroom with a washboard floor that hadn't seen varnish in decades, "The story of the century is mine."

Nobody looked up. The city editor was shouting a story assignment across the room to three reporters gathered around the *New York Times,* which had just come in by train. None of them looked up either. But Temp Dandridge didn't care. He walked straight into Nate Cabot's office, pulled up a chair, and waited for the editor to stop scribbling. Cabot looked even more like a painted Easter egg than usual, principally because he had no neck, a fifty-two-inch waist, and a wide-brim felt hat permanently fixed to his head, even in August and even at ten o'clock in the morning.

"Nate, old man," Temp began, "I got a call last night from someone I haven't seen since Topeka, when I spoke to that law school about the *Star.* Anyway, this kid calls me last night and says he remembers me from the speech, and then he says, 'I want to tell you about my case.'"

Cabot had not yet looked up from his editing.

"'Sure, kid,' I say," Temple continued. "Of course I don't remember him from Adam. But it turns out he's a county attorney in some place out west called Nickerly, and then he tells me the whole town has tarred and feathered their schoolteacher."

Nate glanced up, or at least his hat moved, and Temp pushed on. "This kid is gonna prosecute fourteen guys, not just any guys off the street, but the cream of the town, for pouring a little tar down this lady's dress. Can you beat that for a story?"

"So, let's see your copy," Nate grunted.

"Sure," Temp said, "sure. But boss, I want to go to this trial. We could get a story every day. I want to see this lady who could get the whole town riled up."

"What'd she do?" Nate asked.

"I don't know," Temp said. "The kid says it was gossip. Something about seducing a boy."

"How young?" Nate asked.

"The teacher or the boy?" Temp smiled. "Haven't the faintest."

"Arrests?"

"The trial hasn't been set yet," Temp said. "In fact, they're just arresting people now. I wish I could remember this little county attorney. I can't picture him at all."

"Get us a piece for tomorrow," Nate said. "We'll worry about the trial later."

Temp walked back to his desk, plopped down, and shuffled through the papers stacked haphazardly around his typewriter. Temp's management technique was to write addresses and phone numbers on a scrap of paper, usually a corner of the *Star* he tore off while he was standing at the wall phones installed along the back of the newsroom. He then threw the scraps in the shoe box he kept in the bottom left-hand drawer of his desk. Since the scraps didn't always make it into the box, every couple of weeks he would reshuffle his books and papers, picking out the unfiled scraps of names and numbers, and discarding them or placing them in the shoe box. It wasn't perhaps the most efficient system, but it worked well for Temp.

Temp made a mental note to call this McArdle kid just as soon as he could, and as soon as he found his number. When his desk was almost clean, except for a dictionary with the name "TEMP" written in ink on the side of the tightly bound pages, he found the scrap of paper he needed and placed it in the middle of his desk. It read: "McArdle. No. 3001. Nickerly County, Kansas." If he could get a call through to the Nickerly operators, 3001 translated into three shorts and a long on the desk of W.W. McArdle.

Temp took out his prized writing pen. The pen was an award, given to him by the Kansas City Press Club for a series of stories he did about a nurse who had murdered two of her roommates. Temple lived across the hall from the three girls and had decided to ask one of them out to dinner. He knocked on their door and was greeted by a young woman in white, holding a butcher knife, and sobbing that she had killed her friends. Temp consoled her as best he could, unsure of her mental state, and slightly fearful that she might try to close the gender gap among her victims. He also realized his first responsibility, as all journalists do, to get the story. He only had an hour before deadline. Temp listened as the girl poured out her hatred for her "prettier" roommates and how they had mistreated her. He told her to call the police, checked to see that the victims were indeed in the bedroom with their throats cut, then went across the hall and called Nate Cabot to dictate the story.

"Hell no, I don't have sources," Temp said. "I'm here. The nurse did it. She told me about it herself. And I saw the bodies."

"What about the cops?" Nate asked.

"She's calling them now."

"OK, gimme the story," Nate said. "But you better be right."

Temp was right, and the Kansas City Press Club recognized him with a handsome black pen with his name inscribed in gold letters on the side. Hoping for inspiration, Temp picked it up, opened the bottle of black ink in the well at the top of his desk, and began to write:

NICKERLY, KANSAS, Aug. 10, 1911—Arrests have been made against those accused of the "tar party" in the case of the state against the assailants of Margaret Chambers of Nickerly, who on August 7 was taken to a lonely spot near town where a coat of tar was applied to her body by businessmen and farmers from the surrounding area.

The story contained few solid facts, because Temp didn't know very much. But he was on deadline, and if the *Star* got the story first, it would be their trophy, no matter how rough the reporting. Nate ran the story at the bottom of page one.

The front page of the *Kansas City Star*, the biggest paper between Philadelphia and the Rockies, was a megaphone to the world. Within hours after porters loaded the *Star* bundles on the Western Express headed for Denver, newsmen across the state were reading about the tar party and placing calls to the courthouse in Nickerly, Kansas. First it was Lawrence, then Topeka, then Abilene and Salina. One by one, every town along the rail line woke up to news of the tar party. Reporters were calling Nickerly all morning, but Temp was still one step ahead. He was on the train heading west.

About midnight, Temp stretched out on the seats of Car No. 3, just ahead of the pullman. Nate hadn't approved of this departure, but he would pay the expense anyway, especially if Temp could produce a front-page story every day for God knows how long. He tossed his copy of the *Star* on the seat in front of him, folded his jacket over the arm of the seat for a pillow, and closed his eyes. When he awoke, nearly five hours later, a halo of light was on the horizon, casting a soft yellow haze throughout the train. Several people were seated just ahead of him, no doubt passengers from Abilene or Salina. Just as he stirred himself, sitting up in the seat and peeling his wrinkled jacket from the armrest, he caught a snippet of their conversation.

"Look at this, Charlie. A tarring and feathering. Haven't heard of that in years. Right here in Nickerly, Kansas. Says a whole bunch of town fathers were in on it."

The other man laughed. "I bet those ole boys had a good time. Wish I'd been there."

"You will be," Temp thought. "Through the pages of the *Kansas City Star.*"

Temp felt sticky from the hot train. Even with the windows open, the breeze across the seats was heavy, making his skin feel clammy and raw, as if he had been riding a horse. As the train slowed, he stood up and stretched, then picked his straw hat from the rack at the end of the seat. Though he rarely wore a hat during the winter, he relied on this straw number all summer when the sun threatened his fair skin. It wasn't a panama hat because it was made in Arkansas, and the straw was slightly heavier than the pliable South American variety, but it held its shape in high winds, and the wide brim sat umbrella-like over his eyes, giving him a rakish appearance that he rather liked.

Temp stepped off the train and onto the wooden platform at what appeared to be the outskirts of Nickerly, Kansas. At least it said so on the front of the station, a ghastly yellow building that was blackened by the steam, grease, and oil of the trains. Temp carried only one suitcase, a green plaid cardboard affair with a goldplated latch. A veteran traveler, he had packed several sets of underwear, a razor and shaving soap, two shirts, and two pairs of pants. As long as his hotel arranged for laundry, he could live on that meager supply for a year.

At the end of the platform, Temp got his first look at Nickerly. The town had one long main street of sand running north from the water tower where the train was refilling its tanks. The street was wider than any small-town street Temp could remember and perfectly engineered so that storm water would run from the center to the ditches along the side and be carried to a ravine, that led to a creek, that led to the Saline River. The entire tributary could be mapped from the middle of town. Similarly, from his vantage point at the edge of town, Temp could survey Nickerly's entire collection of businesses, mostly two-story buildings with living quarters above, framed against the horizon. And there, at the far end of the street, was the most imposing prairie structure Temp had ever seen: a limestone giant larger than most of the buildings in Kansas City. It rose up from the earth like an Egyptian pyramid, and Temp wondered how it had been built, how many men with teams of horses had pulled how many sleds of limestone from the quarry to the edge of Nickerly. This was surely the fortress of local government. He decided to go there first.

Temple Dandridge didn't need to introduce himself to W.W. McArdle. His lecture on "The Law and the News" had made a strong impression on the young lawyer. While most of W.W.'s classmates at Washington Law School in Topeka sneered at the idea that public opinion could truly influence a trial, W.W. thought otherwise. He remembered his own father sat on a murder trial jury for a case in which a wife had killed her husband after years of physical abuse. The senior McArdle, an accountant for the Great Western Stockyards on the Kansas side of the Missouri River, was a very precise man who led an ordered life and abhorred violence. During the trial, McArdle read the morning paper's accounts of the proceedings to his family at breakfast. W.W. could see that his father was moved by the paper's accounts of the husband's behavior, his "large hands slashing across her face if dinner were not ready." That kind of description had not been available to the jurors at trial. But W.W.'s father repeated these words again and again to explain why he found the wife "not guilty" of murder. He just couldn't blame the woman after reading those stories about her abuse.

Of course, W.W. McArdle hadn't had much use for the press so far. In the small town of Nickerly, two papers fought for the seventeen hundred readers in the county, competing primarily on the basis of family reunion reports, church picnic notices, and school sports scores. The editors were both deacons in the Presbyterian church, loyal believers in the words of the Reverend Aaron Langston, and never printed gossip or other material that might be embarrassing to individuals or to the town. The local papers were a far cry from big-city journalism in which crimes and trials were magnets for readership, and long columns of newsprint were devoted to the legal machinations of jury selection.

When W.W. McArdle opened the door of his office and offered an outstretched hand to Temple Dandridge, he sensed that an unspoken union was being formed. W.W. was smart enough not to let Temp think he was being used, but he also guessed that the story of a young, single, attractive schoolteacher would be more compelling for readers in Kansas City than the enforcement of moral rectitude by rural businessmen. W.W. knew he was on the right side of the issue, and he sensed that Temp would want the story.

W.W. and Temp sized each other up rather quickly. Temp's suit was wrinkled from the overnight train ride, but his white shirt collar was still starched and straight. He had an open face, light skin with freckles, and he looked quite the innocent for a thirty-four-year-old man in a cynical profession. When he removed his straw hat, his smile looked more like a perpetual smirk, as if all of life were amusing and ironic.

Temp now realized why he had not been able to remember W.W. The man was nondescript. He wore a black suit and tie. His thin shoulders looked like they might have trouble holding suspenders, yet he was taller than Temp imagined. He had to be about twenty-five years old. There was little emotion in his face. It was hard to imagine Mr. McArdle working up great anger over the indignities thrust upon Margaret Chambers, or waving his arms in exuberance to crystallize the jury's outrage. But then Temp had seen lawyers who cast off timidity in front of a jury and became demons of fiery oratory. It would remain to be seen if this young country lawyer could rise to the occasion. In any case, Temp liked him immediately. He especially liked the fact that W.W. McArdle had called him with the scoop of the year.

The two exchanged pleasantries about the train trip and where Temp was going to stay. The town's only hotel, the Adeline, was a three-story limestone building on Main Street with three rooms on each of the two floors over the lobby. Temp could have a front room, which was pricey at two dollars a night, but the *Star* was paying. The average price for a room was one dollar, still a substantial charge for the drovers passing through town or the relatives back for a family visit.

W.W. got right to the point. "Mr. Dandridge, you didn't waste any time getting here," he said. "We just arrested these men two days ago, fourteen of them in all, and all except Jay Langston have posted bond, five hundred dollars. Jay's father is a Bible thumper, and I can't tell whether he doesn't have the money, or whether he's not sure he wants the boy out of jail. But I think his friends are going to loan him the money for bail by tomorrow."

"What happened here anyway?" Temp asked. "Did they hurt her?"

"I can tell you what happened," W.W. said. "But why is another matter."

"Some guy on the train said she was immoral," Temp recalled casually, trying to lead the conversation to Margaret Chambers. "He called her 'that trouble-making tart.' Could that be the case?"

"I don't believe it," W.W. said. "But I'll let you meet her, and you can ask her yourself. You're going to hear some terrible things about her in this town, but none as terrible as what these men did to her. Here's the list."

W.W. handed Temp a list of fourteen names. The men's ages and occupations made it clear even at a glance that this was not a childish prank.

Edward Garvey Jr., 31, miller

Jay Langston, 24, farmer

Edward "Easy" Tucker, 43, farmer and ice man

Herbert Forchet, 29, barber

Ben "Cavity" Johnson, 39, hardward store owner

Ernest "Club" Wilson, 53, quarry owner

Delbert "Red" Romberger, 36, rancher

Abner Polk, 28, farmer

Piney Woods, 35, farmer

Joe Tanner, age unknown, unemployed

John Buckhorn, 28, drover

Hank Simpson, 23, baker

Joe Simpson, 17, unknown

Striper Simpson, 19, unknown

"So these are the town fathers," Temp said, noting their occupations. "What about the town mothers?"

"Well, there's the Civic Improvement Association," W.W. said. "They're the leading wives in town. They meet every Thursday, pray a lot, act kind of snooty about who gets invited to the group, and the word is, they put the men up to this whole thing."

"Because the teacher is a tart?"

"Their claim is that Miss Chambers seduced a student," W.W. responded.

"Any truth to it?" Temp asked.

"I don't think so. I think it's plain old-fashioned jealousy," W.W. said. "You can size all that up for yourself. I'm still collecting evidence, so I don't know everything. But I am certain that these boys pulled Margaret Chambers off a buggy in the middle of the night, assaulted her, tore her clothes, and poured tar and feathers over her body. That is a crime under some statute, it's a crime in the eyes of God, and if it happened to my daughter I don't know what I'd do. But I'll tell you this, I'm going to prosecute this case no matter how much money Ed Garvey has. We're going to show people that men can't get away with this kind of savagery in Nickerly County."

Temp was encouraged by the fire in W.W.'s speech. "What do you mean, no matter how much money?"

"Ed Garvey owns the mill and most everything else in town," W.W. explained. "Everybody says he's an honest man. But I think the blood ran a little thin when it got to Ed Jr. It was Junior who organized the tar party, and now his dad is saying he'll spend every cent he has to keep the boy out of jail. Fact is, of course, nobody here in town thinks any of these boys will ever be convicted by a Nickerly jury. Fact is, most people wanted the girl run out of town."

"When can I talk to Miss Chambers?" Temp asked.

"Tomorrow, if you want. She's at home. But I need time to tell her who you are. Why don't I pick you up at the hotel in the morning, and we'll go out to her house. It's only a short distance."

Temp thanked McArdle for seeing him so promptly and decided to check in at the hotel before sending a teletype to Nate Cabot.

The Adeline was built in the late 1800s to accommodate drovers and cattlemen taking their herds east from Texas to Abilene. For more than a decade, the Santa Fe rail line ended right in the middle of the Kansas prairie, and the town of Abilene sprang up around it instantly, like an oasis around a desert spring. Thousands of head of longhorns were trail driven from Texas, paid for on the spot by the Chicago and

New York buyers, and held in rambling stockyards until the trains arrived to take them to slaughter. The only thing that stayed in Abilene was money, and enough brothels and saloons to satiate several thousand cowboys with big appetites.

Adeline Bowers made one of those cattle drives from Texas, and when she got as far as Nickerly, one day's drive from Abilene, she wanted a good night's rest before hitting the hubbub of the city. She also speculated that if the railroad ever moved on west, it would have to go through Nickerly. So she and her husband sold their cattle and never went back to Texas. Instead they built a limestone hotel to match the courthouse and waited for the railroad to deliver their fortune. The railroad came through Nickerly all right, but it kept right on going to Dodge City. Not only did few passengers going west get off the train to visit Adeline's, the Texas cowboys never got that far east. By 1911, the hotel had changed owners a couple of times, and most of the guests were patent medicine men, hardware salesmen, and settlers trying to reach the Rockies.

The presence of a *Kansas City Star* reporter in Nickerly was almost as newsworthy as a tarring and feathering. The desk man, from all appearances the only employee in the Adeline, was Homer Huffman, a taciturn man known in the community for always wearing a red bandanna about his neck, even in church with his best Sunday suit. When people asked him why, he always gave the same answer, "Jus' like it."

Homer picked up Temp's registration card, read the name of Temp's employer, looked up at the face beneath the straw hat, and offered him the best room in the building.

"Welcome to Nickerly, Mr. Dandridge," he said. "You here about the Chambers girl?"

"Yes," Temple said. "How do people here feel about the tarring and feathering?"

"Just a lot of commotion," Homer said. "I don't think it was anything to get excited about. Just a little tar on her dress. Probably had it coming."

.   .   .

W.W. McArdle pulled up in front of the Adeline about nine thirty in the morning, left the engine running in his new Model T Ford— the car was a luxury purchase he felt he owed his wife after bringing her to the isolation of Nickerly County—and hurried into the hotel to pick up Temple Dandridge.

"Mister, you better not leave that machine running or some of those kids will run off with it," Homer said, as two teenage boys scrambled across the street to inspect the shiny black automobile. W.W. turned to look through the stained glass window in the door and noticed that Temp was coming down the stairs, so he hurried back out to protect his car. Temp followed closely and by the time both were seated, nearly a half-dozen boys were gathered around. Temp wondered how many of them knew Margaret Chambers, or were her students, but those would be interview questions for a later date.

The Chambers place was only about five minutes from town. W.W. pulled into the short lane that ran by the side of the house and widened into a circular area in front of the barn. Around the circle were a water tank and windmill, and a small granary with two bins, one for wheat and one for corn. He drove past the house to turn around so the Ford would be facing the road when they left and to give Margaret a loud warning of their arrival. Chickens scattered in all directions at the sound of an internal combustion engine. Temp brought the machine to a halt, let the engine idle down to a series of uneven sputters, then pushed the switch to still the motor. Margaret Chambers, or at least Temp assumed it was she, appeared at the screen door and watched them untangle themselves from the steering wheel and the black leather seats. She didn't move.

W.W. walked straight to her, with Temp in tow.

"Margaret," he said, "this is the gentleman I was telling you about, Mr. Temple Dandridge of the *Kansas City Star*. May we come in?"

Margaret thought it a strange name, almost like royalty, with too many syllables for a farmer, as if his mother used a last name for a first name.

"Come in," she said quietly. She pushed the screen door open and turned to lead the visitors into the living room. Her mother and father were standing in the kitchen, as if caught in mid-conversation.

"Mr. and Mrs. Chambers," W.W. said, shaking hands with Mr. Chambers and nodding his head to Mrs. Chambers, "this is Mr. Dandridge." He assumed they had heard the earlier introduction to Margaret and saw no need to repeat the name of the newspaper. The two parents stepped back, as if turning the conversation over to Mr. McArdle. They didn't distrust the newspaperman because they had never had any reason to do so. In fact, they had never read the *Kansas City Star* and certainly had no understanding of the reach and impact of a story in this paper. But no matter. If Mr. McArdle asked them to talk with Mr. Dandridge, they assumed it to be at least one new friendship in a community of people pulling away from them. And if it helped Margaret's case, so be it. But still, Mr. Dandridge was a city person. You could see that by the cocky way he wore his hat.

"Please be seated, Mr. Dandridge," Margaret's mother said.

The parents remained standing as Margaret moved to sit in the rocker by the fireplace.

Temp and W.W. sat side by side on the sofa in front of the windows, where the sun behind them cast their faces in darkness, so Margaret turned her chair to angle the sun away from her eyes. Temple Dandridge was struck by her attractiveness. She had said only a couple of words, but she wasn't what he expected. She had a nice figure, but she was too tall to be considered provocative. She was pretty, but her hair was tightly wound in a bun that choked out any thought of frivolity. Her nose was strong, and when she smiled, as she did briefly when Temp sat on a hard cushion that had to be pulled and stored on his lap, her face grew open and warm. Only in her eyes was there any hint of trouble, a mischievousness jailed by fear, as if she knew a threat was at hand but didn't compehend its nature. She seemed wary.

"Mr. Dandridge is here to write about your case," McArdle said. "Could you tell him about the College of Emporia and why you wanted to be a teacher?"

Margaret knew this was just a warm-up question to make her feel at ease, and it didn't really help because she wanted to talk about what these men had done to her. She hesitated, as if bothered with the wasted effort.

Temp picked up on her pause. "Miss Chambers," he said, "I want to write a story about you, about why you went to college, about your life here in Nickerly, and about your interests as a teacher. I want our readers to know that what happened to you, happened to a real person."

"Thank you, Mr. Dandridge," Margaret said. She looked at him squarely. "That's one of the worst parts of all this. I grew up with these men. And Ed Garvey's mother is my best friend. She helped me get into college and to come back to Nickerly."

Margaret took Temp through her college years, the courses, the church parties, the dormitory, the one trip to Wichita with the college chorus to sing at the annual meeting of the United Presbyterian Council.

"Did you have any boyfriends?" Temp asked gingerly.

"I knew the boys at college," Margaret answered openly. "They took me to parties, and sometimes we went to church together. But there was no one special."

Temp thought her answer rather open and unaffected, coming from a girl accused by the entire community of having a low moral character. Either Margaret hadn't picked up on the relationship to today's predicament, or the gossip was wrong. In either case, she betrayed none of the defensiveness he expected.

Temp's article was coming together in his mind. This often happened—that a chance phrase or a quick impression would stir his imagination, and the story would take shape even before the interview was finished. He could see a profile story forming. He would show how an independent girl from a perfectly normal background could find herself ensnared in an iron circle of vicious gossip. But that was getting ahead of himself; this first story would be just about Margaret and her parents.

Mr. and Mrs. Chambers had seated themselves at the kitchen table, which looked directly into the parlor. Temp thought it strange that Margaret's father said very little, although he appeared to be listening carefully to every word. Mrs. Chambers got up to make some tea and set the pot on a silver tray on the small serving table near the sofa. Temp noticed there were few pictures on the wall, except for a likeness of Christ and a faded drawing of the Mount of Olives near Jerusalem.

"Margaret," Mr. McArdle interrupted, "I've asked Mr. Dandridge not to discuss the events of August 7 with you today. When the trial starts, as I'm sure it will, that's the time to talk about what happened. And I would ask you not to discuss that evening with anyone else, even your parents. Is that acceptable?"

"Yes, sir," she said. "And should I not talk about those hateful women either?"

"No, Margaret," McArdle said, realizing that it might be more difficult than he thought to guide his plaintiff. Temp looked up quickly from his notes. What a clever girl, he thought, to introduce the subject of her enemies without actually saying so. He looked forward to their later conversations, when he knew her better.

"Miss Chambers," Temp ventured, "do you know the men who did this? I mean from school, or church, or as neighbors?"

"There were some I didn't know," she said. "Some I couldn't see. It happened so suddenly. I was terrified. I think I know the man in the dress."

W.W. intervened before she could speculate on his identity.

"Have you ever had any trouble like this before?" Temp asked, getting closer to his real question. He couldn't seem to find any basis for the rumors about Margaret Chambers. She seemed every inch a lady, but he did notice that she wasn't afraid of men, at least not of him, and she had touched his arm as they sat down. Some men might interpret that as flirting.

"Mr. Dandridge," Margaret said, "this was hateful violence, not something I am familiar with." Margaret had locked the incident at Emporia in the hinterlands of her mind. Sometimes at night she would recall the rough hand that had invaded her blouse, but she had never uttered a word about it to anyone, and she never would. She understood the adversarial nature of her present position, having to defend her reputation in spite of the violence against her, and there would be no cracks in her armor.

But this was not the trait that intrigued Temp Dandridge. It was her smile, the innocence of her toughness. He scanned his memory of other women he had known, and none could temper an iron will with humility in the manner of Margaret Chambers. Margaret did seem humble, but she clearly would not betray her sense of purpose.

Temp decided to change tack. "Have you ever been to Kansas City?"

"Oh no, Mr. Dandridge," Margaret said with enthusiasm, a broad smile crossing her face. "But I want to. I want to go to the theatre. I want to go to church on Easter Sunday in a sanctuary that is so big a thousand people are there, wearing beautiful straw hats and flowers in their hair. Do you go there?"

Temp was surprised by the question. Not its substance, but that she had turned the interview. In spite of her situation, she wanted to learn, to know about Kansas City. She had a journalist's curiosity, and it excited him.

"I love Kansas City," Temp said. "I will show it to you sometime." Then he caught himself and returned to the subject at hand.

"It is said that you are too familiar with your students," Dandridge said, searching for the right euphemism.

"I am not," Margaret responded quickly. "I respect them, and I have never even touched a boy improperly."

Temp raised his head quickly when he heard her go to the heart of the matter.

"What do you mean?" he asked.

"I know there are rumors about me and young Mr. Swenson," she said, glancing at her sister to see if she recalled any conflicting statements. Of course, Margaret had told Ileen that the boy was cute, but she had never touched him.

"I think that's enough for today," W.W. McArdle said. "I'm sure Mr. Dandridge has enough for his story."

"Thank you, Miss Chambers," Temple said. "I've enjoyed meeting you very much."

.   .   .

On the way back to Nickerly, over the intermittent explosions of the pistons, W.W. McArdle outlined the thrust of his case against the leading citizens of Nickerly, a conspiracy case that would prove fourteen men set about to run Margaret Chambers out of town, at the urging of their wives and with the general consent of the community.

"Five men," the county attorney said, "including that lifeless barber, were directly involved, and the rest were too; they stood around watching like voyeurs at a carnival peep show. There were even some who didn't get there in time to watch, but who wanted to be there; they helped plan the whole thing. Worse, none of them tried to stop it, and I intend to prosecute every one of them."

Sitting in his hotel room at the small writing table between the two front street windows, Temp started to write. He had four hours before the teletype office closed, plenty of time to record his impressions from the morning visit. He took his favorite pen from his coat pocket, dipped it in the hotel ink, and started to write, stopping only briefly after the first sentence. The story began:

NICKERLY, KS.—Margaret Chambers, the eighteen-year-old schoolteacher who was tarred and feathered by leading citizens here last week, has a soft demeanor and says she was terrified when attacked in the shadows on the road.

The attack on Miss Chambers happened August 7, last, near Nickerly, in Nickerly County, where she lives with her parents. Herbert Forchet, the barber, took her buggy riding to a lonely point in the road where several men took possession of her team. Forchet immediately left, it is said, and hid in the ditch along the roadside while a crowd of men pulled the girl from the buggy and applied tar to her body. It is said she was otherwise uninjured.

In the terrifying affair, the men threw the girl to the ground, tearing her clothing partly from her body, and smeared her with tar, a mix for painting barn roofs. One man held her prostrate, another held the tar, a third smeared the black mess over Miss Chambers' body and limbs, from her neck to her knees. Then they emptied the bucket over her body. Then they released her. Forchet slunk from the weeds and helped the schoolteacher back into the buggy. She was so badly frightened that she could scarcely speak, but she was not weeping. The tar dripped from her clothing and her body and smeared Forchet's clothing and the buggy seat. On her bare arms and neck were the tarry prints of the hands of the men who had held her.

The only conversation that passed between the two during the drive home was one question and an answer.

"What did they mean?" Miss Chambers asked Forchet.

"I think," he replied, "they meant the tar as a hint for you to leave the county."

The only excuse for the act was that a number of suspicious, meddling women had whispered evil of the girl and had incited their "menfolks" to punish her.

Herbert Forchet was the first man arrested. It was charged that he entered into a conspiracy to entice the girl to the spot where the gang was waiting to attack. He pleaded guilty and on promise of a light sentence, gave the names of all the others concerned.

Temple Dandridge put down his pen and read the story once more. This would get the town stirred up, he thought, although it was a far cry from the gentle profile story he had intended to write. No matter, he fully intended to see more of Miss Chambers, and the next story could have a more personal touch.

CHAPTER TWELVE

The Reverend Aaron Langston spread the *Kansas City Star* on the kitchen table, poured himself a glass of tea, unbuttoned the white collar that pinched his throat, and sighed. This Sunday's sermon on the sins of avarice was not what the congregation had wanted to hear. He had avoided the only moral issue of any interest, and he felt guilty about it; worse, he didn't have a moral answer. He knew his friends and neighbors were looking to him for guidance. It showed in their faces and in their silence. After the service, the parishioners had filed past Aaron Langston, shaking his hand and repeating the mantra, "Praise the Lord," but they clearly weren't certain of the Lord's position on the men of Nickerly County. There were no picnics after church. Instead, parishioners murmured their good-byes in hushed tones and made a beeline for their buggies, where they were out of earshot and could argue openly about the virtues of Margaret Chambers versus the tar party.

Aaron hated himself for letting them down, and it weighed on his mind all the way home.

"Mother," he said to Ivy, "come read this article with me. We have to decide."

Ivy had gone to the bedroom to remove her black bonnet and jacket. She didn't comment on Aaron's request. She came to the table with her hair in a tight bun, her blouse still stiff and clean despite the two-hour church service and the ride home. When Ivy was angry, her body became a limestone post, never bending, never showing a scratch. She was appalled by the righteousness of the tar party and their wives. Indeed, she had yet to hear a God-fearing explanation from her own son for this act of violence against a woman.

Aaron started to read the story by Temple Dandridge. When he came to the paragraph about tearing her dress and smearing tar on her body, he could not say the words. He pushed the paper across the table so Ivy could read the lines for herself.

"What shameful things to put in the paper," Ivy said, pushing the *Star* back.

The Reverend Aaron found it much more comfortable to discuss these matters in a biblical context, rather than in secular reality. But first things first.

"Ed Garvey and Club Wilson put up the bond for Jay," Aaron said. "We'll have to pay them back the five hundred dollars."

"Jay can pay them back," Ivy said without emotion.

"We must stand behind the boy," Aaron said.

"And he must take his punishment," Ivy replied.

Aaron worried that the iron in Ivy's spine would never bend. He realized she had reasoned out the right and wrong of this matter, but he had not fully decided. Aaron made his own calculations, subtracting the community's responsibility to protect its shared moral values, from his love of his son. The math had slowly come out in the boy's favor.

"There may be a trial, Ivy," Aaron said. "And we must stand with Jay. He will need our support."

"Aaron, I've never trusted those boys, his friends," she said. "I knew they would get him in trouble."

"Mother, those boys are the children of our best friends. Most of them aren't boys at all. They have families of their own, and they were just trying to protect them."

Ivy looked down at her hands and saw the lines of toil, the long days in the fields, picking rocks from the soil so that the hand plow could turn the earth behind their horse. She remembered the heavy stones that hurt her back and the sharp ones that scraped her hands, leaving her fingers rough and aching. She remembered the time she helped Aaron put the harness on a pair of mules, years ago when her parents were still alive. A possum scared the mules, causing them to rear up, pinning her between their haunches. Aaron had yelled at the mules and yanked hard on the harness to get them apart. But the confusion only frightened the animals more. As Ivy fell to the ground, her chest hurting from the collision of moving muscles, she felt a hoof hit her leg, then Aaron's strong hand grabbing her ankle and pulling her under the mules to safety. Her physical damage was mostly bruises, and maybe a cracked rib that the doctor couldn't diagnose for certain. But psychologically, she was shaken by this demonstration of life's fragility. She often remarked to Aaron that if that beast had stepped on her stomach instead of her leg, she would be gone. The myriad of uncontrollable violences in farm life often left her trembling. That's why she hated human violence so much; it was controllable. It seemed so senseless to add another threat to those already abiding.

Finally, she looked up at Aaron. "Let's go for a walk," she said.

Ivy liked to stroll past the barn, through the pasture, and down toward the small creek where the cows stomped to the water's edge, leaving waffle patterns in the mud. Aaron took her hand as they started through the wild daisies, not blooming as vigorously as in July, but bending gently over the natural grasses, as if holding umbrellas for their late summer seedings. The flowers and weeds brushed against the hem of Ivy's dress, reminding her of their intrusion into God's territory.

"Aaron," she began. "I have followed God's law all my life. All the years that you and I have known each other, we have tried to walk the path of righteousness. But there are also our own laws that protect us from our weaknesses, our sins. We must keep those laws. I judge not my son's motives. I know that we must protect the morality of our families and our communities. But we cannot excuse this thing that has happened. Those boys had no right to tear her clothes or to put that horrible tar on her. It's just shameful."

Aaron hadn't heard Ivy talk so purposefully, or at such length, for some time. Her slow, deliberate words made him feel the shame of what had happened. Perhaps his first blush of pride in protecting the community was not quite appropriate.

"I am a leader in this community, Ivy," Aaron said. "My sermons lay out the word of God, the rules to live by, the Ten Commandments that guide our daily lives. I cannot ignore this thing. The community must stand up for itself."

"But not like this," Ivy said. "This was not responsible behavior. Jay did not exercise self-control. Where was the respect for individual life? I am just sick about this."

"Let's go back to the house," Aaron said. "The boys will be home soon."

They turned back, dropping down toward the creek for a few yards, then heading again toward the house. Ivy always liked to walk in different paths when she was in the pasture so as not to flatten the grass, which was so dry it crackled under her feet as the brittle stems broke under each footstep. They walked across the second season of grass, grown in the spring and browned in the summer. Dead leaves from the previous fall, matted in the earth during winter, were covered with mud and cattle hoofprints, and had hardened into the cracking soil. A new crop of leaves would soon be falling. August was an awkward in-between time, buried between the green vibrancy of spring and the orange calm of fall. To Ivy, the deadness of the earth under a barren heat was a time for testing, when God demanded a sacrifice before bestowing the blessings of fall. She wondered if the cool October evenings this year would be truly refreshing.

"What will our family say?" she asked after a few steps. "Jay will wear this shame forever, and so will we. I don't know, Aaron. I just don't know."

They walked on to the house in silence.

.   .   .

Margaret Chambers liked watching the steam-driven trains that rolled past Nickerly, scattering animals and rearranging life on the prairie. She walked along the tracks, in spite of her mother's many warnings against it, and felt the pull of the unknown that the railroad inspired. The tracks were like a hole in the sky that let people in and out of central Kansas. First there were the builders, the crews that noisily swept across the plains leaving the iron trail in their wake. Then came the drifters, always men, jumping the new trains for a free ride west. They came to the Chambers house and offered a day's work for some food, then moved on. But they left their stories behind, often involving the search for a second chance or at least a new dream. The people of Nickerly didn't fear these men, but they did fear their dreams. The hoboes, as they were beginning to be called, spread endless tales of adventures in distant places. In Nickerly, two boys in one year gave up the farm life and disappeared down the tracks. Margaret had no intention of jumping on a train, but she walked the tracks often, wondering about the changes that trains and automobiles were making in their lives. Now the tracks were a refuge, and she walked slowly, stepping on one cross tie after another, wondering how she should handle the swirl of decisions she was now facing.

Margaret thought about the two men she had just met, W.W. McArdle and Temple Dandridge, trying to judge their advice. She had never met a practicing lawyer, let alone a prosecutor. She wondered about his motives. Did he really care about her? Or was this just a chance to make a name for himself?

Margaret approached the trestle over the Saline River and realized she must be a couple of miles from the farm. She was conscious of the time required to get home before dark. It must be about five in the afternoon, which would give her plenty of time. She sat on a plank near the end of the trestle so her feet could dangle over the edge. Margaret was moved to melancholy by the cottonwood trees along the riverbank below her. Their white trunks bent and swayed in the river breeze, fluttering their leaves with a soft rush of noise. She knew these men must be punished, but the thought of sending them to jail tore at her. It would be easier if she knew their motives. It just didn't seem possible that they could have wanted to hurt her, yet they did.

Margaret rested her head on the single guardrail at the end of the trestle. The guardrail was built after John Swartz's cow was picked up by a train and thrown in the river. Margaret thought it stupid. Anyone that far onto the trestle was already in trouble, especially a cow. But the rail allowed her to rest her head on her arm and think.

Someone was coming down the track, and she could hear the tapping on the rail before she heard the voice.

Ileen approached cautiously. "Mom sent me to look for you."

Margaret raised her head. "Hi, Sis," she said casually. "Don't come out here. I'm ready to go."

"Are you alright, Margaret?" Ileen asked. "Mom's worried that you might be depressed or just wander off."

"I'm fine," Margaret said. "Isn't it pretty out here?" Margaret held the guardrail for balance, tucked her feet under her, and stood. Ileen waited and took her arm, guiding her back down the track.

"Mom's worried that you'll have to tell about the tar at the trial, about your clothes being torn."

"Don't worry," Margaret comforted her. "I can handle that. It's just that I don't know what will happen. I can't live here anymore. I don't know these people."

"You mean the boys," Ileen said, referring to the tar party.

"No, I mean everyone. Nothing is the same," Margaret said. "No matter what happens with the trial, Herbie and Ed and Easy have already won. I want Mr. McArdle to get them for it. But what then? I'll have to leave."

Ileen took Margaret's hand, and they moved off the ties to solid ground where the walking was easier. Ileen pulled her sister close as they started for home. She could see that Margaret's eyes were red from crying.

"I'm angry," Margaret blurted out. A tear escaped and ran down the side of her nose. "What right do they have to steal my life? They've held me up to ridicule. I can't go to church. I can't go back to school. What right do they have?"

"We love you," Ileen said quietly. "We'll take care of you."

"I know. I know," Margaret replied, rubbing her wet cheek on the sleeve of her blouse. "But I can take care of myself. I just need to get through this."

CHAPTER THIRTEEN

Judge Thomas Crier had a stern look about him as he strode to the courthouse to hear the guilty plea of Herbert Forchet. He had spent the previous evening poring over the arrest warrants in what the press had already named the Tar Party Case. He reminded himself to be impartial and to maintain that stoic façade that had made him famous in Nickerly County. But he could already sense the community's anxiety about the lurid testimony expected in this case. He was a man of control. He intended to make today's court proceeding swift and certain.

Judge Crier had studied the facts of the case carefully, rendering in his own mind the culpability of various members of the tar party, with a view toward how he might sentence Herbert Forchet. Mr. Forchet had pled guilty to the charge of taking Miss Chambers to a desolate location for the purpose of assault. In exchange for naming all the participants in the scheme, the county attorney had promised some leniency. Herbie Forchet hoped that meant an absence of jail time. It would be up to the county attorney to differentiate the charges between those who actually tarred Miss Chambers and those who stood and watched, but Judge Crier knew that his sentence in this first case would signal to the community his views on the matter, and he intended them to be harsh.

As he sat in his third-floor chambers just beside the courtroom, Judge Crier glanced out the window, expecting to see a few residents of Nickerly walking up the street toward the courthouse. Every court proceeding attracted a few regulars, usually the town lawyers, of which there were a half dozen, and often the family members and close friends of those involved in the case. He had read the stories of the "tar party" in the Kansas City and Topeka newspapers, and he was not immune to the town gossip about the young schoolteacher. He figured the main trial set for mid-November would draw a sizable crowd, but today's proceeding involved only a statement by the defendant and the sentencing.

Thus he was surprised to see—with more than half an hour before the proceeding, and the doors to the courtroom still closed—that a sizable crowd had collected in the yard. The crowd appeared to include half the men in Nickerly and a few strangers as well. Judge Crier surmised that most of them wanted a glimpse of the Chambers girl, even though she would not be in court today. The rest just wanted to hear the charges. Still, maintaining order would be more difficult than usual. He hadn't had a full courtroom since a Nickerly County farmer had killed his neighbor in a dispute over fences nearly five years earlier. In that case, the two families involved had filled the seats, and they got to arguing so violently that Judge Crier had to clear the courtroom. Even so, there was little newspaper attention to the trial, and the community seemed to conclude that both sides were at fault. They didn't condone the murder, but they seemed to understand its inevitability, and since the murderer was eighty-seven years old, most people assumed the old man would die in prison anyway. The people of Nickerly had reasoned all this out even before the trial, so it didn't cause much fuss.

When Judge Crier entered the courtroom to hear the Forchet plea, the bailiff shouted, "All rise," as was the custom, and the audience remained standing until the judge was seated. Judge Crier looked over his reading glasses to survey the room. The audience was entirely male. Of course, children under eighteen were not allowed in court, but it was still surprising that not one woman was present in the courtroom. Not even the mother of the defendant. Judge Crier also realized that at least half the audience was unknown to him. He had spent most of his life in Nickerly County as a lawyer and rancher before being appointed district judge some eighteen years ago. He not only knew everyone in Nickerly County, he knew most everyone in the neighboring counties as well. Indeed, he and Mrs. Crier never missed a Sunday in the congregation of the First Presbyterian Church, and every person named in this case was known to him personally.

Judge Crier had unusually high cheekbones, accentuating a long angular face as hard as limestone, and not structured for smiling. Sixty-three years had carved deep crevasses in his face, and a constant frown reflected the seriousness of his life. His hair was swept from the left directly across the top of his head, thick enough to hide any approaching baldness, but not quite thick enough to hide his age. His complexion was light from years of sitting in a courtroom darkened by the heavy walnut wood of the bench, but it still showed the harshness of the plains that registered itself on the face of every Kansan who had spent his youth in the extreme winds and snows of open fields. Judge Crier was first and foremost a Kansas farmer. He was also tough, some said as tough as an old bird with a new twig.

"Herbert Everett Forchet," he began sternly, "you have pled guilty to taking Miss Margaret Chambers from her home in Nickerly County to a desolate location in said county for the purpose of assault and the application of tar to her body. You did so knowingly and with premeditation. You intentionally put her person in great danger without even understanding the consequences. This court is inclined to treat this infraction with great severity."

Several gasps spread across the room.

"If the defendant has a statement, let him give it at this time," Judge Crier stated.

Herbie Forchet, who had spent his life in the middle of a large French family, or in a barbershop where friendships and conversation were central to his success, slowly rose from his chair. He stood alone. It seemed he had been alone since the first invitation to join the tar party. In the weeks since his arrest and incarceration for assaulting Margaret Chambers, he had been wrestling with some futility over the reason for his involvement and for the charges against him, especially since he had not assaulted the victim. But the reality of his situation had slowly fixed in his mind, and he realized he had few options.

Herbie faced the judge. He had gone over this speech last night in his jail cell with Paul Rinker, his attorney from Ellsworth. Rinker had advised him to apologize to Miss Chambers and to her family with as much sincerity as possible. Herbie assured him that task would not be difficult. He was sorry he had ever gotten involved in this whole mess, and he knew how cowardly his actions must appear to his friends and family.

"Your Honor," he began, with just a small break in his voice, "I am the humblest of men today. I know what I did was wrong. I don't know why I did it. I always liked Margaret."

Herbie's words started with a sense of formality, as Rinker had instructed. But they quickly gave way to the fearful emotions of the moment. Herbie realized he would probably go to jail.

"I'm sorry, Judge. I'm so sorry," he reiterated as tears began to stream down his face. "I didn't want to hurt her. Please don't send me to jail."

Mr. Rinker, sitting directly at Herbie's elbow, tugged at his client's coattail, signaling that he had probably said enough. Herbie collapsed in his chair. The courtroom was still, as everyone waited for the next move. Even the judge said nothing, as if waiting to be sure that Herbie was finished. Finally, as every spectator examined the judge's face trying to detect a sympathetic glance or a disapproving frown, Judge Crier folded his arms and placed his elbows on the bench.

He spoke quickly. "Herbert Forchet. I hereby sentence you to a fine of five hundred dollars and one year in the State Prison in Topeka."

Another gasp echoed through the room. Someone uttered above the others, "Holy Cow."

Judge Crier stood almost immediately, turned on his heel, and disappeared into his chambers. The whole thing was over in a matter of minutes. Most people had expected a sentence of thirty days, or perhaps just a fine and probation. Sitting in the back of the room, Ed Garvey Sr. grew red with rage. He wanted to spit in disgust on the floor of the court, but decided better of it. He swallowed hard and got up to leave. Temple Dandridge was sitting just behind Garvey and stood when he did, hearing him utter to all those around him, "My boy will never spend a day in jail. That judge can rot in hell."

CHAPTER FOURTEEN

Something had clearly happened to Easy Tucker. Ever since the night of the tar party, he seemed to work harder. Not longer hours because that would be impossible, but at a more feverish pace. Even his neighbors were beginning to notice. There were some whispers in the community about Easy's gloves, although gloves weren't that uncommon, especially with all the fencing that was going up lately. Digging holes for the limestone posts was a callused undertaking, not to mention handling the spools of barbed wire that had to be loaded onto wagons at the train station. It took two strong men to run a post through the center of each spool, lift it high enough to roll it into the back of the wagon, then climb into the wagon and drag the spool on the bed to make room for more. Several spools were needed to run three strands of fence around even a small field of fifty or so acres. One mistake in handling the wire could put a long gash in your hand or arm. Gloves weren't a fail-safe protection, but they were a basic essential. In addition to stringing the wire, just handling the posts or chopping wood for the approaching winter would be adequate reason for wearing gloves. But still, people noticed that Easy held his arm in a funny way, as if he was tensing his hand muscles. Every so often he grabbed one hand hard with the other.

It was late in the afternoon when Tiny Tucker brought the buggy home from the first Civic Improvement Association meeting since the arrests. She pulled the mare up to just a few feet from the woodpile where Easy was chopping wood for the winter. She brought the rig to a halt, but didn't lay the reins along the mare's rump as she might normally do. Instead, she held the reins tight in her left hand, adjusted her bonnet so she could see Easy without obstruction, and said, "Forchet was sentenced to a year."

Easy looked up, but said nothing. Tiny shook the reins ever so slightly and turned the horse toward the hitching post by the front of the house. She knew Easy would put the horse and rig in the barn later.

Easy had just started slashing a log, and he tore into it with renewed determination. First from one angle, then another. The chips flew, and the work felt good, as if each whack would drain another drop of sobriety from his being, leaving various parts of his body numb with exhaustion. He wanted numbness. He wanted not to feel his arms and legs, especially his right hand. He ached so badly to be rid of it, to put the itch on his finger in another place, to free his mind from the knowledge that held his finger captive. But no matter how numbing his work, the itch always returned.

As the final log cracked under his ax, Easy rubbed his gloved finger against his leg, and it made no difference. "One year in jail," Tiny had said. The thought left him weak. He could not raise the ax. He set it on the ground and felt himself engulfed in an enormous cloud of hopelessness. He let the ax topple over as his eyes filled with tears.

He walked toward the house and turned slowly to the task of caring for the mare, unwrapping the reins from the post and leading the

horse quietly to the barn. He tied her to a post where years of experience indicated the buggy would fit fully inside. He closed the outside door, sliding it along the overhead rail until it almost filled the
opening, then slipping his body through the open crack and pushing the door the last few inches. Even with the doors closed, the barn
had suffered enough rot in its timbers to let in shafts of evening light.

Easy leaned against the milking stanchion and rested, letting the
tension release, thinking about what Tiny had just said. A year in
jail. First, it meant a trial, with maybe hundreds of people watching
and listening as someone described his cowardice—wearing a woman's
bonnet, hiding behind the skirt of a woman, hoping not to be recognized. And then it would come out somehow, maybe from Margaret Chambers herself, that he had ripped her clothes, and then, oh
God, had touched her breast, and he could never face his church again.
He could never ask God's forgiveness again. The feel of her flesh had
already led to nightmares, and worse, desire. He had felt himself in the
night and knew that in spite of all his shame, the lust was there, and
he was too weak to banish its ugly portent of life in the future. It
hurt. It ached. It drew him. It ran his life. As his tears turned to anger,
he knew he must rid himself of this curse, strike it from his body, drive
it from his mind with the force of his will. Easy screamed at his own
agony. He stumbled to the corner where he kept his axes and machetes,
and picked one with a short handle. Turning furiously to the stump
in the corner of a stall, he tore off the glove on his right hand, placed
his little finger on the stump, and swung the hand ax with a purpose
and direction that could not be stopped by all of the angels in heaven.
He clenched his teeth but did not scream as the small hatchet tore
through his finger. It didn't move an inch. It lay still on the stump as
the blood started to gush from Easy's hand.

Easy looked at what he had done, but he felt nothing. No change.
No relief. He still felt her nipple, and he jerked his hand away. How

could this be? The finger was gone. He stuck his hand with its bleeding nub into the ground, and put all his weight on it. The soil was fresh and cool. The finger was unmoved on top of the stump, like a chip of wood that remained after the chop, to be flicked away before the next swing. Then Easy began to feel the pain.

He lowered himself to the dirt floor, hardened by years of trampling by man and beast. The floor was covered with straw to provide warmth and soak up moisture. He had pitched the straw out of the loft above at regular intervals and now was thankful for the softness as he sat next to the wall, leaning back against an interior post. He stuck his finger back into the ground, at an angle so he could lean back and rest his head. Then Easy Tucker, an entirely physical man who had defined his life in work and fights and strength, began to cry.

He thought about going to jail and having to leave Tiny, the one person who had made him feel loved and needed, who had nursed his body and his soul. He had deserted her on a dark road with cowardly friends and a schoolteacher he hardly knew. Hopelessness rushed through him, driving a pain through his arms and legs. Yet strangely he could still feel his finger at the end of his hand and at the same time see it lying where it had fallen, like a small mouse perched in the shadows.

Easy's eyes rolled back toward the sky. He could see up the ladder to the loft where a shaft of light illuminated a canvas of right angles, formed by the hundreds of rectangular bales of hay stacked to the roof. Easy had created the picture. As he threw each bale down to the waiting cattle, he had created moving patterns in the stack. It was a game, like the game he had played in the loft as a child, moving the bales to form endless tunnels that climbed to the rafters, high above the floor. He used to sit in the openings with his legs dangling thirty or forty feet above the ground, and he felt safe because no one could reach him. No one knew the tunnels. He had built a fortress that could not be penetrated.

Easy tried to follow the light to its source at the pitch of the roof, but his head could not bend far enough back, and he wasn't sure whether it was sun or moon, how long he had been in the barn. Then the light was gone.

.   .   .

Tiny had been working in the kitchen, cooking a large ham from the icebox, cutting off the fat and some extra pieces of meat for the pea soup that was slowly coming to a boil. She knew Easy would be hungry from the chopping, and dinner might be difficult. They had to discuss the Forchet sentence. She did not look forward to it, angry with herself for even suggesting to Easy that he might have wanted to touch that girl. She knew he hadn't. Indeed, she had urged him to participate in the tarring for the good of the community. It was the will of God, and now it had come to this. A good hot dinner might help.

When the sun went down Tiny began to worry. She had seen Easy walk the mare and the rig to the barn well over an hour ago, but hadn't heard any commotion since. She hadn't realized till now how the sounds of Easy's work filled her world, his chopping wood, or the clang of metal as he hitched the horses to the plow, or the whipping of the reins as they splatted against one another in the fields. She always knew he was there, as surely as rolling up against him in the night and feeling his toes or his shoulders. She listened for those sounds, and hearing none, she moved to the door. She gave a shout and received no response. Suddenly seized with panic, she raced across the yard to the barn. She smelled the fear that every mother has for her family, knowing that something had happened. Had he fallen under the horse, or down the ladder, or nicked himself with the ax? She heaved the door aside, stuck her head into the darkness, and called Easy's name. And then she saw his shadow, propped against the wall, almost as in prayer, with hands folded across his chest.

Tiny ran to Easy and took his head in her arms, shaking him and begging him to wake up. Then she saw his hands, clasped tightly around the wooden handle of the long ice pick. It was buried deep inside his chest.

CHAPTER FIFTEEN

Margaret walked erect but felt like she could wilt at any moment. She clung firmly to her mother's and her sister's hands as they walked toward the Nickerly courthouse for the first day of trial. W.W. McArdle had advised them to arrive early, in case there was a crowd, and to wear light-colored clothing and breezy summer hats. He wanted them to appear confident and innocent. Though she was nervous, Margaret certainly felt innocent. Even her few flickerings of guilt had vanished in the days since the tarring and feathering.

There seemed to be some effort in the community to blame her for Easy Tucker's death, but Margaret didn't see why. It was traumatic to have such a gruesome act of self-destruction take place in Nickerly, and Margaret did dream of Easy once, out there in his barn, getting more and more depressed, seeing the shadows of evening bounce off the trestles, intensifying the demons in his mind. Her most vivid image was of Easy standing in the dark, his large frame looming like a bald eagle before the moon, with one arm rising above his head, its shadow shooting through the roof, and then coming down on that tiny finger. She could almost feel it, not the physical pain, but the desperation that must have been a product of Easy's guilt. She awoke thinking Easy was in her room, and it scared her. At least this new dream had replaced the nightmare of being pulled off Herbie Forchet's buggy.

The Chambers family didn't attend the funeral, of course, but the gossip around town was that Mrs. Wilson said Margaret Chambers did it—she had killed Easy Tucker with her charges against the men. Mrs. Wilson had circulated at the graveside like a stray cat looking for a home, searching for sympathy to her grievance, and finding a willing audience. Margaret had brought the tarring and feathering on herself, the mourners reasoned, and now she had brought destruction on the community. There was one death. And everyone knew that the Reverend Aaron Langston and his son had had an angry exchange, with the boy charging out of the house, saying he wouldn't mind living in jail for a while. Better than living with a preacher who wouldn't defend his son or a mother who defended that girl. The general feeling was that the Chambers girl would try to destroy them all before this matter was over.

Margaret suspected the whole town would be against her, and she had steeled herself for a possible confrontation at the courthouse, but she hadn't expected to have so many faces peering at her, judging her and condemning her with their open stares. She had told herself that she would not look, she would not catch their eyes and give them the satisfaction of knowing that their disdain had been conveyed. She would rise above them. She would pick a spot above the courthouse door and stare at it the whole way through.

But as she turned the corner a block from the courthouse, Margaret could see the people milling around, little children playing hide-and-seek in their mothers' skirts. A gaggle of men had gathered near the steps dressed in suits as if this were a church service, and bicycles sprawled in the grass where young gawkers had left them, anxious to see the courthouse or even Margaret Chambers herself. It looked like a celebration, Margaret thought. But the crowd hushed as she neared, and the children just stood and stared, some clutching their mothers' hands. Strangely, the women started moving closer to each other as if for protection. Almost imperceptibly they were edging nearer the steps, some glancing at each other, some staring straight at Margaret as if trying to make their hatred penetrate her discipline, trying to make her look at them, to recognize their right and role as the moral enforcers of community standards. And she would not do it. Without a word or a glance, Margaret Chambers climbed resolutely up the courthouse steps and strode through the open door.

It startled Margaret that even the hallways were filled. As she moved out of the sun and into the building, she was momentarily blinded by the darkness, hearing only a jumble of voices around her but feeling a hand take hers away from her mother. Then W.W. McArdle's voice said, "Don't be afraid, Margaret; everything's fine." She looked in his eyes, the first she had made contact with, and they were reassuring, the eyes of a man who knew his way around the building, and presumably around the law. After a brief stop to convince the bailiff to open the door, McArdle directed the Chambers family into the empty courtroom, seated them in the front row just behind the small table designated for the prosecutor, and asked them to make themselves comfortable. They wouldn't have to say or do a thing. This would just be opening statements.

The first surprise was a line of women who marched into the courtroom like legionnaires, dressed in black ankle-length skirts, black high-button shoes, and stern black felt hats with only the smallest bent of the brim as a nod to stylishness. The crowd dissolved to let them through the minute they appeared. The Civic Improvement Association of Nickerly, Kansas, was not to be trifled with, and of all the residents in court that day, only Margaret Chambers seemed not to know it. She observed them out of the corner of her eye, but she did not turn to look. W.W. McArdle, however, sitting at the prosecutor's desk, spun around immediately upon hearing them shuffling down the aisle. He watched as the principal attorney for the defendants ushered them into the second row of benches, just behind the Chambers family.

After the folderol of getting the judge seated, the call to order, and the entrance of the fourteen leading citizen defendants of Nickerly—a smattering of applause and light chatter of support spread through the courtroom—the trial seemed about to begin.

John Engle, the attorney hired by Ed Garvey Sr. from among Salina's finest criminal lawyers, stood to address the judge. Engle had coal-black hair, slicked back. It looked wet, as if the lawyer had just stepped from a shower, and it set off a red face that suggested a life of field work, although Engle's black vest and gold watch hinted that few of his forty-five years were spent in manual labor. But the name Engle was known in these parts for integrity, for a family that had served on school boards and county commissions. Whether you were trying to get a loan at the bank or shocking wheat, you could count on the Engles for help.

"Your Honor," John Engle began, "before we start any other proceeding this morning, I would like to address a special appeal to the court on behalf of the Civic Improvement Association of Nickerly. These leading ladies of the county respectfully submit to the court, on behalf of the defendants in this case, a request for a change of venue."

A rustle spread through the courtroom.

"All quiet," the judge ordered, using his gavel for the first time. "What possibly can be the reason for this?"

"Your Honor," Engle began again, "our petition maintains that the defendants cannot get a fair trial in Nickerly County. There has been so much rot printed about this case in Nickerly County that any man ought to know these defendants cannot get a fair jury here. The population here has been so prejudiced by a salacious press against my clients that all manner of lies are now a part of the public mind. We will submit to the court stories of the most extreme nature, all without foundation, that openly accuse these good men of Nickerly of every misdeed known to man."

Mrs. Wilson virtually leapt to her feet, screaming, "Read these, Your Honor. Blasphemy against our husbands." She waved a half-dozen newspaper clippings over her head. They were Mr. Temple Dandridge's articles from the *Kansas City Star*, his entire serialization of the tar party case since his arrival in Nickerly. "These are lies," she screamed. "Fodder for the damnation of Margaret Chambers."

"That is enough," the judge shouted, bringing down his gavel with a loud crack.

John Engle quickly moved in front of Mrs. Wilson, telling her to please sit down. Club Wilson, sitting among the defendants, also rose to attend to his wife, but Engle intercepted him and guided him back to his seat.

The judge could see that this trial was getting out of hand, a situation he did not intend to allow for one more minute. He brought down his gavel again and said, "Mr. Engle, Mr. McArdle, I will take this petition under advisement. The trial is adjourned until nine o'clock tomorrow morning." He immediately got up and returned to his chambers, leaving behind a stunned audience.

Temple Dandridge, however, was not surprised, and he made a fast move around the benches, across the front of the court, and stood at John Engle's side even before the lawyer had picked up his papers. "When can I get a copy of that petition?" Temple asked.

"Now," Engle said. He had a carbon copy ready, already in an envelope marked *"The Kansas City Star"*. When Mrs. Wilson saw Temp reach for the petition, she unleashed an attack of the kind never heard at the monthly meetings of the Civic Improvement Association.

"You unspeakable vermin," she hissed. "How dare you accuse our men of following prurient interests? They were defending our families, our children, and God's divine principles. That woman is a harlot. She enticed our men and seduced our children, and she's done it before. You tell the truth for a change, Mr. Kansas City Star."

Temple stepped back, just in case the woman decided to lash out with more than words. He took the envelope with the petition and headed for the door. Nearly everyone in the courtroom had witnessed the tongue lashing, and when Dandridge turned to leave the room they closed in behind him. They wanted to exit as quickly as possible to tell their friends and neighbors about the remarkable turn of events.

W.W. McArdle took Margaret by the arm and whispered close to her face, "Don't say anything till we're in my office."

.   .   .

When Margaret and her family returned home from the courthouse, Temple Dandridge was leaning against their front door, petition in hand, his straw hat tipped on his head to shield the sun, which had just angled over the noon hour. His tie was undone, and his jacket was slung over his right shoulder. Margaret had seen a lot of Temple during the past few weeks and had come to enjoy his company. She didn't fear his newspaper's motivations the way her mother said she should, and she had not tried to manipulate his thinking the way W.W. McArdle hoped she would. She liked talking to Temple about events outside of Nickerly County, even though he kept bringing her back to the subject of her prosecution. Temple had never before seen a case like this, in which the victim appeared to be the one on trial.

"Margaret, I have the petition," he began. "I'd like to talk to you about it."

"Sure, Temp," she said brightly. "Come in."

She turned to her mother, who seemed more upset. Temp thought she might have been crying, although it was hard to see her eyes because of the sun.

"Mother, may we have some tea?" Margaret asked. "Temp and I want to talk."

"I assume W.W. went through the petition with you after court," Temp began after wedging himself on the parlor couch with two needlepoint pillows. This was his favorite spot because he could see through the open living room into the kitchen and nearly to the back door. It gave him a sense of control, a sort of "back to the wall" defense that made it possible to know where Margaret's family was at all times. They were always there, listening, peering in at the conversation, but seldom interfering. Temple was surprised at how deferential the family acted toward Margaret, treating her more like an honored guest than a member of the family. And Margaret seemed comfortable with that role, always respectful of her family but ready to make her own decisions about the trial and about Temple Dandridge. She liked him. And so far his articles had been favorable. Indeed they had started to turn public opinion against the defendants, and against the community, as Mrs. Club Wilson had pointed out that morning.

"Margaret," Temp said, "this petition says the press has already condemned the defendants because they are portrayed as wanting to hurt you. It says that they have already been judged guilty and can't receive a fair trial here. Do you agree with that?"

"Temp, they did want to hurt me."

"Do you think the press has been unfair?"

Margaret noticed that Temp never referred to his own stories, but rather "the press." Several other papers were covering the trial. In fact, the Adeline was full of reporters from the Universal Wire Service, the *Topeka Capitol*, and other newspapers across the state. Temp had explained to Margaret how a wire service story might appear in papers as far away as New York City, and indeed, several other big-city newspapers had publicized the case, including the *New York Times*. Margaret had never actually seen the *New York Times*, but she knew that New York was the largest city in America and presumed that its newspaper would also be the biggest. And just in the last few days she had received many letters from New York, from people she didn't even know. All were sympathetic to her plight, and some even included money. She had three checks for five dollars each that her father had taken for safekeeping. He said she shouldn't mix this money in with her regular money because she might have to give it back or something. Margaret and her father were both slightly stupefied by this phenomenon. Why were people sending money?

"I don't think so, Temp," she said. "Your stories have been fair. You told what happened. I don't want to have this trial someplace else. We would have to move there, or get a hotel room, which we can't afford. That would be unfair."

That was the quote he needed, so Temp tried to change the subject, to ignite a more personal relationship. W.W. McArdle had endorsed the relationship between Temp and Margaret, but other reporters were seeking interviews with Margaret as well and the competition seemed to be increasing daily. He needed a personal rapport to keep his advantage. More importantly, he really liked Margaret. This was a problem he had encountered before as a journalist. It was often hard to separate his personal and professional role in his friendships. He found himself consumed by Margaret, even thinking about where she might go when this trial was over. No matter what happened to the tar party men, Temp assumed Margaret would have to leave Nickerly. Indeed he could foresee that even if everyone were convicted, they would win their first objective by driving Margaret Chambers out of the county. She couldn't stay. Of course, it looked to Temp as if the attitudes of outsiders, the readers of the *Kansas City Star* and even those of the *New York Times*, were beginning to have an impact on the citizens of Nickerly. They were starting to feel a little isolated in their moral conclusions. And that's the impact he wanted his stories to have.

The scene in front of the courthouse the next day was even more outlandish than before. Word of the change-of-venue petition had sparked even more interest. Of maybe Margaret just hadn't noticed the jugglers yesterday. There they were today, two men in clown costumes throwing bowling pins back and forth between them. There was no reason, no sign, no indication of their purpose. Margaret had heard that a carnival was appearing in Russell, and maybe the jugglers were from the show. They did give the trial a more festive atmosphere than yesterday. The Civic Improvement Association was clearly not amused, and the ladies of the club marched right past the entertainment with total disdain printed on their faces.

In addition, the crowd outside was perhaps twice as large as yesterday, with many people Margaret didn't recognize. Buggies were lined up on both sides of Main Street, and the occasional Model A Ford with a popping engine scared the horses and caused much anxiety. Clearly, all these people couldn't fit into the courtroom.

Judge Crier took less than one minute to dispose of the change-of-venue petition, ruling that the defendants could indeed get a fair trial in Nickerly County and that trial would start just as soon as the jury was sworn in, possibly even today. And that was that. The jury questioning was slightly limited because every prospective juror was a neighbor, they all knew both the victim and the defendants, and they all had children at one time or another in the school system, except for Indian Smith, who never had children and had never been inside a schoolhouse. Judge Crier accepted the first twelve jurors presented, all men, and swore them in by mid-afternoon.

As the last juror was sworn in, and before the judge could turn to the business of adjournment, the lawyer for Hank Simpson stood in the front row and said in a near shout, "Your Honor, my client wants to change his plea."

Pandemonium broke out, even though most of the people in the court weren't sure just who the lawyer's client was. But the judge knew. He also knew that the county attorney had spent several days in intense interviews with Mr. Simpson, trying to get him to turn against the others. Perhaps the interrogations had worked.

"Your Honor," the lawyer said in a calmer voice, "my client, Mr. Hank Simpson, of this city wants to change his plea to guilty."

Mr. Engle leapt to his feet. "Your Honor, what kind of tomfoolery is this? We have not been notified of any change."

Judge Crier ruled Engle down, turned to Hank Simpson's representative, and accepted the guilty plea. The judge pushed his wire glasses up the bridge of his nose, looked squarely at the row of defendants, then addressed the room, "Although I have accepted the guilty plea, sentencing will be withheld until after the pending trial. Court is adjourned."

Again Temple Dandridge was the first person at Mr. Engle's side as the courtroom rose in exclamation. "What's this mean?" Temp asked, knowing full well that it meant Hank Simpson was going to be a witness for the prosecution.

"I don't know," Engle snapped. "We'll see tomorrow."

Once again the crowd was elbowing its way out of the courthouse, eager to spread the news of another surprise. Temp joined the bulge through the door, edged his way to the side of the group, and darted into W.W. McArdle's office. McArdle was standing behind his desk, waiting.

"Can I interview Simpson?" Temp asked, still breathing hard.

"Not right now," McArdle said. "Come back tonight about six o'clock."

"That's too late," Temp said. He recognized that the county attorney didn't want everyone to know about his close relationship with the press, but he also wanted this story. "How about four thirty, after everyone's gone? I have to dictate a story before six p.m."

W.W. paused, wanting to say no, but he also wanted this story badly. He knew it would scare the pants off the defendants as well as show the prosecutor's initial success in getting two guilty pleas. "Okay," he said meekly.

Temp left the room without even saying good-bye and hurried down the front steps of the courthouse. He needed to collect his thoughts and make a list of questions. He wondered fleetingly if Margaret understood what a big break this was.

W.W. McArdle was as good as his word, bringing a squirming and agitated Hank Simpson to his office about five o'clock under the watchful gaze of the deputy sheriff. Temp decided he really didn't need much from Mr. Simpson, just a confirmation that he was going to testify against his friends and a basic retelling of the tar party night, both of which Hank was willing and eager to provide.

Temp Dandridge thanked everyone and hurried back to the hotel, excited about his story for the morning paper, but more interested in what Margaret Chambers might say in her own defense. Temp was a talented reporter, the kind who thought ahead, sorting through the facts of a story and making some educated guesses about where it was going. Reporters called it "following the string." Temp figured this trial was going to hinge on whether the defense could establish any black marks on Margaret Chambers's character.

Temp had written a half-dozen stories about Margaret and hadn't detected any moral fallibilities yet, but he hadn't asked her

directly. His gentle questioning was designed more to build a relationship than to elicit dramatic new information. Not only that, he
found himself seeking her company because in spite of her problems,
she seemed so alive, and relatively fearless for someone under attack.
He remembered a conversation he once had with Tiny Tucker about
Margaret, and Tiny remarked, "She's so bold." Temp liked Margaret's
boldness, but he realized that Tiny viewed the quality differently. Margaret's strength made her stand out from her surroundings, like a pink
building in the middle of a block.

After dictating his story by telephone to the *Star*, Temp decided
to take an evening stroll, perhaps out past the Chambers place. Early
November puts Kansas on the cusp of changing seasons. The air is cold
at night but rises to the sixties in the daytime, burning off the dew and
lending a crystal vibrancy to the air, which seems to almost sparkle like
a freshly washed glass. The fields were plowed and black, still free of
the winter weeds that would have to be disked again in the spring. And
it was dark, especially where the rich loam soil met the line of the
sky. Walking toward the distance made it seem endless, but Temp
knew he would reach the Chambers place well before the night chill
penetrated his jacket. He could see their house already, or at least a
light where the window should be.

Temp hadn't been out for a long walk after dark in Nickerly before,
and it gave him a sense of stillness that was different from the day,
as if one set of life had gone to bed and another got up. It was like
the day shift of his newspaper going home just as the night shift came
on duty, or like a factory gate where smudge-faced steelworkers fil-
ter in and out. Temp wondered if the raccoons felt that way, emerging in the night to rummage among the refuse of somebody else's
day in the fields, or the seagulls that searched the clods turned up by
the plowshares during the day. These were just idle rambling thoughts,
of course, but they made him realize the urban nature of his perspec-

tive. Could he, a city boy, really understand this town? He allowed himself a brief moment of hesitation—was he seeing Margaret Chambers with the wrong eyes? But he was not a man given to self-doubt, and having ruminated, he walked on.

Temp found Margaret and Ileen sitting on their porch swing, wearing bulky sweaters over their dresses, letting the freshness of the evening cleanse away the day's events. If not for their rhythmic movement, and a slight squeak in the swing, he might have been startled by their sudden presence. But he saw them in time and called out, "Margaret, it's me, Temp, just out for a walk. Can I come in?"

"Oh, Ileen, it's Temp," she answered. "Come in." Margaret's hand was lying near Ileen's in the fold of her dress, and as she welcomed Temp she also moved her fingers just enough to press against Ileen's, silently telling her sister to stay.

Temp walked to the porch and sat down on the top step. "Good evening, Ileen," he said. "How is your sister holding up?"

"I'm just fine, thank you," Margaret said, picking the conversation out of the air as it travelled past. "Ileen and I were just enjoying the evening, wondering why bad things happen to good people in such a peaceful place."

"I thought you wanted the hubbub of the city, to travel the world," Temp teased.

"I do," Margaret responded. "But I'll always want to come back to Kansas. Even with all these terrible things that have happened, I'll always want to see Ileen, to catch the fireflies, and to feel the freedom of the long sky."

"Well, Margaret," Ileen said, "if you're going to get poetic, I'm going in the house."

"Would you tell Mom and Dad that Temp is here?" Margaret asked.

Temp moved up to the porch swing and sat beside Margaret. His leg touched hers as the swing gave a sudden move backward under his weight. She did not move. He realized they had never been this close before, or this alone before, and he had a strong urge to take her hand, but he didn't. He had to keep his senses, and he wanted to talk about the trial.

"Were you surprised by Hank Simpson today?" Temp asked.

"No," she said. "He's a weak person. I'm glad he pled guilty because it will make the trial go faster."

"Tomorrow, you will have to testify," Temp ventured. "Are you ready?"

"Yes," she said. "I want to tell my side." Margaret looked down at the narrow interlocking slats of the porch floor, worn from years of stomping and footsteps by friends and neighbors. She remembered playing with her sister on the steps, talking to their dolls and pretending to be adults. She remembered watching her grandmother sit in the porch swing, dying of some terrible internal disease, and withering away with each passing day. She marveled at Grandma's determination to stay involved, to always ask the children about their day in school, and to ask Margaret what she thought of things—like the cost of linen, or how windmills worked, or why houses should face the south.

Temp said nothing, letting Margaret's contemplation play out, knowing from many interview experiences that these kinds of reflective moments might lead to other, more revealing flashes. Good reporters needed the patience to wait.

"Temp," Margaret began, turning her head in the swing to look him squarely in the eye, "will you not repeat something if I tell you?"

"Yes," he said cautiously.

"I mean really not tell," she said.

"I promise," Temp said, knowing the many ways of getting around promises without actually reneging on his words.

"I have to stand up to these men," she began. "I can't live my life in silence. I can't live a lifetime of knowing that people are talking about me; that they think I'm the kind of teacher who would seduce a student. These boys don't know what that means. Maybe Tiny Tucker and Mrs. Wilson know how gossip hurts, but I doubt it."

Once more there was silence.

Temp Dandridge had come to believe in Margaret Chambers, that she was a headstrong young woman, unafraid to break the fashion but sincere and sensitive as well.

"One other thing, Temp," she said looking out into the dark. "I've never admitted this before. But I know my mother and father have lived under a cloud of gossip for years and years, since before I was born, and it has changed them, driven them into a life of artificial walls. Their fear of what people will say has defined how they live, their friends, their church, their attitude toward others. I couldn't stand it if that happened to me."

Temp wanted desperately to ask what had happened to Margaret's parents but decided to wait and see if she would tell the story. He also figured that if he could keep this little secret, she would tell the rest later.

"I'm sorry," he said. "I think you'll do just fine tomorrow."

"I will," she said. "And I'm not wearing that pretty little bonnet and light dress either. From now on I'm wearing my best suit with a felt hat. It's winter, for heaven's sake. And I'm also wearing a black boa that hangs around my neck and down the full length of my coat. When I walk past those old ladies, I might even twirl it."

"I would recommend against that," Temp said.

"I won't, silly," Margaret laughed.

"It's getting late," Temp said reluctantly. "I better get back to the hotel."

The next day's *Kansas City Star* led with Temp's story, upper right-hand corner with a large typeface. The headline read, "Tar Party Member Pleads Guilty."

The text read:

NICKERLY, KANSAS, Nov. 5, 1911—What the attorneys for the state regard as a major victory in the Nickerly County "tar party" case came this morning when Hank Simpson, the town baker, entered a surprise plea of guilty. Sentencing was suspended until after the trial of thirteen others accused of carrying out the "tar party" affair.

CHAPTER SIXTEEN

County Attorney W.W. McArdle was resplendent in a black pinstriped suit with lines that seemed to run from the top of his head to his toes, where the crease of his trousers hit squarely in the middle of the tongue of his highly polished shoes. And even when he walked, the pants hung steady, like a compass that never changes course. He stood directly in front of the jury and came right to the point.

"It becomes the duty of the prosecution at this time to impress you with a clear statement of the facts in this case, together with the evidence upon which the State of Kansas hopes you will find these thirteen defendants guilty of the crimes as outlined.

"The state will show, first, that a plot, scheme, and plan was entered into by the defendants in this case for the purpose of assaulting one Margaret Chambers.

"Second, that it was carried into effect. On the afternoon of the seventh of August, last, one Edward Tucker, now deceased, drove up to the Garvey Mill with a load of corn to sell to Edward Garvey, the miller at that place.

"When he arrived at the mill he sold the corn to Edward Garvey and engaged in conversation with several other men, including six of the defendants. One of them said to Edward Tucker, known as Easy, 'Have you heard about Margaret Chambers,' mentioning gossip which had been set on foot in the town concerning her. Finally they said to another of the men at the mill, John Buckhorn, 'Won't you take Margaret down to the river tonight, where we can take her out and singe her?' Buckhorn answered, 'No, fellows, Margaret never did me any harm.'

"Jay Langston, also at the mill, then went to put up his horses in the livery stable and returned the same afternoon to Nickerly. In Nickerly, he came across his friend Herbert Forchet, sitting in front of the barbershop where he worked.

"'Gee, I wish I had a date tonight,' Forchet said.

"'I know where you can get a date and have some fun,' Langston replied. And he told Forchet how the men at Garvey's Mill were waiting to waylay Miss Chambers that night but could not find anyone to take her out.

"'Well, I'm game,' Forchet said. 'I'll take her out,' and he made an engagement over the telephone with the girl to take her to a fictitious dance at a barn above Nickerly."

McArdle's voice was rising in strength and tone. "The evidence will show," he said, "how Forchet went in his buggy that night and drove Miss Chambers out to the appointed ambush. But to return to the conspirators: Jay Langston had ridden back to Garvey's Mill on his bicycle. He saw Ed Garvey and said, 'Herbie Forchet is going to take your girl out for you.'

"'That's good,' Garvey said. 'Better go and tell Piney Woods and Easy Tucker.'

"In the meantime, some of the young fellows of Nickerly, the 'dirty dozen' of the town, had got wind of the plan and decided they wanted to see some of the fun, too. They all gathered at Garvey's Mill early that evening and completed their plans for the crime.

"The evidence will show that although only two men put the tar on Miss Chambers's naked body, all thirteen defendants were conspirators in the crime.

"The evidence will show that Miss Chambers was frightened when she saw the motorcycles at the top of the hill where she was waylaid. She was frightened and asked Forchet what that was, and that Forchet declared he did not see anything.

"We will show that one man, Herbert Forchet, has already pled guilty; that it was the defendants who originally paid his bond; and that these same defendants conspired, participated, or tried to participate in the assault on Margaret Chambers. They are all guilty. And furthermore, Mr. Hank Simpson will corroborate their guilt.

"Finally, Your Honor, we will show that the conspiracy to harm Margaret Chambers had its seeds in the community, fanned by the flames of gossip and jealousy, justified by a righteousness that was totally misplaced. No greater sign of this conspiracy could exist than Esther Ennis's pillow, a bag of feathers contributed at the last minute by a widow who readily joined her Nickerly sisters in community malice."

McArdle's sparse and sharpened words had left their mark. The courtroom audience had never heard the word "naked" uttered by a public official, and couldn't imagine their friends and neighbors standing in the middle of a road watching, indeed leering, as a girl's clothes were torn off. McArdle turned to move behind his table when he caught the eye of Margaret Chambers's mother, one of only two women in the entire courtroom. She was burning with anger. It was an anger of many years.

．　　．　　．

Although several of the defendants had private attorneys, John Engle was selected to present the opening rebuttal. In marked contrast to McArdle, Engle had the blood of central Kansas in his veins. His suit was the color of earth, basic brown, and his shoes were so recognizable in farm country that you could almost hear people look at them and murmur, "I'm Buster Brown, I live in a shoe." He knew the men on trial, and he knew their ancestors and all their neighbors and how they lived their lives. His voice started slow, as if carrying the weight of truth, as if he knew that this brave jury would never convict anybody for protecting the community from a misfit. He began with the town.

"Your Honor, members of the jury, this is a good and decent community, where people praise the work of the Lord, and spend their days in honest labor. The people of Nickerly immigrated to this great state from Europe, or from the East, in search of religious freedom, the freedom to raise their families in a God-fearing atmosphere where citizens respect each other. We respect each other's property, their person, their right to live and pursue a meaningful life. These are a people bonded together against the elements of nature, against the tyranny of evil in all its manifestations. And that's what happened in this case. We will show that no harm was done to Margaret Chambers; and that this community stood up for its values and principles.

"We will show that the events described by the prosecution were harmlessly carried out and that they expressed the will of the community. The county attorney himself has stated that Nickerly was a God-fearing community trying to protect its children from the moral degradation of their schoolteacher.

"We will show that several of the defendants were not even on the road to Twelve Mile Run on the night in question, and still others had no participation whatsoever in the events of that evening.

"We will show that these upstanding citizens of Nickerly—the miller, the quarry owner, the restaurant owner, our minister's son, and our best farmers—are not guilty of any crime. They were protecting the community. They should not be prosecuted. They should be honored.

"And finally, we will ask the jury to set these men free so they can return to their families and return to the betterment of Nickerly and the State of Kansas."

It was not a particularly long or stirring rebuttal, but the people in the courtroom murmured their approval. John Engle thought the jury would agree. But he hedged his bets. He did not attack Margaret with specific charges of misconduct, he did not claim the incident never took place, and he avoided inflaming the audience with accusations. In the back of his mind was the knowledge that Margaret Chambers had contacted a lawyer in Kansas City about the possibility of filing charges for civil damages once the trial was over. If the defendants were acquitted, she could battle on. She intended to win either way, John Engle thought, and she was a very smart girl.

The next morning's *Kansas City Star* carried the prosecutor's opening statement almost verbatim. Little mention was made of the defense.

.   .   .

After hearing Mr. Engle's opening statement, McArdle made a quick strategy change and called Jay Langston as his first witness. He would make it clear at the outset these boys were not avenging angels, and the words would come straight from the minister's own son.

McArdle led Jay Langston through a series of questions that established his identity, portraying Jay as a fervent religious disciple of his father's teachings. Jay was obviously uncomfortable with the description, but he couldn't deny his own father, and besides, his own lawyer had suggested a religious defense. By the time McArdle asked for a description of the tarring and feathering, Jay was very uneasy, not quite sure how to present himself.

"After you talked to Forchet, what happened?" McArdle asked.

"I went back to the mill and told Ed that Herbie would get the girl for them."

Jay explained. "Some of the boys in town had heard of the plans. We gathered at the mill. We decided to wear masks and Club and Piney were selected to hold the buggy up. We were a little late getting to the place, and when the buggy appeared, we had the tar ready and held her up. Forchet jumped out of the buggy and hid. Then we did it. That's about all."

"Were all of the defendants there?" McArdle asked, realizing he was going to have to lead Langston through the details.

"No," Jay said. "Some of them were walking, and some were on motorcycles, and they were late."

"Did you have anything on besides your ordinary clothing?" McArdle asked.

"I had a handkerchief around my face," Jay said.

"What were the others wearing?"

"Ed Garvey had a bag over his head," Jay responded. "Club had a gunny sack over his head. Piney was wearing some kind of apron."

"What about Easy Tucker? What was he wearing?"

"Easy had on Tiny's fishing bonnet," Jay said, "and one of her dresses. The flowered one."

"Tell me about what these men did to Margaret Chambers after they took her off the buggy," McArdle continued.

"They took her back behind the buggy to the side of the road."

"Then what did they do?"

"They sat her down on the ground."

"In a sitting position, was it?"

"Well, I don't know as to that. I couldn't hardly tell from where I was."

"You were around in front of the horses?"

"No, sir. I was around to the north side at the time."

"What were you doing there?"

"I was holding the gun on Forchet."

"Was it a toy gun?"

"No. It was real."

"Did Ed Garvey say anything to you?"

"He said to hold the gun on Forchet."

"Then what happened?"

"Well, Easy took the tar while the other two held Margaret."

"Where did he get it?"

"Out of the buggy."

"Then what was done?"

"As near as I could see they went to putting the tar on her."

"On what part of her body did they put the tar?"

"On her lower limbs, as near as I could tell, and her chest."

"Then what did you do?"

"Easy walked off so I poured more tar on her. Then someone threw the feathers."

McArdle stopped for emphasis, to let the courtroom catch up with the questioning. He paced back and forth twice in front of the judge, as if pondering his next question, giving it gravity.

"Mr. Langston," he said for added importance, "isn't it true that you pulled down Miss Chambers's undergarments and applied the tar to her lower limbs?"

Jay was stunned. He couldn't believe he was being forced to describe this act in front of his father. He looked at the floor, even as he heard the commotion throughout the courtroom.

"Yes," he said quietly.

McArdle paused again, and then continued, "Who threw the feathers?"

"I don't know. One of the boys from the wagon."

"Did Miss Chambers say anything during all this, or make any sounds when they took her?"

"Yes, sir."

"What?"

"She asked what they were going to do with her."

"That was before the events you described, when she was in the buggy?"

"Yes."

"Did she make any sounds after she was taken from the buggy?"

"She said, 'Oh, oh. Herb,' as near as I could hear."

"Did she call loud?"

"Yes. Rather loud."

"How did she get back in the buggy?"

"We put her there," Langston said in a low voice. He had gone over this scene many times in his mind, but in the privacy of his own soul this scene was carried out with a sort of missionary zeal, a sense of righteous indignation, that somehow W.W. McArdle had stripped away. For the first time, Jay felt the shame of it all. He left the witness stand without looking at his friends or his family.

The next witness was Herbert Forchet, by now a sniveling little man in the eyes of his former friends. McArdle led him through the events of the evening. Herbie's account at the scene didn't add much of value because he was hiding in the ditch, crouching among the shoestring and ironweed. He couldn't really see. When Herbie was done testifying, he was led out of the courtroom by sheriff's deputies amid muffled whispers of "shame, shame." He never looked up.

Everyone in Kansas knew that Margaret Chambers would take the stand the next day. Even the two local newspapers, while not reporting on the actual trial, did mention that certain Chambers relatives arrived in Nickerly for the testimony of Miss Chambers and would be staying with friends of the family. The Adeline Hotel was fully booked for the week, and the front parlor had been transformed into a bar where strangers, patrons, and Nickerly residents alike could gather after dinner to discuss the trial. The revelers were mostly men because minors had been barred from the trial by Judge Crier, and the Civic Improvement Association had decreed that no self-respecting woman of Nickerly would attend such a spectacle. None had so far. Although women and children had gathered outside the courthouse to see who was attending, and to show their displeasure to Margaret and her family, they believed that listening to the sordid testimony of the trial would be sinful. According to Temple Dandridge, more than two thousand people had gathered outside the courthouse. The gathering reminded him of "a convention of the old Populist political party." Politicians stood about in groups, watching their constituents flock in from all over the county. Solicitors, photographers, the idle and the curious, all contributed to the strange scene.

Except for Margaret's mother, no women were in the courtroom on the day of Margaret's testimony. Margaret sat impassively as the courtroom filled to beyond its capacity, with spectators standing around the edges of the rows and crowded onto the benches. At one point an elderly man in overalls with a long brown beard and wire-rimmed glasses made it to the front of the courtroom. Then seeing no empty seats, and all the aisles blocked, he simply sat down on the steps leading up to the judge's dais. As Judge Crier entered, a bailiff helped the old man to his feet, escorted him toward the door, and told him to wait outside, then closed the heavy hasp and padlock on the swinging doors so no one could enter without permission.

W.W. McArdle took his usual spot in front of the prosecution table, turned directly to the jury because he wanted to see their faces, and called his first witness of the day. Temple Dandridge later wrote in the *Star*, "When she was called, Miss Chambers rose unsteadily, her hand upon her mother's shoulder, and ascended the steps to the witness box. She faced the defendants while the oath was being administered; her eyes wandered over the faces of the attorneys, defendants, and men at the press tables."

McArdle paced to give Margaret time to compose herself. During those few minutes she placed her gloved hands together in her lap, raised her chin almost imperceptibly, and looked confidently about the room.

The county attorney took her through the details of her family and where they lived, her education and where she taught school, her phone call from Herbert Forchet, and where he took her. Then he came to the crux of the matter.

"Now," McArdle said, "you may tell what occurred when you arrived at the top of the hill."

"Five masked men came out of the hedge and stopped the buggy. Two of them pointed revolvers at us."

"Forchet?"

"Herbie was pulled out of the buggy on his side. Two of the men took me out of the buggy, and I was carried around behind it, where they threw me down in the road."

"Then what?"

"They raised my clothing and rubbed tar all over the lower part of my body and lower limbs."

"How many men took part in lifting you out of the buggy?"

"Two."

"Masked?"

"Yes, sir."

"Did you recognize any of these men?"

"No, sir."

"How long were they in taking you out of the buggy, throwing you down, and rubbing the tar on your body?"

"About ten minutes."

"How did you get back into the buggy?"

"I don't know."

"I will ask you if you were made lame by being thrown down?" McArdle continued.

"My back and body hurt for more than two weeks after that," Margaret said.

"And you cannot tell who helped you back into the buggy?"

"No, sir."

"When you got home, did you speak to any of your family?"

"No. I went around the house to the barn. I didn't want my mother to see me."

"Why not?"

"The tar was all over me. I just couldn't face her."

"You may tell us to what extent your clothing was daubed with that tar."

"All around."

"Was your outer dress daubed with it?"

"Yes, my dress was daubed with it."

"Tell us the condition of your waist."

"It was a one-piece dress," Margaret said. "It was tarred all down the skirt, and the waist was tarred all around."

"What underclothing did you have on?"

"I had on two underskirts and a union suit."

"What was the condition of your corset?"

"The corset was tarred all around."

"You may state whether this tar was rubbed onto your body and lower limbs."

"Yes, sir."

"Margaret, I have to ask you this," W. W. said with effect. "Did these men rip your clothes and expose your naked body?"

"Yes, sir."

"And did they touch your naked body?" W.W. asked gently.

Margaret did not immediately answer. She shivered slightly, clasped her hands together for strength, and answered in a steady voice, "Yes, they did."

McArdle said nothing. He stood looking directly at Margaret, as if directing the gaze of the courtroom. He gave the jury enough time to fully absorb the implications of her answer, then paced across the room and resumed questioning.

"What did you do with your ruined clothing? You did not keep it to show to the prosecuting authorities, did you?"

"No. My father burned it."

"Do you mean to say your father burned all the ruined clothing?"

"No. There was a handkerchief I used to rub off my hands while going home in the buggy."

"Would you recognize that handkerchief again if you should see it?"

"I will remember how it looked all my life."

"Is this it?"

"Yes, sir."

"If the court please, the state will now introduce this handkerchief in evidence," McArdle said. The defense's objections were in vain.

The county attorney wrapped up his questioning of Margaret Chambers by asking her about the somewhat elusive motives of the tar party. None of the defendants could actually come up with a specific charge against Margaret Chambers. The charge that Miss Chambers had lost her license to teach in neighboring Saline County had been proven false even before the trial began, when the Saline superintendent of schools sent a letter to the Nickerly county attorney and the *Kansas City Star* saying Miss Chambers had never had a license in that county. That left them with the charge that Miss Chambers was sweet on the Swenson boy. W.W. McArdle had gone to the Swenson farm to interview the boy, and found him to be a lad of such innocence that even the question of relations with his teacher sent him to his mother's apron, asking her the meaning of "relations." McArdle was convinced that whatever the boy's fantasies, he simply didn't have the courage or understanding to carry them out, and whatever Margaret's fantasies, this boy could not have kept it secret or have handled its emotional effects. The more the young man proclaimed his innocence in the midst of tearful answers, the more McArdle realized that he could not put the young man on the witness stand. But he had to ask Margaret.

"Miss Chambers," he began, "have you ever seduced one of your students?"

The courtroom gasped and seemed to hold its air in, as if no one would ever breathe again until the answer was heard.

Margaret was ready. "No," she said in a strong voice, her eyes glued to the county attorney. "I have never seduced a student. I have never harmed a student in any way."

She paused to let the answer sink in, then couldn't resisting adding, "That is just vicious gossip by the women of this town."

Almost as an exclamation point, the courtroom started to buzz. They were leaning over, whispering to each other about which women Margaret Chambers was referring to, when McArdle quickly said, "Thank you, Miss Chambers," and helped Margaret down the steps.

The trial moved rather quickly through the defendants. Some of them were called to testify about their own participation and whether they could implicate others. Langston, Garvey, Wilson, and Woods all admitted to their participation in the tarring and feathering, but pleaded for mitigation on the grounds that they were upholding community morals. They hadn't hurt Miss Chambers; she couldn't even produce the dress to show damages, and their only purpose was to deliver a message on behalf of the community. The other defendants claimed not to be a part of the tarring, although they were in the bushes watching or sitting on their motorcycles. The three men walking up the road to Twelve Mile Run as Forchet and Margaret galloped home claimed their innocence because they were too late to witness the tar party. They admitted wanting to be there but claimed no participation.

As the last day of the trial opened, and County Attorney McArdle was about to start his summation, John Engle rose to inform the bench that four of his defendants wanted to change their plea to guilty. Once again the court was thrown into turmoil. The first defendant to stand and say he was guilty was Ed Garvey. Garvey had vowed to fight the charges to the bitter end, but after hearing the testimony, he knew that public opinion had turned against him. His father had to agree. By most accounts, Ed Jr. was considered the instigator of the whole affair.

"These *Star* stories have whipped the whole damn country into a frenzy," Ed Sr. told his wife the night before. "We can't possibly get a fair verdict, even from that no-account jury. They're all sitting there pious and all, listening to that girl tell about a little daub of tar as if her whole life was on the line. And yesterday that tinhorn lawyer from Atlanta shows up and offers to help McArdle, just so he can get this name in the paper."

"Calm down, Ed," Mrs. Garvey said. "You're not helping matters. Those boys did a terrible thing. And I feel worse for Margaret now than ever."

"You and every other weak sister in town," Ed said. "I believe that boy would be better off with the judge than with the jury."

Mrs. Garvey was at a loss for words. She hadn't been able to reason with her husband since the trial began. It was better to just be quiet.

"I think the boy should plead guilty and let the judge decide," Ed said. "I've known Judge Crier all my life. He's a farmer, and he knows how these things happen. Let's just ask for the mercy of the court."

"Talk to Mr. Engle, Ed, and see what he says," Mrs. Garvey said, ending the conversation.

The next morning, all four boys directly involved in the tarring offered a guilty plea. Almost as surprising as the new pleas was Judge Crier's immediate announcement of a five-hour recess so he could consider the case, and his stated intention to announce a sentence at four o'clock the same day, not only for the four who pled guilty today, but also for Herbert Forchet and Hank Simpson.

"My God," the man next to Temple Dandridge said as the courtroom leapt to its feet. "The judge is going to sentence even before the trial is over. What about those other guys?"

Dandridge raced for a telephone to call Nate Cabot. "Hold the front page," he yelled down the wire. "The main guys have pled guilty, and the sentence is coming at four. Today's the day. I'll call you back after four." He hung up the phone and headed for McArdle's office to find out what the heck was going on.

·   ·   ·

The Reverend Aaron Langston sank into the family's Victorian couch and closed his eyes. The couch had long since lost its spring, leaving it the softest and most comfortable seat in the house. He rubbed his temples. He was tired from the courtroom, from worrying about his son, from not knowing what to tell his congregation about the trial. But he knew he had to talk with his family about the day's events. Jay had pled guilty and Judge Crier had done the unexpected, imposing a stiff sentence of one year in the county jail and a five-hundred-dollar fine, the maximum possible for assault and battery. The courtroom, filled with family of the defendants and mainstays of the town, had responded with shouts and tears. As Judge Crier walked off his dais after sentencing, the audience fell silent and watched the defendants console each other with brave admonitions to "get through this." The strangers in the room, including the press, were surprised by the stunned reaction of the audience, but immediately began moving for the doors so they could run down the street to a telephone or teletype to report their headlines: "Six Go to Jail, Tar Trial Continues."

The first journalist through the swinging doors was a reporter for the *Salina Journal*, who shouted to the crowd in the hallway, "One year in jail." His words were passed through the crowd and out to the front steps where a stranger cupped his hands over his mouth like a megaphone and repeated the verdict to a front-yard crowd of more than a thousand. Aaron Langston, who was just emerging from the building, was stunned to hear a great shout of celebration rise from the crowd. People could be heard almost screaming, "They got what they deserved. Let 'em rot in jail." A woman shouted, "That'll teach 'em."

As Ivy Langston, Ray, and the girls gathered in their living room, it felt like every stitch in their lives was frayed and breaking. Jay was gone, at least for a year, and they were left with his debt as well.

Ivy examined her husband, slumped in the couch. He seemed unbearably tired. His long white beard hadn't been trimmed in weeks, and it hung limp upon his vest. Ivy noticed that his hair seemed whiter, at least around the ears where it was beginning to curl, and she worried for his health.

"Ivy, children," Aaron began, "Jesus taught us there is a time for every season. This is our time of testing, and we must not be found wanting. We must take our direction from the scriptures where God directs his followers not to give up their faith. He rewards those who are loyal to his cause, and he forgives those who trespass against him. Now we must trust in the Lord."

"But the judge was right, Aaron," Ivy said quietly. "What Jay did was wrong. He must pay for his sins, and we will pray for him. Then we will welcome him home."

"God bless you, Ivy," Aaron said. "And may God bless our family."

Aaron thought maybe that would suffice. His family's love of God and each other would bring them through this terrible nightmare, but he wasn't so sure about the community. He couldn't erase from his mind the sounds of those shouts, those celebrations just outside the courthouse when the people heard the sentences. There was no sympathy for the defendants, only ridicule and derision. It was impossible to know who was in the crowd, but many of them must have been from Nickerly, many of them from his own church. And there were many women among them. One thing was clear, this trial had changed the community, and it wasn't over yet.

.　　　.　　　.

The next day, Judge Crier made it clear that the trial of the nine remaining defendants would continue to its conclusion, and he left it to the prosecuting attorney to clarify the nature of the charges. W.W. McArdle argued with great vigor that a conspiracy to tar and feather was just as damning as committing the act, and that these men were all part of the conspiracy. Three of them took the witness stand and pled their innocence on the basis of nonparticipation. They argued that they only watched, and it was even hard to see anything in the dark. Some of them said they remained in the hedge and saw nothing. Two of them said they were still a mile away from the incident because they were walking and couldn't get there in time. But all were forced to admit that they knew about the tar party, did nothing to stop it, and probably would have participated if circumstances had not intervened. It was their gamble that no jury would convict on such a flimsy charge as conspiracy, especially when it amounted to nothing more than a few boys showing up to see some excitement.

W.W. McArdle had practiced his final argument at home, pacing across his small living room, reading his longhand words with as much emphasis as he could muster. He changed several of the formulations that seemed too legalistic. He knew this jury well, and they would not listen to lawyer talk. They were propelled through life by a fear of the Lord, and the Lord's simple words had given their lives meaning. But this morning he would give them another set of moral tenets, the laws of the State of Kansas that embodied the great commandments themselves. And he would deliver those laws with a fervor that courtroom had not heard before.

McArdle seemed to have grown during the trial. His somewhat stiff and formal appearance had given way to a certain nobility, to a sense of correctness, born of the conviction that his argument was strong and his position correct. He knew he was right and that knowledge made his eyes sparkle and his spine stretch straight. He began his closing arguments with an unsparing denunciation of the defendants:

"In my practice I have sent men to the penitentiary for felonies, but I have never had a case that could equal the one before us in the enormity of its cowardice and brutality.

"I regret indeed that our laws are so lame, our legislatures so lax, that we must be content to send the offenders of such a crime to jail or heap upon them an insignificant fine. Certainly an offense of this nature will never be committed again and be subjected to a similar punishment. And yet our legislature, our people, our students of political economy doubtless never dreamed that a law of this nature would be found necessary to put into effect.

"Tar and feathers! A relic of ancient times. Tarring a girl! Think of it. One of our own girls; one of our own citizens; right here in the center of civilization. I have heard of such things taking place in barbaric times, but I never believed it. I have heard that they would some-times take a man and tar him and ride him on a rail. But did you ever hear of a bunch of men tarring a helpless girl? One who cannot defend herself? It is simply awful. Why, Robin Hood and his gang of des-peradoes would start at such a thing. They, who made their liveli-hood by forage, by highway robbery, would blush to do such a thing as this band of desperadoes did the night of the seventh of August, 1911.

"It has been intimated throughout the conduct of this trial that Miss Chambers is not a girl of good reputation or character. This I would challenge most strenuously, if it were necessary; if her reputation were an issue in this case. But it is not an issue.

"I care not who Miss Chambers is, nor what she is. That matters not. She may be the vilest character on top of the earth, yet she is just as much entitled to the protection of our laws as if she were an angel. No matter how grievously she has broken the moral or legal laws, her punishment is not a coat of tar. If she did that which is improper, let her be brought before this same tribunal that is trying these defendants. There she would get her just punishment, if she deserved it.

"But where in the name of God and all reason did those men, who on this dark night so desecrated our laws, customs, ethics, get the all-important right to judge her without a trial; to take her ruthlessly and forcibly out of the conveyance in which she was riding and thus chasten her? Why, even a dog deserves better treatment than was given Margaret Chambers that night.

"Gentlemen, this girl is our sister! This girl is one of the daugh-ters of Kansas. This girl calls for the protection of our laws and our state. It is your duty to give it to her. You can if you will. Will you, in your verdict today, blot from the spangled banner the bright star that glitters to the name of Kansas and leave the stripe behind, a fit emblem of her degradation? Or will you, by the word 'guilty,' continue to make it one of the brightest stars that shines upon the broad field of our national flag?

"Margaret Chambers was tried, condemned, and punished before a force worse than Pontius Pilate. I hope by your verdict you will triumphantly punish her unjust treatment. I will leave the case in your hands."

·   ·   ·

After Judge Crier gave final instructions to the jury, he called for a recess, and Margaret and Temp went down to the basement of the courthouse hoping to find some privacy. Some clerks were working in the file rooms where court records were stacked in wooden cabinets, but the two found a small wood bench in a quiet corner. The stone walls were painted white, as were the iron water pipes coming through the walls from the two wells in the yard, giving the place a hospital feeling, exacerbated by the pervasive smell of Lysol.

Margaret was distinctly nervous, glad to have the arguments over, but worried by the judge's instructions.

"My God, Temp," she said. "How can the jury ever find them guilty after hearing those instructions? They were there. They all did it. Why did he go over and over that conspiracy business?"

"It's the law, Margaret," Temp began. "He has to tell them the law."

Judge Crier had delineated fifteen different points of instruction to the jury, which he had written himself in longhand. He checked off each point as he read it, writing "Given" and scratching his initials beside it. Temp had taken notes as fast as he could, figuring he could get the full text later from the clerk, but catching the main points: that no evidence showed the remaining defendants had actually participated in the tarring and feathering; that the mere presence at the crime does not make the defendants participants; that counseling others is not participating; that "reasonable doubt" meant no conviction; that even if the men were on their way to the scene of the crime, they were not guilty, and presumed innocent. Even Temp found it remarkable that the only statement of reason for guilt came in item thirteen. The judge had said, "Although you should believe from the evidence that Margaret Chambers was tarred and feathered, and if you find that these nine defendants did not actually participate in the act, then I instruct you that the defendants cannot be considered parties to said plan or responsible for any assault upon the said Margaret Chambers, and unless you should find and believe beyond a reasonable doubt that the defendants advised and counseled the perpetration of the last named assault, you should acquit them."

"And even then he went on to emphasize that silence or assent doesn't mean they approved," Margaret said with some resignation. "How can this jury, half of whom can't read or write anyway, possibly convict? The judge gave them every way out."

"That's not all true, Margaret," Temp said. "I'm told the foreman is the smartest man in this county, has written a book, and speaks two languages."

"He's still a farmer who thinks these men should be out plowing the north forty," she said.

"Margaret," Temp said, switching gears, "you can't stay here when this is over. What are you going to do?"

"I don't know. Maybe go to Kansas City. Maybe join the suffrage movement."

Temp rolled his eyes, but said nothing. He would like to have Margaret in Kansas City, but those suffragettes were not his cup of tea.

"Temp," Margaret said pleadingly. "Why do women get so little respect? Why aren't there any women in that courtroom? They don't even think they have the right to come. Even Mrs. Garvey isn't here, and her son's on trial. Why do we leave everything to the men?"

Temp was looking for a way out of this conversation when W.W. McArdle came clattering down the steps to join them.

"I was told you two had slipped down here," he said. "Now people will be talking about that. At least you're sitting out here in the hall-way."

"Oh, Mr. McArdle," Margaret said with a smile, "I can't take another scandal."

"I just wanted to let you know that the jury may be out for a while," W.W. said. "They have asked to see the handkerchief and the can of tar they found at the mill. Don't leave the courthouse without checking with me. I still think this may be over tonight."

McArdle turned and trotted back up the steps.

"My mother went on home, Temp," Margaret said. "She was so upset by all of this, but now I think she wants it to happen."

"You mean the verdict?"

"Yes, I think she has come to see this as her trial, and she's been the victim a lot longer than I have."

"I'll have to go back to Kansas City soon," Temp offered. "I hate to leave you."

"You'll be fine, Temp," Margaret said. "I'll come see you. I'm almost famous now. Maybe I can travel. At least I know I'm not going back to that school."

"Six men are in jail already," Temp said, bringing the conversation back to the trial. "Herbie, Garvey, Langston, Wilson, Simpson, and Woods. The maximum penalty. How do you feel about that?"

"The only one I feel sorry for is the one who did the most harm to me, Easy Tucker," she said. "At least he knew it was wrong. And his guilt killed him. These others still think they were railroaded."

Margaret's hair was beginning to droop under the strain of the day. A handful of pins and clips were unable to hold the weight of her curls, and perspiration undermined the strength of their construction. She rubbed her forehead, wanting to let her hair down. Even her corset began to pinch and itch, and she rubbed her sides for relief, but she knew it was a weariness of the mind that took her strength, so she excused herself to go home. Temp offered to walk her, but she declined, asking him to stay at the courthouse and call when the jury came in.

·   ·   ·

When the jury convened at nine o'clock the next morning, after deliberating until past one o'clock the night before, it took them another seventeen ballots to reach a final verdict on all nine of the defendants. They had taken a total of forty-two ballots in two days of arguing about the conspiratorial role of each man, with over two hours of debate just on the subject of the can of tar found at Garvey's Mill. Since six men had already pled guilty to assault and battery, it wasn't clear to the jury that this evidence was relevant. And none of the conspirators had been directly connected to the physical evidence. It all depended on their intentions, and the jury was reluctant to put men in jail for that. The part that stuck in their minds was the testimony by Herbie Forchet that these men just stood around and watched. They had indulged in a kind of voyeurism particularly repulsive to practicing Presbyterians, as most of the jury were, and a sexual sin of far worse proportions than tarring and feathering. The act of watching was indeed a form of participation. The jury also called for two readings of the testimony by Margaret Chambers about her clothes being torn and her body exposed. Once the jury consensus formed that these men were involved for reasons of sexual stimulation, rather than moral convictions, the verdicts were much easier. Thus the jury spent a great deal of time reviewing the testimony to figure out where each man was standing and what he was trying to see.

.   .   .

Rumors started flying about two o'clock in the afternoon that a verdict was coming, and spectators began pouring in from every corner of the county. It was a clear, early winter day when sweaters were adequate against the chill, and the sun gave a bright sheen to the grass. The crowd outside was larger than ever, swelling to well over two thousand. The trial regulars, including the press, had never left the courthouse, and they took their seats in the courtroom at once.

The earlier guilty pleas had come in such a way that they had deprived the crowd of any surprise. The spectators had not witnessed the blunt force and finality of a jury decision, and they seemed to ignore the fact that these remaining verdicts were about conspiracy, not the actual assault. The boys at the Adeline Hotel were giving ten-to-one odds that all would be found innocent.

The one difference in today's crowd was the presence of the wives and children of the defendants and a large group of Civic Improvement Association members. The latter bustled up the sidewalk like a gaggle of geese, dressed in their finest overcoats, a black hat on every head, and a certain lockstep gait that suggested days of marching practice in the church basement, although that seemed unlikely. Mrs. Club Wilson was in the lead, perhaps realizing that with her husband in jail for a year, the association members might be her only companions. She had asked Tiny Tucker to lead the group, but Tiny had declined, even saying she might not want to meet with the group again. Her reasons were not clear, but Mrs. Wilson assumed she was overcome with grief and did not pester her further.

Curiously, and in contrast to the first day of the trial, the crowd gathered around the front steps of the courthouse saw the ladies marching toward them and shrank away from the sidewalk, as if afraid the hems of their dresses might burn them. Mrs. Wilson sensed the change in attitude, but it did not deter her. She marched right into the courtroom, dislodged her youngest son, who had been sent ahead to save the row, and ushered the Civic ladies across the front of the courtroom. Mrs. Wilson was determined that the defendants, the men of Nickerly, would see the ladies of Nickerly as soon as they entered the courtroom. Maybe the spectators in this courthouse, or the readers of the *Kansas City Star*, or the citizens of New York had changed their moral values to accommodate the actions of Miss Chambers, but the Civic Improvement Association's values would not budge, no matter what the verdicts.

The last person to enter the courthouse was the only one with a reserved seat, Margaret Chambers. And she was alone. After McArdle's call, she dressed according to her plan of the morning, told her mother and sister that she wanted to walk alone, and struck out for the courthouse. The crowd was waiting, as if all the preliminaries were over, and it was time for the star to appear. When they first saw her, two blocks away, she was just a blur, although something seemed different about her appearance. It wasn't her dress, which was a long and gray gabardine with black buttons from her neck to her waist, or her black coat with the boa that she had worn the day before. It was her head and feet.

The ladies began to gasp as each step brought her more clearly into focus. "My heavens!" they said, and not under their breath. Margaret was wearing black shoes with her ankles showing. No high tops, no laces as were the norm, but open-throated shoes of a kind never before seen in Nickerly, open from the crown of her foot all the way to the hem of her dress. Her ankles were bare.

And on her head was the most incredible sight of all, a large black hat with a brim bent rakishly to one side under a silver band. "A silver band," the crowd repeated as if they were reading a fashion review in the Sears magazine. And finally, the item that made the women put their hands to their mouths, a single long white feather. It stuck in Margaret's hat like a plume or perhaps an enormous specimen from Esther Ennis's pillow. When Margaret walked into the courtroom with her long strides and commanding figure, every head and eye moved in her direction and stuck. She was like a figure from another time, oblivious to her surroundings, alive to another set of customs, and as self-contained as a pirate ship. She sat without comment.

The big Irish foreman stood before his jury of eleven and began to read the verdict slowly and with determination: "We find the defendant John Buckhorn not guilty."

A chorus of "Thank God's" and "Bless the Lord's" went up from the ladies in the second row, and the judge had to rap his gavel and ask for quiet. Mrs. Wilson smiled. Margaret did not change her expression, and the feather did not dip; it held itself erect and proud.

"We the jury," the foreman began again, "find the defendants Ben Johnson, Delbert Romberger, Abner Polk, Joe Tanner, Joe Simpson, and Striper Simpson guilty of assault and battery as charged in the information filed in said case, and that they and each of them spend a maximum of ninety days in the Nickerly County Jail, and that they each pay a fine of two hundred dollars to the County of Nickerly in the State of Kansas."

The feather bobbed briefly and pandemonium broke out.

CHAPTER SEVENTEEN

Still a little groggy from a poor night's sleep, Buck Lamb pulled his copy of the *Kansas City Star* off the pile at Callahan's drugstore in Salina, where nearly seventy copies arrived by train each morning for designated buyers. The story about W.W. McArdle was spread across two columns at the top of the front page and even the headline proclaimed his victory: "Country Lawyer Avenges Tar Party." And the subhead in smaller type read, "Even Conspirators Convicted." No regular *Star* reader needed further explanation, having followed the tar party stories in more than fourteen front-page articles by Temple Dandridge, the most widely quoted journalist in the state.

The minute he saw the article, Buck Lamb had an idea about how to save the Democratic Party of Kansas. Brushing off his sleepiness, he rushed out of the store and headed toward the Farmers Bank and Trust at the main intersection of town, the paper folded haphazardly under his ample arms. His cowboy boots with his initials embossed on the side hit the boardwalk with a rapid thud, and his bolo tie with the silver clasp in the form of a "B" dangled from his neck so that the silver ends bounced off his belly as he walked. Buck was a political leader who often said, "If William Howard Taft can live big, so can I."

As the Democratic chairman of the state party, Buck was searching for a candidate for the United States Congress, a spot soon to be vacated by the seventy-three-year-old incumbent, who had recently fallen off his horse and broken his hip. Buck did not expect the old man's return to Washington, and worse, the Democrats had lost the governor's race in the last election. In addition, both U.S. senators were Republican. The state party was demanding a turnaround. At least Buck had more than a year before the election. So far there had been no panic about a new slate of candidates.

Buck Lamb's first name was actually Horatio. A few people around town called him Lamb, but mostly it was Buck, a no-nonsense, manly name that was easy to shout over the wailing and whining of cows and horses at Buck Lamb's Auction Barn every Thursday afternoon. Buck had started the auction in 1902 by bringing in buyers from Kansas City and matching them up with local farmers who brought their livestock to his pens for sale and shipment east. As soon as he realized the market between farmers for each other's livestock was just as great as selling for slaughter, Buck built an auction shed. It consisted of a twenty-foot-square cow ring surrounded by bleachers. Young Buck would stand on a podium he modeled after the pulpit at the First Presbyterian Church, introduce each cow and owner as the livestock was driven from the pens into the auction ring, tell a few stories about the owner to loosen up the audience, and start the bidding. It wasn't long before every farmer within a hundred miles wanted to take his cattle to Buck's both because Buck produced good prices and because the auction had become a social event, with Buck's wife Hettie selling ham sandwiches and homemade ice cream right from the back porch of their home. Buck could look out over his customers and see forty or fifty men in overalls, leaning back on the wide bench seats, adjusting their felt cowboy hats. Their children sat beside them in fascination, waiting for the day when they could raise their finger, or tip their brim, and buy the prancing muscles of a fine new stallion.

Many of Kansas's finest young men learned the ways of manhood at Buck's just by listening to the men's conversations, watching their fathers spit tobacco and measure cattle for their value. Buck's auction was also the best breeding ground in the state for politics, with arguments flying left and right about prices, presidents, family gossip, and certainly about the tar party trial. The boys at the auction barn gave it a prime beef rating for high drama, legal wrangling, and sex.

The auction was every Thursday at one o'clock in the afternoon, and Buck would hold his meetings of the state Democratic Party in the morning. That gave him a chance to show off his operation to the bankers and landowners from other parts of the state, who would drive to Salina the day before and spend a little money in the town. Finally it let his local boys at the auction barn do a little hobnobbing with the party leaders in the afternoon. Everybody benefited, especially Buck, and about all he had to do to maintain this cushy situation was pick Democratic candidates who could win elections. He thought he saw a sure winner in W.W. McArdle.

"Charley," Buck said to Charley Hundley, the bank president and major Democratic money raiser, "I got us a man for the fourth district." And he tossed the *Kansas City Star* down on Charley's desk with an exaggerated motion. Charley said nothing, looked down, looked back up at Buck, and said quietly, "Do you think you could get that schoolteacher to campaign for him?"

"Let's not go too far," Buck said, plopping down in a chair and wiping his forehead with the handkerchief he took from his back pants pocket. "We don't want a bunch of suffragettes coming in here. We don't need any women marching in the streets. But I bet that girl would support him."

"Well, she ought to," Charley said. "He not only gave her respectability and sympathy . . . Did you know that I'm holding money here at the bank for her that was collected by two of Taft's cabinet members, agriculture and interior? They call it a legal defense fund, and the schoolteacher wasn't even the defendant. That trial didn't cost her a penny."

Charley was so worked up about the money aspect that it took him a moment to finish his thought.

"McArdle also got convictions," he added. " I still can't believe that nearly ten people went to jail just for watching."

"That alone would make him a good candidate," Buck countered. "It would be good for some of these cowboys to know they can't just shoot the first thing that makes them mad."

Buck had a rather unusual countenance. His potbelly was surrounded by a three-inch-wide leather belt and a massive silver buckle given to him by a pig farmer in lieu of his sales commission. The buckle was polished with the imprint of a wild boar, which Buck rather liked, perhaps because it reminded him of himself. In spite of his girth, Buck's face was angular and strong, without a trace of fat or a double chin, and some of the church women had remarked on this handsome quality. It was even rumored that some of the farm wives came to the auction just to see Buck in action.

"How about going with me to see McArdle over at Nickerly next week?" Buck said. "I bet we can talk him into running."

"I've never seen a young lawyer yet that didn't dream of spending a little time in Washington, no matter how dreary that swamp of a city is," Charley said. "They can't resist the power. Sure, he'll go."

. . .

W.W. McArdle stepped onto Margaret Chambers's porch the day after the trial, expecting her to be a little down. His other clients always were. They became so engrossed in the trial that it became their lives;

it changed their perception of themselves; it made them special in some unseen way; and often, even when they won their case, they experienced a period of depression as they returned to routine life. W.W. wanted to help Margaret through this period, especially in view of the circuslike environment she had endured over the past three months. Indeed, she had become famous, if not recognizable in person, at least recognizable by name throughout the state and in many parts of the nation.

Margaret opened the door, threw her arms about the startled McArdle, kissed him on the cheek, and exclaimed, "I love you, sir. Thank you. Thank you. Thank you."

Margaret was sorry that she had rushed out of the courthouse yesterday without thanking anybody. The minute she heard the verdicts she stood up, adjusted her hat and feather, and walked with dignity right out of the courtroom. When she got through the swinging doors, she walked out the courthouse's front door, down the steps, to the end of the sidewalk. Then she turned and waited. She wanted to be outside, vindicated, free, and in the midst of a courthouse crowd that was stunned by the verdict. She wanted to meet them at the bottom of the steps and see their reactions.

"Oh, Mr. McArdle," she began, "it was so amazing. A couple of women actually came over to me and said, 'I'm sorry.' Others just hurried away. And Mrs. Wilson was spitting and sputtering mad. She came over to me and said, 'Miss Chambers, you've sent all these fathers to jail and left their wives and children home alone. You should be ashamed.'"

"I just laughed, Mr. McArdle," Margaret said. "Not at those poor women without their husbands, but at Mrs. Wilson. She's home alone because of what her husband did to me. I don't hate her; I just think she's nuts."

That made McArdle smile. He took his gray fedora off and followed Margaret into the house, his black hair indented along the sides where the hatband had rested. He was still dressed as elegantly as black would allow, with a long black topcoat to guard against the November winds which were starting to carry a foreboding chill. The first snow usually hit Kansas before Thanksgiving, and the perennials had already wilted under an October frost. He was thankful the trial had ended before a hard winter.

As W.W. greeted Margaret's parents and accepted the offer of hot tea, Margaret began to see the county attorney in a different light, as a man with his own life, family, and ambitions. Until yesterday he was just her prosecutor, the man who would exact justice, the legal force that would guide her through the process, and a rather one-dimensional character at that. Margaret had met his wife, of course, but never his daughters, and she had never been in his home. Now she wondered about those matters, especially his little girls, and what they might think of her. As W.W. moved to the living room, set his cup and saucer on the corner table, and tugged at his vest before sitting, Margaret realized she not only owed this man a lot, she really liked him.

"Margaret," McArdle began, "I wanted to talk with you about a couple of matters. First, I think it will take a little time for you to adjust to things now that the trial is over."

"Well," she said, "I know I don't want to teach anymore."

"I hope you don't rush off somewhere," he said. "Unless, of course, you know what you want to do."

"I don't, sir," she said. "I haven't thought about my future for the past three months."

W.W. was a little hesitant with Margaret because he didn't want to take advantage of her, or even have her believe that he would try, but he had to raise this new subject anyway.

"Margaret," he said, "I got a call today from Buck Lamb over at Salina. He's the chairman of the Democratic Party in Kansas, and he wants to come talk to me this week about politics."

"What does he want?" she asked.

"He says he wants to talk about me running for the United States Congress."

Margaret's eyes flew open. She took her cup of tea from her lap and slid it onto the table, then clasped her hands in front of her, and exclaimed, "That would be wonderful. Would you go to Washington?"

"There's a lot that would have to happen, Margaret," he said. "The election is a year from now. I'd have to campaign, maybe even quit my job at some point. But there is another problem I want to discuss with you."

"Oh, I think it's wonderful," she said hurriedly.

"This is about you," W.W. said. "I'm at least wise enough to know that Buck Lamb wants me because of your trial and all the publicity. I also know that if I run for Congress, this tarring and feathering business might not die down so fast."

"What do you mean?" she asked.

"First of all, I'll be known as the 'Tar Party Prosecutor,' so you'll see that name in the newspapers, maybe even on campaign posters. How would you feel about that?"

"I don't mind," she said. "We won. Those men were convicted, and I don't mind at all if this town is reminded of it."

"Yes, but the Civic Improvement Association won't like it."

"I don't care a whit what they like."

"There is one other thing," W. W. said. "Someone will run against me. And those boys from Garvey's Mill are never going to like me. You could hear some pretty nasty rumors, or even public charges, if I run."

"Like what?" Margaret asked.

"They could say your whole trial was just trumped up to make me famous, to get me into Congress," he said.

Margaret said nothing.

"They could say you're going to Washington with me," he added, avoiding the more direct charge that he really feared, which was gossip that he and Margaret were romantically involved. W.W. had talked this over with his wife last night, and she was reluctant to put the girls through that kind of campaign, although she assured him she would never believe such malicious mudslinging.

"Margaret," W.W. said. "I have to tell you that this trial has not been easy on my family. Louise has received the cold shoulder in church. And she knows how people look at her on the street. I've been the center of attention, but Louise is trying to make new friends. It hurts to have a store clerk throw her change down on the counter without even saying hello."

"But people like you, W.W.," Margaret suggested. "They're taken with how you stood up for me. People in this county have never heard a speech before like the one you gave in summation. It was glorious."

"It may have sounded that way to you," W.W. said. "But it didn't sound that way to the families of the defendants."

"And it shouldn't," Margaret jumped in. "They should feel scorned. But people here should know you'll fight for them. You'll uphold the law. And when we all get to Washington, I bet Louise will have more friends than ever."

"Margaret," he said, "we shouldn't be presumptuous about Washington."

"That's OK," Margaret said. "I might just go to Washington with you, if you'll take me."

W.W. was a little nervous about Margaret's tendency to blunder ahead, even if she hadn't thought through all the consequences. Going to Washington might be in that category. But he also knew that he couldn't run for Congress without her. His fame was her fame, and that's why the party wanted him to run. At least he was pleased that she supported him and that her family voiced no objections, although her mother and father listened to the entire conversation from the kitchen with a worried look on their faces. As he left, Mrs. Chambers said only, "Good luck, Mr. McArdle, and thank you for taking care of our daughter." So far, this matter had gone much better than he expected.

·   ·   ·

The campaign of W.W. McArdle for Congress started on the front steps of the Nickerly County Courthouse with a rousing speech by Buck Lamb in his best auctioneering crescendos, his voice rising and falling with each sentence until the small audience of local citizens and three or four reporters were suitably impressed, as was the candidate. W.W. wished he could speak like that.

W.W.'s summation speech to the tar party jury was the most forceful, pointed, and emotional speech he had ever given, and all the passion of his soul had been engaged in that presentation. How would he ever muster that kind of enthusiasm for a simple political speech in the middle of winter on cold courthouse steps in front of a crowd that mostly hoped he would fall on a patch of ice? Buck had said he had to announce his candidacy at home, at the scene of his legal triumph, even if the crowd didn't like him. Buck said the rest of the fourth district, which included eight counties, would love him because he was famous. Furthermore, they applauded his prosecution of the men of Nickerly, a group whose circle of supporters had shrunk considerably during the trial. Buck had told him that after this first day, the campaign would get better and easier.

W.W. felt insecure in his trial victory. He felt some strange new forces in his personality, like the love of attention. He had never considered himself a public figure before. Now, he often saw groups of men congregated along the street and would hear his name mentioned as he passed. People were talking about him, and he liked it. But he also feared that it was false pride. It made him wonder if he could sustain his newfound fame. Or was he just a product of the trial glare, a man left diminished when the spotlight moves on? Putting himself before the people and asking for their support would test his confidence. He would need a lot of help from Buck Lamb, and maybe from Margaret Chambers as well.

But strangely enough, Buck was right about campaigning. It did get easier. In fact, after a few appearances, W.W. began enjoying it. The endless speeches and meetings were exactly what he had trained for as a lawyer, and he even enjoyed meeting people, to the point that he abandoned dark suits and started wearing buckskin cowboy boots. He joked to his wife that he was becoming a man of the people.

·   ·   ·

The letter from the First Presbyterian Church of Nickerly to the Reverend Aaron Langston didn't have a printed return address or a letterhead on the stationery. When Ivy opened it, as she did all the mail, she noticed that it was written on tablet paper. Her eyes went immediately to the scrawled signature of the head deacon of the church. The two lines above it read: "Dear Reverend Langston" The letter began, "The deacons of the Church must inform you that we will no longer need your services as minister. Thank you for your service."

Ivy sat down at the kitchen table and pulled the corners of her shawl tight around her neck. There was still a chill in the house from last night's sharp wind. Several tree limbs were strewn about the lane, their bright broken ends a testament to the force of the gales. The last of the elm leaves were scattered on the ground. It would take until noon for the sun to soak a little warmth into the ground. Ivy usually liked the fall, but these days were lonely. Nearly every part of the Langstons' life was suffering. Jay was in jail. Their oldest girl had gone into service with the Watkins family in Ellsworth. She would be well taken care of by the Watkins, with free room and board, and her income would help pay for brooder chicks or repairs for the reaper. Ivy missed her, though.

At least she knew Ray was going to be a good farmer—he had good hands that could gable a barn as easily as knitting a sweater—but like the rest of them, he would have to live with the shame of Jay. It would probably drive Ray to another part of Kansas. As she gazed across the corn fields with the brown stalks left by a machete harvest, Ivy thought of the sheer work involved in living, in having to always forge ahead with another season. She knew work was God's way to salvation, but she was tired, and she didn't want to give Aaron this letter—another piece of bad news, another hill to climb. It was just in her mind, this tiredness from wrestling with forces beyond her control.

When Aaron opened the door, he let in a blast of cold that had rolled down from the crest of the Rockies, skipped across the western prairie, and settled down like a stray dog waiting to be driven away. Aaron took his sheepskin coat off, slung it over the wooden hook beside the door, and set the bucket of milk on the table. The milk was still warm.

"Aaron," Ivy said, as she rose to take the milk from the table to the counter, where she would pour it into a glass pitcher. "We received a letter from the church today. It's there on the table."

Aaron returned from the bedroom with a clean shirt. "I leaned up against that heifer, and she had something on her. It's all over my shirt. Must have been some tree sap she picked up in the pasture, all sticky."

Aaron sat down, put his hand around the glass of warm milk that Ivy had poured, and unfolded the letter.

"Doesn't say much," he muttered, staring down at the writing, trying to detect all the hidden reasons and motivations behind the words. "Deacon Sims's writing sure is hard to read."

"His intent is clear enough," Ivy said. "They don't want us back."

"Now, Ivy," Aaron said. "We're all God's children. There's other places to preach, and when the weather warms again, I can go back to the river."

"Aaron," Ivy started, "what about Jay? Sitting there in that jail. People talking. How can we preach the Lord's work when our son is in jail? I still can't get over what he did to that girl. No wonder the church doesn't want us."

"My ministry is for everyone, even unto the smallest sparrow," Aaron said. "And certainly to my son."

"I just don't understand him," Ivy continued, sitting next to Aaron, and gazing out the window at some distant point.

The sky was as gray as rotting wood. They were both silent, contemplating their son, weighing the conflicting passions of family and religion. Then Ivy began again.

"I remember once when Jay was here at home, while he was out on bond," she said. "I noticed him through the window. He was out on the porch watching a big brown spider starting his weave. Jay never moved as that spider dropped down from the roof and started his design. The spider moved up and down his strands of silk and then he moved sideways from one strand to another. His web sparkled in the sun. Jay was fascinated. He just sat there, never moving his eyes, as that spider put out another anchor to the mulberry bush beside the house. And when the spider moved through the air, against the backdrop of the open sky, it was like a painting. A beautiful thing. After almost an hour, Jay got up and walked over to that spider, clapped his hands, wiped them on his trousers, and walked away. He just killed it. How could he do that, Aaron?"

"It's the forces of the devil, Ivy. They're in the boy. Maybe the jail will help him see that."

.   .   .

Buck Lamb managed the campaign of W.W. McArdle like a veteran coach with a traveling prizefighter. The two men went from town to town together, calling on farmers and ranchers who had been to Buck's auction barn, walking down the main street of every town in the district, visiting the dry goods stores and the livery stables where people tended to congregate, and following Buck's hard and fast rule: Never go in a saloon. If folks saw you coming out of a saloon, you would be branded a drunk in the eyes of the town. No politician could recover from that stigma.

Buck's other rules were: Never appear alone with Margaret Chambers; never unbutton your shirt no matter how hot it gets; kiss the babies and pet the dogs but never nuzzle the horses. Buck had elected a lot of politicians with these simple dictates and one other: Only promise people what you know they want. W.W. was having a little trouble with this last rule.

During Margaret's trial, Margaret and W.W. had spent a lot of time together, waiting for court to resume or having lunch, and several times he had engaged her in conversation about teaching, just to take her focus off the events at hand. And it got him to thinking about the problems of education. He was troubled by Margaret's description of how her one-room school operated, with only one or two students in each grade, and even then with a shortage of books. The children had to listen to their classmates recite lessons of no use to the other grade levels. It struck W.W. that consolidation of schools was the answer, even if it meant the children couldn't all walk to school. They could be driven by buggy, and it would allow so many efficiencies in terms of books, teaching materials, and shared experiences by children of the same age. He realized there were a lot of complicating factors in this plan, but it seemed they could be worked out if parents realized the value of a better education. His one mistake, however, was in not recognizing the effect consolidation would have on the parents themselves. Simply put, consolidated schools meant more power for some, and a lot less power for those who no longer had a school nearby. As some parents put it, "I'm not turning my kids over to strangers." But this was just a code for their real fears: that they would no longer have control over their own school. Nevertheless, W.W. believed this was an important issue, and despite Buck's pleading, he brought it up at every rally.

He did follow Buck's advice concerning Margaret, which was to have her appear only at events outside Nickerly County. Buck reasoned that while many local citizens still held Margaret responsible for the tar party, strangers found her fascinating and pretty. Buck arranged for W.W.'s first major speech outside of Nickerly to be held at the auction barn in Salina, and posters for the appearance featured a drawing of Margaret Chambers, advertising a special appearance by the Tar Party Schoolteacher in support of her fearless prosecutor. The barn was packed with political supporters and curious onlookers. Mrs. Lamb ran out of ice cream.

W.W. climbed into the auction pulpit after a rousing introduction by Buck and began his regular speech, starting with his complete history, his law school training, his love of the state and the country, and finally, the need for better education. As he got to his stemwinder education finish, a number of hisses and boos sounded from the back rows. Consolidation was not popular. Still W.W. forged on, announcing: "Now, my friends and neighbors, I want you to meet one of my greatest supporters, a young lady known far and wide as a great teacher with the courage of a hundred men, a young woman who stood up for herself and for the law, a young woman who showed the people of this state that bullies will not prevail. I give you the Tar Party Schoolteacher, Margaret Chambers."

At that point, Buck Lamb pulled open the sliding gate between the cattle pens and the auction arena, and in rode Margaret Chambers on a sidesaddled black stallion that Buck had borrowed just for this appearance. She was sitting perfectly erect in a green velvet dress with brown leather high-top shoes; her waist was made of fine pure linen, with large plaits on either side stitched to her bustline, giving her a graceful fullness, with laundered collar and attached cuffs. But no amount of starch could hide the ample bosom that jarred just slightly with every step of the horse. She kept her eyes on the top row of the pavilion, rode once around the ring, stopped in the middle, and then reached up to remove her famous hat with the white goose feather. She held it high over her head and rode out of the ring. The crowd was stunned. The entry, the horse, and the schoolteacher's beauty were so unexpected that everyone just gaped. Then as the gate closed behind her, they burst into applause and whistles, with every boy in the barn putting his fingers to his lips and letting go.

W.W. McArdle stepped to the podium and literally yelled, "Thank you, Margaret, and thank you, good citizens of Salina." He hoped that at least some of that applause was for him.

CHAPTER EIGHTEEN

It had been a long year of campaigning, but with only two weeks left before the election, W.W. McArdle had established himself as a formidable politician. According to Buck Lamb and most of the other party leaders, McArdle held a comfortable lead over his opponent. His reputation as a prosecutor had provided large and enthusiastic audiences for his political messages. W.W.'s opponent, a loyal farmer who had chaired the Republican Party in Ellsworth for decades, was seen as a nice fellow, but hardly in the same league as W.W. McArdle, the nationally known prosecutor with big ideas about education. The election, still months away, looked like a shoo-in.

W.W. was up early this morning, ready to get started. His wife and the girls were still asleep when he heard horses in the yard and then a knock on the door. He expected Buck to join him for a day of campaigning in Ellsworth, knocking on doors and handing out the flier that read: "Vote for Winton McArdle, the fighting prosecutor." But when he pulled the door open, it was Sheriff Graves, standing beside a young girl. The girl was perhaps fifteen or so. She wore a long red flannel dress under her traditional school coat. There was no greeting.

"Is this the man?" the sheriff said, looking down at the girl's straight brown hair, not unkempt but not recently washed either.

"Yes, sir," she said, looking harshly at W.W. in his stocking feet. "He's the man who tried to rape me."

W.W. staggered back, trying to comprehend what this was all about. His knees weakened as he looked the girl square in the face, trying to recognize her, to put her in some context that made sense. She stood there expressionless, strangely passive, neither fearful nor aggressive, and as the sheriff put his hand on her shoulder, she made no response, no effort to seek reassurance. She simply made the charge and waited.

"What is this all about?" W.W. asked the sheriff.

"I'm sorry, Mr. McArdle," the sheriff said. "Francis has filed charges against you, saying you came to her uncle's house and forced yourself upon her. Is that true?"

"True?" W.W. repeated incredulously. "I don't even know her. I never saw her before in my life."

"I'm sorry, sir," the sheriff said again. "But I have a warrant for your arrest, based on her statement given to the new county attorney, Mr. Dunfee."

W.W. had resigned as county attorney more than six months earlier when it became clear he could not campaign for office and do his job as prosecutor. Since then his life had changed immensely. He was being paid by Buck Lamb out of campaign funds raised by the party, and he started using his first name, Winton, instead of his initials. Ironically, he had always used his initials because they sounded more formal and distinguished in his role as an attorney. Now Buck had coached him to act less formal in order to relate to the voters, and Winton it was. Buck even suggested W.W. shorten the first name to Win, which would fit nicely on window posters. But W.W. had drawn the line at Winton.

"I'm afraid you'll have to come with me," the sheriff said, "down to the courthouse."

"Can I tell my wife?" W.W. asked.

"Certainly, sir," the sheriff said. "We'll wait right here."

W.W. was still reeling from the confrontation at the door when he found his wife sitting on the edge of their bed, trying to hear the conversation with the sheriff. She stood and touched his arm.

"What is it?" she asked anxiously, knowing only that the sheriff usually means some kind of trouble and that this sheriff was a longtime friend of Ed Garvey Sr. She had never liked or trusted him, remembering his general reluctance to arrest the members of the tar party. And although she couldn't see who was at the door with him, she had heard a female voice. She searched W.W.'s ashen face, gray as day-old embers. His eyes looked confused. She had rarely seen him like this.

"There's a young girl," W.W. began, stammering. "I don't know her. She's making charges against me."

"What kind of charges?"

"I don't really know," he said, not quite up to a fuller explanation. "But I have to go see Dunfee with the sheriff." They had talked about Dunfee often, primarily because he was W.W.'s successor, and also because the governor had appointed him, the same governor who was a buddy of Ed Garvey's.

"I shouldn't be gone long," W.W. said. "Will you tell Buck when he comes that I've gone to the courthouse?"

She nodded.

"And one other thing," W.W. said. "Call John Engle and tell him I need his services immediately."

"Oh, no, Winton," she said. "Why? What is this?"

"I still don't know," he said. "But I'll be back soon."

W.W. returned to the kitchen for his shoes. As he started to tie them, he looked back at the bedroom door to see his wife standing under the jamb, staring through the living room at the sheriff. Down her cheeks streamed the large, quiet tears of the threatened.

.   .   .

A week earlier, Ed Garvey, the last of the tar party to be released from jail, had invited some of the boys to stop by for a swig from his father's jug. The time in county jail had passed quickly, punctuated every two or three months by the release of one or more of the tar party. With thirteen men under sentence, some of them had to go to the Ellsworth County Jail. Nickerly only had eight cells. So it seemed like someone was always being transferred in or out, or being released, and friendships among the group grew even stronger than before. The cells were not comfortable. Each one had only a small cot pushed against the concrete wall. The only bathroom was in the sheriff's office, and a trip to the toilet required a deputy escort, a task as degrading for the deputy as the inmate because it virtually defined his job. But the conversation between cells was almost like a meeting of the Civic Improvement Association, which incidentally disbanded when the membership dropped to three. Mrs. Club Wilson still met every week with Hettie Woods and Minerva Simpson to sew and talk about their old friends, but their unmitigated bitterness toward the community made even those sessions awkward and joyless. The eight inmates, however, grew closer in the absence of any books or magazines. They discussed their lives and loves over and over and detailed their plans for the future, mostly dreaming of getting far away from Nickerly. For Ed Garvey, the future took him two miles back to the mill, with several scores to settle.

When Garvey walked out of jail, escorted by his father, people on the street stared at him, but no one shouted hello, as would have been the case in the past. He could feel the difference in attitudes, but everything looked the same—the long main street of limestone buildings and a few more automobiles on the still unpaved street. He wanted to go back to the mill with its familiar surroundings and within a day he sent word that the tar party was invited to stop by for a visit.

Jay Langston's release from jail was more typical of the others. No one came to meet him. Jay stood outside the jailhouse, relishing his first taste of freedom. He looked up and down the street, searching for his parents or at least a familiar face. His extra clothes were in a pillowcase thrown over his shoulder. Oh well, he thought, a long walk home on the open road would do him some good.

Jay knew his father wasn't preaching at the church anymore, and he suspected that his welcome home might be chilly. But he hadn't expected a cold shoulder. Jay had spent a lot of time thinking about his family and had decided that fate had cast him as a minister's son, but that it was not a proper fit, and he would escape as soon as possible.

When Jay entered the house, only Ivy was there to meet him. She seemed not to know how to act. But she put her arms around him and murmured, "Thank God you're home, Jay."

"Your room is ready," Ivy said, releasing him.

"Thanks, Mom," he said, tossing his pillow bag on the floor beside the table. He didn't know what to say either. He didn't even ask about Aaron or his brother, Ray. And he didn't want to start an argument with anyone in the family. So he said little, greeting each of them with this same spartan hello as they returned to the house. When he went to bed that night, his first night home in a year, he was thankful to be out of jail, and thankful that the Reverend Aaron and his mother had not greeted him with a biblical lecture. Maybe time would heal their differences.

Jay Langston was the first to arrive at Garvey's Mill, riding his father's dapple gray horse and still wearing the smirk that had always spelled trouble. Jail hadn't changed his appearance one bit. He wore a blue plaid jacket over his blue workshirt and brown trousers. A shock of thick brown hair fell cockily over his forehead. He jumped out of his saddle, tied the horse to a hitching post beside the mill, and bounced into the office. He had been out of jail only three days and was still plain old thrilled to be free.

"Ed," Jay said, "good to see you back behind the scales. How's your mom and dad?"

"They're fine," Ed said. "Although Mom is more nuts than ever. She acts like nothing ever happened."

"My mom and dad are the same way," Jay said. "They watch me like a civet cat. I think Dad blames me for the fact that he can't preach at the church anymore."

"My old man blames McArdle for everything," Ed said. "We're going to get that son-of-a-bitch."

The stove in the center of the office was warming up fast from the three logs Ed had brought in earlier. Jay walked around to the side, held his hands over the front of the stove for a few minutes, then unbuttoned his coat, and sat on the bench along the wall. It had all started right here more than a year ago, he thought, and he felt a brief chill.

"What are you going to do to McArdle?" Jay asked. "Hell, he's going to be a U.S. congressman."

"Not when we get done," Ed said.

"Now what?"

"My dad's working on something," Ed replied.

"Don't get us in any more trouble," Jay offered. "I don't like McArdle either, but I sure as hell don't want to go back to jail."

"Don't worry," Ed said. "My dad's got this all worked out with that orphan over at Russell that he's been taking care of."

"Are you crazy?" Jay exclaimed. "Not another tar job."

"No, no, no." Ed said. "This is something else. We don't do anything."

"What's gonna happen?"

"I can't say everything," Ed said. "But we'll get McArdle out of that race, that's for sure."

It didn't take more than a few minutes for Jay Langston to figure out what Ed Garvey was up to. He had never met, or even seen, the orphan girl, but he had heard about Ed Garvey supporting her and visiting her in the orphanage. Jay thought Garvey would take the girl to McArdle's political rallies and get her to ask embarrassing questions of some kind, a mischievous plan he rather liked.

"Where are the rest of the boys?" Jay asked, wanting the others to hear this story. He was as game as the next guy for a good time, but not another stint in jail. Truth is, Jay hadn't grown particularly fond of Ed Jr. while in jail, concluding that the miller was less than astute, had an exaggerated sense of self, and was more or less a kept man through his father's largess. Jay had no such backup, certainly not in the religion business, and he spent a lot of time thinking about how he could make money with cars, the shiny new black machines that were changing the landscape.

"I don't know who's coming," Ed said. "It's still early. Won't be dark for another hour, and I'm not sure Club Wilson or Piney Woods will ever get away from home again. Their wives got them chained to the barn door."

But Piney did show up. His glasses were still perched high on his nose, and he appeared skinnier than ever, with his overalls looking all legs. Piney had been out of jail for more than six months but had some trouble readjusting to life in Nickerly. For one thing, Ed Garvey didn't know it, but Piney's wife had left him, a doubly shocking development since the Woods family went back so far with never a break in the generations. Piney responded by taking to the jug. He only worked about three hours a day on the farm, starting late with the milking and stopping early with the plowing so he could get a running start on the moonshine. He arrived at Garvey's Mill carrying a brown porcelain jug of corn liquor that would knock your head off. If you could survive the first couple of swallows, it got to tasting pretty good. After that, you went directly from dizziness to oblivion. Piney was in the first stage when he said hello to Jay Langston.

Jay moved to the back of the room so he could prop his feet on the corner bench. Seeing Piney made him think about jail, and it bothered him that Piney seemed in such a diminished state. Jay also worried about himself. He feared that confinement had marked him in some way, like leather straps across the rump of a horse. Jay was the kind of guy always looking for shortcuts, a faster way to shock corn, a quicker way to chop wood. He knew he was impatient. When they painted the barn, Jay never bothered to paint the underside of the wood, even when his father explained that the purpose of paint was to prevent rot, not just to improve the barn's appearance. If a shortcut was possible, Jay would find it. As a result, he had a reputation for never doing a job well. Jay had examined these characteristics a thousand times in jail, but the examination didn't lead to any particular transformation. Rather it left him with the simple hunger to get away, to start anew.

"I'm ready to get out of here," Jay said to Piney Woods. "There's nothing for me in this county. Maybe Kansas City."

"You can't leave yet," Ed Jr. interjected. "You don't want to miss the day we nail McArdle. That'll be a good one."

.   .   .

Judge Thomas Crier presided at the arraignment of W.W. McArdle and knew immediately that something was fishy about the charges.

But he had seen stranger things in his life, like perfectly normal bankers who turned out to be embezzlers, so the charges stood: one count of felonious assault and abuse and a second count of attempted rape. Judge Crier was particularly skeptical of the assertion that this crime took place at the home of the plaintiff's uncle, who apparently had left the state of Kansas with no known whereabouts, at least none that his niece could identify.

The judge did make one concession to his private concerns; he scheduled the trial for one week hence, thus preserving the possibility of a resolution before the congressional elections. John Engle arranged bail for W.W. and agreed to the expedited trial, against his better judgment. W.W. thanked him for his work, saying he wanted a quick resolution of the matter, and furthermore, he intended to serve as his own lawyer. Engle argued against this course, but W.W., still hoping to save his fledgling political career, was adamant that he could quickly prove his innocence.

Meanwhile, Buck Lamb was in a quandary. Word of W.W.'s arrest was spreading quickly, and with only two weeks to go before the election it was impossible to hunt up another candidate, certainly not one that could win. He discussed the matter with his fellow members of the State Democratic Committee, but they were of little help, throwing up their hands in frustration, some of them even urging W.W. to withdraw immediately from the race. Not one of them wanted to stand behind a candidate charged with rape. Even if W.W. were absolved of all charges, the scandal was enough to ensure defeat. But to Buck's credit, he didn't see any honor in retreat. So he placed two calls to the only people he knew who owed W.W. a significant debt: Temple Dandridge and Margaret Chambers.

Margaret Chambers met Temp at the train station, as they had agreed over the phone, and embraced him warmly. They had exchanged letters over the past year, but the pace of W.W.'s cam-

paign kept Margaret from going to Kansas City, and although Temp
had asked his editor if he could do a story on the McArdle race, the
assignment had gone to the *Star*'s Kansas political reporter. As Temp
looked at Margaret, he noticed a certain change in her face. In spite
of the anxiety about this latest legal problem, she seemed to have a
tranquillity that added to her beauty, which Temp noted, held the same
attraction as a year ago. She seemed calmer and more mature. He
was instantly drawn to her. He took her hand and led her into the
station.

"Margaret, I've really missed you," he said, then quickly added,
"How are your parents?"

If Margaret were in any way embarrassed by his attention, she
didn't show it. "My mother is well," she said. "She's started going to
church again, and we even had the neighbors over for dinner. Dad's
the same. Just keeps on working."

Temp turned to pick up his suitcase that was on the cart being
pushed into the station. "I didn't pack much 'cause I figure on a short
trial," he said. "Tell me about this whole mess."

"I don't believe this for a minute," Margaret said. "Winton has the
most wonderful family. He would never do such a thing. Somebody
put that girl up to it."

"The wire services carried the story," Temp said. "And they were
pretty specific about what happened. Are you sure?"

Temp considered himself a good friend to W.W. McArdle, but
the newsman in him couldn't help feeling skeptical. Temp never quite
believed anything without knowing the facts for himself.

"Let's talk about this later," she said. "It's so wonderful to see you.
Let's walk to the Adeline. I left the buggy tied over there."

As they started down Main Street, Temp put his free arm around
Margaret's waist, and she did not move away, indeed he thought she
moved closer to him. He liked the way she added to his confidence,

making him feel taller and stronger. He was trying to figure out if he could talk with her at the Adeline, drive her home in her rig, walk back to the hotel, and still be ready for tomorrow's trial. But she enveloped his mind, crowding out all those pesky thoughts of deadlines and interviews. As he felt her hips move under his hand, all thought of the trial vanished.

.   .   .

Judge Crier wasted no time convening the trial and impaneling the jury. It was clear to Temple Dandridge, who accompanied Margaret to the courthouse, that this was to be a sober affair. There was none of the celebratory atmosphere associated with Margaret's trial, and in fact the courthouse seemed almost deserted by comparison. Temp and Margaret were a little late because of a last-minute call from Nate Cabot in Kansas City, asking for thirty inches on the trial and the congressional campaign. When they walked through the courtroom doors, a reappearance Margaret approached with some apprehension, the surprise was waiting. In addition to Mrs. McArdle, who sat alone directly behind W.W., the only other people in the room were all fourteen members of the tar party, including Herbert Forchet. Only Easy Tucker was missing.

Margaret squeezed Temp's hand, not as a request for support, but as a challenge. He could feel her leading him down the aisle to sit right beside Mrs. McArdle, every tar party eye watching her proceed through the courtroom, without expression or comment, as if in secret confrontation.

Margaret leaned close to Temp as Judge Crier ordered the trial to begin and murmured, "Most of those guys I don't even recognize."

The first witness was Francis Ferris. W.W., acting in his own defense, intended to end this trial as quickly as possible, and that meant

establishing the facts immediately. No character witnesses. No effort
to establish an alibi, although he could do that if he had to by calling Buck Lamb, who would testify that he was on the campaign trail
with W.W. almost every day. Francis had made it difficult to refute
her charges by offering very few details. The charges as read into the
court didn't even specify a date for the attempted rape; the uncle at
whose house the abuse allegedly took place had vanished, if indeed
he ever lived there; and no reason was even given for why McArdle
would have been at this location. It was just Francis charging that it
had happened.

She was only fifteen, but dressed to look five years younger, and
when she entered the chambers with Ed Garvey Sr., she seemed confused about where to sit, until County Attorney Dunfee motioned her
to his side. By the time she was called to witness, she seemed frightened, glancing nervously at the jury as they stared at her, fidgeting with
her small purse, a natural leather bag cinched at the top. Her dress was
long, almost to the floor, with white lace cuffs and a starched collar.
Her hair, which W.W. had noticed as straight and dark, was now
curled and lighter.

But when W.W. McArdle, who treated her with careful respect,
asked where her uncle lived, she knew it was near Ellsworth but little else. She didn't know where the uncle was now or even when he
had gone; she had been living at the orphanage for several years and
only visited her uncle occasionally; and she felt she had to tell the sheriff her story. Every question W.W. asked her drew an ambiguous or
negative response.

W.W. was careful not to ask about the physical aspects of the
attempted rape, in spite of the written charge which said McArdle
"asked her to have sexual intercourse" and "did then and there lay upon
a bed with the said Francis Ferris, and did then and there hug, fondle, and kiss the said Francis, and did then and there place his hand

upon the body of said Francis Ferris, and being in a partially disrobed condition, did then and there embrace, fondle, and hold the said Francis Ferris in his arms for the purpose and with the intent to then and there unlawfully and feloniously carnally know her, contrary to the statute in such case made and against the peace and dignity of the State of Kansas." Not a murmur was heard when these charges were read to the jury at the opening of the trial, and W.W. did not intend to ask Francis to repeat them. He didn't think it would be necessary. And he didn't want to make it look like he was trying to embarrass or intimidate the girl.

The prosecution did ask Francis to repeat the charges, but all she would say was: "He tried to rape me." County Attorney Dunfee wanted to paint his victim as a sympathetic person, but every time he tried to lead her into a description of McArdle touching her or hurting her, she simply repeated the charge that he had raped her.

W.W. rested his defense thinking it had been clearly demonstrated that the crime simply did not occur. The jury lived in the county, knew the tar party boys at least by reputation, knew the saga of Margaret Chambers, and also knew about the defendant's candidacy for Congress. He could not imagine a more public case or a more obvious outcome. And he was right. The jury took just seventeen minutes and one ballot to acquit W.W. McArdle of all charges.

CHAPTER NINETEEN

"Son," the Reverend Aaron Langston began, the day after the acquittal of W.W. McArdle, "our family must gather itself this morning to bless the Lord, to bear witness to His life, and to restore the integrity of our family in following His dictates. We cannot ignore our responsibility to our family and our Lord."

Aaron had fashioned his own religious beliefs through many years of different churches, congregations, and meditation on the teachings of Christ. His family had started as Quakers, believing deeply that some of the divine God lived in each person and that each person had a personal relationship with God. Aaron's personal savior was a loving God, not a fearful one, and even though Aaron could spit fire and brimstone on the evils of sin with the best country preachers, he began early in life to move away from the harsher realities of Quaker tradition. He especially rejected the punishments of the church against its parishioners, such as the whipping of mothers for illegitimate births, fines, community jail for missed church services, and the expulsion of parishioners for adultery. Aaron and Ivy believed in punishment for sin, but they also believed that God should be man's judge. Now they were returning to an earlier set of rules.

Pain settled over Aaron's face as he looked across the living room at his pious and hardworking wife, Ivy, a woman who had never asked for worldly goods, but who had demanded that her family be loyal to the most basic tenet of her religion. Ivy believed that the integrity of the family grew out of their life and the land. Their lives should be a testament to their beliefs. She was a good woman. And this family gathering was surely the most difficult she would ever face.

Aaron glanced at his daughters, demure and perhaps woven of a strong fiber he had not yet seen. He hoped so, because he knew his actions today would not be easy to understand.

Finally, he looked at Ray and Jay, thinking of the pain he would cause by separating these boys who had played together with so much innocence, worked together with so much strength, and yet pursued lives on such different courses. Aaron didn't like to think of Jay as a bad boy, but he could not ignore the pain Jay had caused, the denial of God's direction, and his seeming inability to do the right thing. Now it had come to this.

As he had done once before, Aaron let the *Kansas City Star* make his charges. He held the paper before him, standing like a monument in the middle of the room in his black suit with its vest pocket chain hanging from his stomach. His white beard was trimmed and just dried, as if he had dressed up for the occasion.

"Let me just read the first two paragraphs of this story by Temple Dandridge, so we all know how the world sees the recent events in our life," he began.

The headline read: "Jury Believed McArdle Charges a Conspiracy to Wreck His Character." This was the story Buck Lamb had hoped that Temp Dandridge would write, and the story they would need if W.W. McArdle was to have any chance of winning the election.

Aaron moved to the third paragraph. He read it slowly. "Jurors, after the verdict had been returned, said that it appeared to them that the case against McArdle was part of a conspiracy to blast his character because of his prosecution of the tar party case."

Then he turned to address Jay directly: "Son, we prayed that your actions against Margaret Chambers were inspired by the holy word of God, that you believed you were protecting our neighbors and our children from her sinful ways, but the trial proved other motives were at hand. We prayed that during your time away"—Aaron could not bring himself to say "in jail"—"that you had repented. That you had seen the wages of vindictiveness and hate. We know this is a time of religious toleration, and people are shamelessly moving away from the word of God. And we must remain a community of the faithful. But it is not loyalty to the faith that corrupted that poor orphan girl and forced her to bear false witness against another person. In the tarring and feathering of Margaret and in this matter, you played a part. You could have stopped them both. You have ignored your responsibility to God and to our family."

The room was deathly quiet. Ivy clung to the knitting in her lap as if it were an anvil, praying silently while staring at the floor. The girls reached for each other's hands, not fully understanding what was happening, glancing at each other nervously. Only Jay looked directly at his father, fighting to keep his inner anger in check. Only a twitch of his cheek betrayed his fear.

Aaron stood like marble, as if waiting for some last-minute reprieve, perhaps a plea for forgiveness, perhaps the admission of guilt that he had never heard from his son, perhaps a commitment to a new life, a promise. But it did not come.

"Son," Aaron began slowly, "you must leave our family today and never return. You must leave the state of Kansas and start life in some other place. For our part, we will never speak your name again, or speak of the shame you have brought to our family. We will pray for you always, but in the silence of our hearts."

Jay stood to address his father, his legs trembling and his arms hanging loosely at his side. Ivy and the girls began crying quietly. Ray bent over with his elbows on his knees, holding his head. He could not look at any of them.

"Father," Jay said, "I am ready to go." He swallowed, thinking of other things to say, angry things, but he knew they would not help. He considered throwing himself at his father's mercy or begging his mother to prevent this act, but those were not his real sentiments. He was, in fact, ready to be done with Nickerly, Kansas, and that might as well include his family. He said nothing else.

"Your mother has packed your clothes," Aaron said, pointing to a carpetbag near the door. "And you can take the mare. She's ready."

Jay Langston turned, stepped over to Ray, and briefly shuffled his hand through his brother's hair. Then he walked out the door. He was not followed.

.   .   .

In the few days before the election, Winton McArdle, Margaret Chambers, Temp Dandridge, and Buck Lamb traveled to every corner of the district. Two of them rode on horseback and two rode in the wagon that carried a trunk of clothes, two boxes of posters, and a large cloth banner that could be strung across almost any street, reading "McArdle for Congress."

W.W. could feel a change in his audiences. Some hadn't heard about the acquittal and clearly wondered why he wasn't in jail. Some wanted to make their own judgment of the man and stared at him suspiciously. Only two weeks earlier W.W. had been a shoo-in to win. People had trusted him, had brought their kids down to the train platforms to meet him. Now they acted cautious. They did not cheer so loudly. They did not crowd around to shake his hand. They felt betrayed. Nothing angers an electorate more than a betrayal of their beliefs.

"I know this is a long shot, Buck," W.W. said, sitting in the lobby of the Sunflower Hotel in Russell, "but I can't let the Garveys beat me. If I can just talk to enough people, I can make it."

"You're doing great," Buck said. "Get some sleep. We head for Tescott early tomorrow, and then it's home for election day."

Margaret and Temp had gone for a walk along the main street of Russell, with its new buildings painted in bright cheery colors. The boardwalk was worn, but it wasn't splintered. The Indian summer air was warm around them. She held his arm as they walked.

When they came to the River Brethren Church at the end of the street, Temp said, "Let's sit a moment."

He knew he had to return to Kansas City as soon as the election was over. It would be his last story from Nickerly.

"Margaret," he said, "you have been wonderful these last few days, getting up in front of everybody and talking about W.W. No matter what happens with the vote, you have done your best."

"I owe him so much," she replied. "It's still so sad that he should have to pay for what happened to me."

"He was just doing his job," Temp said. "And it was you who gave him the chance to run for Congress. So I'd say you're about even."

Temp put his arm around Margaret's shoulders. The first shadows were falling from the church steeple, creeping across their faces like a veil.

"Margaret," he began, "I've come to feel so close to you. It seems like whenever we get close, I have to leave."

"I missed you when you were gone, Temp," she said. "But I didn't know what to do about it. It seemed I was in the middle of so many people, all pushing me in different directions."

"I know," he said. "Even now we've gone from a trial to an election in just days. Fortunately, as a newspaperman, I'm used to it. But I can understand your confusion."

Margaret wasn't sure that Temp did understand her. She admired him, but she was wary of his ability to wall off his emotions, to write the story he wanted no matter who was involved. She knew, of course, that his stories had been sympathetic to her, and perhaps not as objective as he liked to pretend. She was thankful for that. Of course, she also thought her position was the objective one. She hadn't given a lot of thought to falling in love with Temp Dandridge. But he could not say the same.

"I don't want to leave without you, Margaret," he said. "Will you come to Kansas City with me?"

Margaret drew close to his face. Her gloved hand touched his cheek. She could feel his body quivering.

Margaret pulled away slowly. "I like you very much, Temp," she said. "But we have to get through all this first. I can't come to Kansas City with you now. But I will come later."

"Why?" he asked. "What do you have to do here?"

"I need some time with my mother and father, even Ileen. I need to be with them without some calamity hanging over our heads," she said. "Also, Buck says I should use my fame while it lasts, maybe travel. Wouldn't that be great?"

"Come to Kansas City," he said again. "We can travel wherever you like."

"I will, Temp," she said. "I'm just not ready now. Buck says I have opportunities. Women should use their opportunities, like getting to vote. I have to see what happens."

Temp turned to face her in the thickening darkness of the night. He put his arms around her waist, and she confidently touched both sides of his face as they kissed. He withdrew slowly and murmured, "I love you, Margaret."

Margaret did have strong feelings for Temp, and she cared for his feelings, but she could not quite bring herself to return the commitment to love. "I guess we had better return to the hotel," Margaret said, "before somebody catches us." The destructive force of gossip was never far from her mind.

.　　　.　　　.

Jay Langston arrived on the outskirts of Topeka on election day. He felt deliciously free—free from family and friends, free from laws and courts, free from newspapers and records of the state, and most importantly, free from his father's religion and all the restrictions on his innate sense of joy in life. He was heading for a new life in the north, across the prairie and beyond the farms to a land where trees were as thick as locusts, and the water could carry him to big cities or remote islands, whatever his whim devised. Perhaps he would go to Michigan or even Minnesota. Jay had not planned where his feet would wander. He was just happy to be going.

On the edge of town, he stopped at a lone boardinghouse with fading gables to spend the night. He tied his horse near the trough next to two other horses and stepped onto the porch, when he noticed a flier attached to a board where church notices were posted. It was printed on thick paper and appeared to have been nailed up that very day. The word "MARCH" was printed in six-inch letters across the top, and below it read: "We Want the Right to Vote. Join Your Sisters and the Tar Party Schoolteacher, Sunday on Main Street."

"Jesus," Jay said as he yanked the flier off the board, crumpled it in both hands, and threw it into a muddy pool of water collecting near the porch. "How far do I have to go?"

This story is based on a series of events involving my great-uncle Jay Fitzwater and my great grandfather, the Reverend Levi Fitzwater. The events of the story track many of the facts of the actual "tar party" case. All of the names have been changed; some of the characters are totally fictional; and all of the motives, dialogue, descriptions, and relationships in this novel are fictional, with the exception of some language taken directly from newspaper accounts of the "tar party trial" of 1911.

On August 7, 1911, a schoolteacher from Shady Bend, Kansas, was tarred by several of the leading citizens of the area for allegedly seducing one of her students. At the subsequent trial, no evidence was presented in support of that assertion. Seven of the men were found guilty of assault and abuse and received varying sentences of up to one year in jail. The Lincoln County prosecutor ran unsuccessfully for Congress. He was accused of attempting to rape a young girl on December 24, 1911, and was found innocent in a trial that lasted only thirty minutes. All members of the original tar party were in attendance. The schoolteacher later married and lived out her life as a wife and mother in Illinois. The prosecutor continued to practice law in Lincoln, Kansas.

In writing this story, I am indebted to my family, especially my uncle, Everett Fitzwater, and my aunt, Veve Fitzwater, and my brother Gary. Mr. and Mrs. Ted Webb of Beverly, Kansas, helped with local information. I thank many people at the *Kansas City Star,* a distinguished newspaper that covered the actual tar party case extensively; the Lincoln County Historical Society; the Lincoln County Clerk of the Court; and my agent, Robert Barnett. My editor at PublicAffairs, Kate Darnton, is wise beyond her years. I am immensely grateful for her guidance.

My great friends Andy and Kathi Card, Carol McCain, Leslye Arsht, Clare Pickart, and Beth James kept up my confidence during this project and read various drafts. Richard North Patterson provided advice and encouragement. And the boys from Shannon's Restaurant, including the late Henry Burroughs, Dr. Francis Wenger, and Thomas Abercrombie, kept me writing. I also thank my wife, Melinda, for constantly asking, "How's that book coming?"

Finally, the family search goes on. The whereabouts of my great-uncle Jay Fitzwater or his descendants is still a mystery.

MARLIN FITZWATER
Deale, Maryland

PUBLICAFFAIRS is a new publishing house and a tribute to the standards, values, and flair of three persons who have served as mentors to countless reporters, writers, editors, and book people of all kinds, including me.

I. F. STONE, proprietor of *I. F. Stone's Weekly*, combined a commitment to the First Amendment with entrepreneurial zeal and reporting skill and became one of the great independent journalists in American history. At the age of eighty, Izzy published *The Trial of Socrates*, which was a national bestseller. He wrote the book after he taught himself ancient Greek.

BENJAMIN C. BRADLEE was for nearly thirty years the charismatic editorial leader of *The Washington Post*. It was Ben who gave the *Post* the range and courage to pursue such historic issues as Watergate. He supported his reporters with a tenacity that made them fearless, and it is no accident that so many became authors of influential, best-selling books.

ROBERT L. BERNSTEIN, the chief executive of Random House for more than a quarter century, guided one of the nation's premier publishing houses. Bob was personally responsible for many books of political dissent and argument that challenged tyranny around the globe. He is also the founder and was the longtime chair of Human Rights Watch, one of the most respected human rights organizations in the world.

·　　·　　·

For fifty years, the banner of Public Affairs Press was carried by its owner Morris B. Schnapper, who published Gandhi, Nasser, Toynbee, Truman, and about 1,500 other authors. In 1983 Schnapper was described by *The Washington Post* as "a redoubtable gadfly." His legacy will endure in the books to come.

Peter Osnos, *Publisher*